My

MOTHER'S
CHILDREN

My
MOTHER'S
CHILDREN

ANNETTE SILLS

POOLBEG

Published 2021
by Poolbeg Press Ltd.
123 Grange Hill, Baldoyle,
Dublin 13, Ireland
Email: poolbeg@poolbeg.com

A catalogue record for this book is available from the British Library.

ISBN 978178199-421-4

www.poolbeg.com

About the Author

Annette Sills was born in Wigan, Lancashire, to parents from County Mayo, Ireland. Her short stories have been longlisted and shortlisted in a number of competitions including The Fish Short Story Prize, *Books Ireland Magazine* Short Story Competition and *The Telegraph Magazine* Short Story Competition. Her first novel, *The Relative Harmony of Julie O'Hagan*, was shortlisted in Rethink Press New Novels Competition 2014.

Annette writes contemporary sagas set in the Manchester Irish Diaspora. She is fascinated by migration and belonging, and the dynamics of family life.

She currently lives in Chorlton, Manchester, with her husband and two children.

Acknowledgements

Heartfelt thanks to:

Lyndsay Hollingshead and Claire Winstanley for reading the early drafts, Dr Rob Boon and Dr Anita McSorley for their medical expertise, Jenny Raddings for her vast gardening knowledge, Nicola Doherty and Emily Hughes for their beady-eyed comments and editing.

To the wonderful team at Poolbeg – Paula Campbell for taking me on and Gaye Shortland for her impressive editing skills.

To the Manchester Irish Writers group, and to Liam Harte and John McAuliffe from the Creative Writing Dept at Manchester University for the thought-provoking discussions on writing, migration and belonging. It might have been a different story without those evenings in the Irish World Heritage Centre in Cheetham Hill.

To my Short Story Club ladies for keeping me laughing throughout lockdown and for keeping the stories coming.

To my extended family in County Mayo and the US, whose true-life dramas will always top my fiction.

And to my lovely Nick, Jimmy and Ciara for their constant love and support xx

Dedication

For the survivors of the Irish Mother and Baby Homes and the women and children who perished in them.

Author's Note

On March 3rd 2017, the Irish Mother and Baby Homes Commission of Investigation announced that human remains had been found during a test excavation carried out, between November 2016 and February 2017, at the former site of a Mother and Baby Home in Tuam, County Galway.

Tests conducted on some of the remains indicated they were those of children aged between 35 foetal weeks and 2–3 years. The announcement confirmed that the deceased had died during the period of time that the property was used by the Mother and Baby Home and not from an earlier period, as most of the bodies dated from the 1920s to the 1950s.

The remains were found in an "underground structure divided into 20 chambers". The remains were not thrown into a mass pit or sceptic tank as previously reported in the press.

Chapter 1

Mikey was always late. He'd turn up at weddings, birthdays and funerals hours after everyone else. I could see him as clear as day, perched at the end of the bar, laughing and running his fingers through his shaggy blonde hair, as handsome as hell.

Karen nudged me. She was air-drumming to the refrain of Siouxsie's "Happy House" floating in from the main function room. I joined in. Joe rolled his eyes, so I drummed harder. We were only having a laugh, for God's sake. And tonight, of all nights, I needed a laugh.

For once the lounge bar at Chorlton Irish was busy. There were rumours the club was closing. The older

Irish were dying out and the young Irish were no longer coming over like they used to. If they did come, they frequented the tapas bars and Indian restaurants across the way. These days the club relied on outside events, fundraisers like this one, to stay open. Tonight's crowd was a mix of locals and people from previous fundraisers. The auction of promises was under way in the main room, raffle tickets were flying and I was optimistic the Heart Foundation would reach the target they needed for the scanner that government cuts had denied them.

Our crowd were gathered at a long table near the bar under a Mayo GAA shirt depressed in a glass frame and a poster advertising a film about women in the Easter Rising. I was touched by the turnout: friends from his clubbing days, colleagues from the gym, neighbours from the old house on Brantingham Road.

I sat with my head in my hands sometimes and asked myself if it was true. I still couldn't quite believe he was gone.

A rangy bloke approached the table carrying a pint of Guinness. He grinned at our drumming and I dropped my imaginary sticks in embarrassment. Then someone knocked into him from behind and he lurched forward, dousing our table with the black stuff. A few minutes later he was mopping up the tar-like puddles, his long arm circling across the table like an eagle wing. He looked in his late forties. He had a craggy face with lines etched around moss-green eyes, like well-worn paths on a mountain side. His strawberry-blonde hair was tied back in a ponytail and a long scar ran along his forearm.

"You missed a bit." I smiled and lifted up a soggy pile of Stena Line leaflets so he could clean underneath. Then I pointed at the scar.

"War wound?"

Karen kicked me under the table. A therapist, she knew better than to ask people where they got their scars.

He grinned. "I'm Dan, by the way." He couldn't keep his eyes off Karen. "Sorry about this. Let me buy you all a drink."

Karen sat upright and threw him the haughty look she kept for attractive men. "A glass of Sauvignon Blanc would be lovely."

Joe frowned down at his white shirt which had taken the brunt of the dousing and shook his head.

I nodded. "I'll have a Sauvignon too, thanks. I'm Carmel Doherty. This is my husband Joe and this ..." I waved my hand in the air, "is my amazing friend Karen."

He smiled and I watched him walk back to the bar, a straggle of hair slipping from his ponytail onto his neck.

When I looked back Karen was cocking her head and smiling.

"What's so funny?" I asked.

"You are. You are so drunk."

"Yep." I knocked back more wine. "My only brother died a year ago today. Why wouldn't I be?"

By the time Dan had arrived back with our drinks Joe had moved to the other end of the table to talk to a friend of Mikey's who'd just arrived on his own. Karen had gone to the bathroom after placing a glass of water in front of me and telling me to get it down my neck. Dan looked around, disappointed as he put the drinks down on the table. I gestured at him to take the chair next to Karen's. He didn't need telling. He sprang towards it like a gazelle, pulling it back to make room for his long legs before he sat down.

3

Picking up a Guinness beer mat, he cartwheeled it between his forefinger and thumb.

"I think I met you briefly before at another Heart Foundation gig."

"Probably. My brother passed last year and Tess – that's my mum – and I used to come to some of the fundraisers in his memory." I reached for my wine. "And to get bladdered. It's what he would have wanted."

He smiled. "Sounds like a good man."

"Most of the time."

"I think I met your mum too. She said she was from County Mayo, like my family."

"Tess passed in November too."

He dropped the beer mat. "I'm sorry. That's very tough."

"I'm a walking talking tragedy at the moment." I gave a brittle laugh and raised my glass. "Anyway, here's to beautiful Mayo!"

He lifted his glass. "To Mayo. My wife's family are from Achill Island."

I gulped my wine. "I know Achill well. We used to go to Keem Bay all the time when we were kids."

He downed his Guinness, the liquid barely touching the side of his mouth, just like Mikey used to. Then his eyes travelled around the room and he picked up the beer mat again.

"Why did you call your mum by her first name, if you don't mind me asking?"

"She was more of a girl-woman, I suppose. Vulnerable. I looked after her more than she looked after me." I sighed. "Anyway, how come you hang out at Heart Foundation gigs?"

"I raise funds. My son's been in and out of the children's

hospital for a while now. He has heart problems."

At that moment Karen arrived back from the bathroom, hair and lipstick refreshed. Like most men, Dan stared at my best friend of thirty years like he was shielding his eyes from a blinding sun. Five eleven and willowy, she had the startling combination of her Scottish mother's translucent blue eyes and the brown skin and ebony hair she inherited from her Nigerian father. When we were teenagers, people used to stop and stare at her in the street. It's never been easy living in her shadow. I was the ugly friend, a tall scraggy bottle-blonde with bandy legs and no chest. I've always been full of nervous energy and, as much as I tried, I could never put on weight. Joe always told me I had beautiful eyes, though. Cat-like, he said.

Karen and I were approaching forty but she looked ten years younger. In the past year grief had ravaged my face as well as my heart. Burgundy half-moons hung under my eyes, my skin was pockmarked and lines had started spread across it like an expanding Tube line.

The three of us chatted. Dan was good company. I couldn't place his accent. It was a curious mixture of educated London peppered with Mancunian. It was like listening to a symphony with a quirky guitar thrown in.

The wine started to make my thoughts wander. I kept thinking I could see them in the corner of my eye. Mikey was chatting up a random girl at the bar and Tess was sitting in her corner seat, smiling her enigmatic smile. I felt myself welling up. I missed the bones of them.

Dan and Karen were getting on like a house on fire, so I left them to it and looked around for Joe. He was chatting to Bryonie Phillips by the door. She was standing behind a table stamping hands and selling raffle tickets under a heart-shaped helium balloon. Bryonie knew everyone and everything going on in Manchester's grooviest suburb. She was a gossip and her daughter Tallulah was one of my first-year students. She waved and threw me a tight little smile. Little did I know how much grief those prying eyes would cause me later.

I waved and gestured at Joe to join me at the bar. It was closing time at the pubs so people were flooding into the club and the small space was heaving with sweaty bodies.

"Karen's copped," I said, as he joined me.

He glanced over the table where Dan and Karen were engrossed in conversation and frowned. "He's married. Didn't you see the ring?"

"I did. That's never stopped her before, though."

My recollection of the rest of the evening is hazy. I remember drinking every glass of wine put in front of me, singing Mikey's favourite "Cigarettes and Alcohol" with everyone around the table, crying a lot and telling strangers I loved them.

After the raffle, Joe and Karen had to take me outside and pour me into a waiting cab. It was still early. Joe said he'd come back home with me but I insisted he stay. I could tell he wanted to. It was a warm evening and a large crowd had gathered by the smoking shed. Above their heads nicotine and vape-clouds drifted over the Chorlton chimneypots into a mauve-and-pink sky. I slumped back on the gashed leather seat and wiped a circle of condensation from the window. My face wet with tears, I looked through my porthole, searching for Mikey's face in the crowd.

Chapter 2

I uncurled my legs and sat upright on the armchair.

"She said what?"

"She said you tripped over her table and knocked the raffle prizes flying."

"Christ." I shook my head. "I don't even remember. What else did she say?"

Karen chewed the inside of her lip.

"Come on. Spit it out, woman!"

"She said it wasn't really fitting behaviour for a university lecturer."

My jaw dropped. "She did not."

"Afraid so."

"Jesus, Mary and Joseph!" I leant forward and put my head in my hands, closing my eyes briefly then opening them and raising my head. "You know her daughter is in my class?"

Karen nodded, her lips suppressing a smile.

I gave her the finger. "Get lost, Obassi!"

We both started to laugh then I shook my head. "I really can't remember any of it. So when did all this happen, exactly?"

"In the toilets not long after you'd left."

"God. And who was she talking to?"

"No idea. The hand-dryer came on and I couldn't hear anything else. I waited inside the cubicle until I was sure they'd gone."

It was Saturday, the morning after the fundraiser. Karen and I were in her "white room", the inner sanctum at the back of her Old Trafford terrace house where she practised yoga and mindfulness. A beige leather sofa in front of French windows overlooked a long narrow garden. Apart from a matching armchair, a pearl rug on white painted floorboards and a rolled-up yoga mat propped against the wall, there was very little else in the room. Chet Baker was playing on a lonely iPod on the grey marble mantelpiece and the lingering smell of fresh white paint was starting to make me queasy.

I preferred the rest of the house, a happy chaos of books, colourful retro and eclectic second-hand furniture. The walls were busy with posters of gigs, art exhibitions and anti-racism marches, many of which Karen and I had been on together. Recently a shrine had appeared in the kitchen dedicated to my lovely goddaughter Alexia. She was a language student at Sheffield. Old trophies, photographs and random objects like shoes, schoolbooks and cinema tickets lined the windowsill.

"She's not dead, you know," I said when I first saw it. "She's only gone to Sheffield Uni."

Karen raised an eyebrow and gave me a look that said, 'You don't have kids, so how would you know?' At which I yawned inside. To be fair, Karen wasn't half as patronising about my childless status as some of my other friends were. The pitying looks, the comments about my clock ticking and what a wonderful mum I'd make. Some of them were driving me bonkers. What business was it of theirs whether I had kids or not?

At thirty-nine, I still hadn't decided. But I had good reason. Dad died when I was ten. Tess's mental health deteriorated considerably afterwards. I had some help from a neighbour but I had to rear Mikey singlehandedly a lot of the time. He was four when Dad died and, believe me, being a child carer for a rumbustious four-year-old was no easy task. I bathed my brother, changed him, fed him and played with him. If he got sick, I stayed off school to mind him. I knew how hard it was to raise a child so having one of my own was never going to be a decision I'd make lightly. I loved my uncluttered life, the freedom I had to travel now that I didn't have Tess to care for and I'd worked hard to secure a permanent post at the university. I wasn't sure I wanted to give up all that for a baby.

The floor suddenly shuddered beneath my feet. I clutched the chair-arm as the room began to vibrate. Karen rolled her eyes, Chet Baker got drowned out and I put my fingers in my ears as the eleven thirty-two to Piccadilly screeched past at the end of the garden.

Karen and I had both wanted to buy houses in Chorlton but by the time we were ready we'd been priced out of the working-class suburb where we were raised. In the nineties, fancy wine bars, cosmopolitan restaurants and a vegan food cooperative moved in and it transformed into Manchester's bohemian suburb. House prices rocketed and locals like Karen and me were elbowed out. We both ended up buying a mile away in the arctic hinterland of Old Trafford, streets from the roar of the stadium. Karen bought her terrace house at a knockdown price when the railway track at the bottom of the garden was rarely used but now she endured a minor earthquake every half hour. Tragic circumstances and a windfall allowed Joe and me to return to Chorlton, but Karen remained out in the cold. She'd been trying to sell for years.

Now, not long back from a run, she was lying across the sofa in cream joggers and a black vest top. Her golden curls had come loose from her ponytail and were spread across the cream leather. Honey-coloured April sunshine poured over her from the French windows, an endorphin halo hovered above her head and she glowed. Like Joe, Karen was a fitness freak. She ran five kilometres at weekends, worked out at the gym at least three times a week and did yoga at home.

Springer Bell yelped and scratched at the kitchen door. He was a lively beast and Karen always locked him in there whenever I visited because I got nervous around jumpy dogs. He yelped again and I winced. I was hungover. My head was throbbing and the inside of my mouth had the texture and smell of a nightclub carpet.

I reached into my bag for my bottle of water. "Tell me about Dan. You looked pretty cosy when I left."

Karen flipped on her side and propped herself up on an elbow. "We were just chatting. He's married. Nice bloke, though."

10

"Chatting, my arse."

I started to sing "Danny Boy". She laughed and threw a cushion at me. I threw it back. For a brief moment I felt the old warmth return. For some reason that I didn't understand, our friendship of almost thirty years had waned recently. Karen used to be like family. We saw each other at least twice a week, often turning up at each other's houses unannounced, we swapped clothes, went on mini-breaks and holidays together and spoke on the phone for hours at a time. Our relationship had ebbed and flowed when we were younger, but I was confused about why she had distanced herself from me now. I suspected she was fed up with me offloading my grief on her. I was hardly a bundle of laughs anymore. The pain seemed to consume me sometimes. She was so supportive in those first weeks and months, but I guess she got weary. Her clients vented to her all day at her clinic. Why would she want to listen to me unburdening my grief when she got home as well?

She picked up the cushion from the floor and hugged it to her chest. "Don't worry about Bryonie Phillips and Tallulah, Carmel. It'll all be forgotten in a day or two."

I threw my hands in the air in mock horror. "Don't worry about Bryonie and Tallulah? You're supposed to be a therapist. I'm an angsty nail-biting neurotic. Of course I'm going to bloody worry about them!"

I laughed it off but I knew I would worry about that night and my shameful behaviour. The racing thoughts would keep me awake. At breakfast Joe had told me I was a disgrace. He was laughing at the time but I detected a serious undercurrent. He looks after himself and doesn't drink that much nowadays. And now, on top of everything, I had to worry about Bryonie Phillip's daughter Tallulah spreading rumours at the university about me being a drunk. I knew what students could be like. Especially ones like Tallulah. She was a sly little madam who'd had it in for me ever since I'd called her out for plagiarising chapters in one of her essays on Chaucer.

I slumped back into the armchair. Karen swung her legs off the sofa, sat up straight then pulled an elastic band from her wrist and tied her hair back. She turned and looked out into the garden. It was long and narrow and bursting with colour in the sunshine. Cabbages and carrots sprouted in the vegetable patch, flowerbeds were alive with cerise tulips and daffodils and hyacinth and blowsy red-and-white shrub pieris crept up a side wall. She sat perfectly still and strummed her fingers on the top of the sofa, humming along with Chet to "I Fall in Love Too Easily".

I wondered what she was thinking about. Had something happened with Danny Boy that she hadn't told me? It was more likely she was thinking about Simon Whelan, though. She swore it was over between them, but I didn't believe her. I'd noticed she was wearing a bracelet I hadn't seen before. It was lovely, gold with the two ends shaped in the form of a snake's head with tiny emeralds for eyes. When I complimented her on it, she said it was new. Simon must have bought it for her. He was always surprising her with presents like that. It wasn't like she was ever going to tell me though. She'd stopped talking about him. She knew how much I disapproved.

Though Karen and I had been friends since we were eleven years old, she was still an enigma in many ways, especially when it came to men. None of her relationships had lasted longer than a year and the minute any boyfriend hinted at commitment, she kicked them into touch. The list was long and it included Alexia's father Marco, a gentle Brazilian musician. When she fell pregnant at twenty he was desperate to stick around and play a part in his daughter's upbringing. Karen was having none of it. She wanted to go it alone and she played cruel games over access. Marco, stung, moved to Leeds and started another family.

Men fell at Karen's feet at every opportunity. Maybe she just hadn't met the right one yet but it struck me that she had attachment issues.

She glanced down at her watch. "Sorry. I've got to get changed. I'm meeting some friends at the anti-austerity march in town."

Slightly piqued she hadn't asked me to join her, I grabbed my bag from the floor and followed her into the hall. A silence hung between us like taut elastic. She opened the kitchen door and scooped up Springer Bell into her arms.

As I went to open the door, I stopped in front of a new poster at the bottom of the stairs that I hadn't noticed on my way in. It was a framed black-and-white photograph of Maya Angelou. She looked elegant and stately and across the bottom it said: "*Love recognises no barriers. It jumps hurdles, leaps fences, penetrates walls to arrive at its destination full of hope.*"

I turned round. "Very romantic," I said.

She was kissing the top of Springer Bell's head and I noticed she was blushing. I found it a little odd as Karen Obassi rarely did coy.

Chapter 3

I found the letter the following Thursday and nothing was ever the same again.

I'd spent most of the week fretting about Bryonie and Tallulah Phillips. Of course I had. I was a champion fretter. I ruminated for days about things most people wouldn't give a second thought to. Neurotic, highly strung, skittish, a born worrier – I'd been described as many things over the years. Apparently now my way of being had a name. It was called "mild to moderate anxiety". I'd been both bemused and relieved to learn it had been classed as a medical condition. I traced its roots back to Dad dying. I was a happy little thing before then. Life with Tess afterwards was unstable and chaotic, and the world was no longer a safe place without him in it.

I lay awake every night replaying the events of the fundraiser, thoughts racing round my head like greyhounds on a track. Bad thoughts. I worried about Joe. He'd been keeping his distance. He'd opted for a boxing class at the gym instead of our usual Sunday-night curry and he'd barely said goodbye when he left for a meeting in Warsaw on Monday. Was he as ashamed of me as I was of myself? That was all we needed. Our marriage was going through a rocky patch. I tossed and turned and sat up in bed, imagining Bryonie embellishing tales of my inebriation to Tallulah in the huge kitchen of their mansion in Chorltonville. I saw Tallulah surrounded by first-year students, cackling and tapping on her phone with her pink talons, flinging off messages to more students on WhatsApp groups, Facebook and Twitter. Why oh why did I do it? I drank too much when I went out because I was socially awkward and nervous. This led to me to do idiotic things and then I beat myself up about it for ages afterwards. As the week went on I managed to work myself into a right state. There really was no end to my fretting talents.

I offloaded to my friend Mary at work on Wednesday. We were in the staffroom having lunch and trying to get some marking done. I couldn't concentrate. I was fidgeting, constantly checking my phone and sighing loudly.

Mary looked up from her laptop. "Everything OK, hen?"

Barrell-shaped and Glaswegian, Mary Duffy had a doll-like face with large baby-blue eyes, a mane of soft black curls and rosebud lips. But there was nothing soft or innocent about her. An expert in the twentieth century novel, she was bawdy, brilliant and as tough as rawhide.

"Remind me never to drink again, Mary."

15

"I'll do no such thing. Why? What did you do?"

I glanced furtively around the room. "Tell you another time."

"Sounds intriguing. Tell me now."

I leant over and lowered my voice. "I got really bladdered at Mikey's anniversary do and made a show of myself. Tallulah Phillips' mum saw me. I fell on top of the table where she was selling raffle tickets but I can't remember a thing."

Mary hooted with laughter and a couple of the other teachers glanced over.

Then her face fell. "You don't mean Tallulah 'you better give me a first or else' Phillips?"

I nodded.

"Christ."

"I know. I've really got to stop this drinking malarkey. I'm nearly forty for God's sake."

"Och, bollocks to that!" She tore the wrapper off a Mars Bar. "As the man said, '*Ageing can be fun if you lie back and enjoy it'*."

A cheer erupted from the corner of the room. Someone had got the photocopier working.

"Oscar Wilde?" I asked.

She bit off a large chunk of chewy chocolate and shook her head.

"Irvine Welsh?"

"Close.

"Martin Amis?"

"Nope."

"I give up."

"Clint Eastwood." She grinned and showed me her caramel-smeared teeth. "How's Joe?""

16

"Alright. He's a bit mardy by times."

"How so?"

"Tell you another time."

I didn't want to go into my marital problems in the staffroom, but I knew I could tell Mary anything. She was a wise old owl and I found myself increasingly confiding in her about a lot of the things I'd normally tell Karen. Joe and Mary got along well. Joe was a United fan, Mary a Liverpool season-ticket holder and they slagged each other about football. Mary's long-term partner, a Swiss lawyer called Monika, was serious and introverted and preferred tennis.

I put my head down and got on with my marking. Little did I know that by the end of the week all my anxieties about Bryonie and Tallulah Phillips and Joe would be completely forgotten. What I was to discover would blow everything out of the water and make my all my fretting look trivial and insignificant.

Thursday was a strange, unsettling kind of day. As I drove to Tess's house in Brantingham Road, a weak sun dipped in and out of slate-grey clouds and half-hearted gusts of wind rose and fell away. I put Morrissey's "Back to the Old House" on the CD player – a mournful tune about someone who has mixed feelings about revisiting their past – and the song was still echoing around my head when I parked outside at about eleven. Armed with black binbags, I was about to do a final sweep of my childhood home before the house-clearance people arrived and I was dreading it.

The red-brick thirties semi where I was raised was the sick old lady in a healthy-looking street of identical houses.

17

Luckily for us, Tess and Dad had paid off the mortgage early on, which meant we always had a roof over our heads after he died. But there was never any money for maintenance and the place had been in a state of ill-repair for decades. Clumps of concrete had fallen from the porch, the frosted glass in the front door was cracked and tiles were missing from the roof like gaps in a row of rotting teeth. The one thing Tess had taken care of was her beloved garden. She'd have turned in her plot at Southern Cemetery if she'd seen the state of it now. Hailstone was sweeping through the cherry blossom, and takeaway cartons and crisp packets littered the lawn. Someone had thrown an old chair over her cuckoo flowers and the Sherlock Homes SOLD sign was impaled on the rosebush she'd tended with such care.

As I entered the gate, I narrowly missed treading on the corpse of a half-formed baby bird that had fallen from the cherry blossom. I stared down at it. A bulbous eye stared back. It was lying in a coffin of fuchsia petals, its pink jellied belly turned on one side. I took a tissue from my bag, scooped it up and as I was burying it by the rosebush I heard someone calling my name.

I turned to see Samira Kahn herding two shiny-faced grandchildren into the back of her Ford Galaxy on the other side of the street. Samira lived at Number 28. Her eldest son Adeel had recently bought Numbers 34 and 36, and coverted them into a huge six-bed detached. The result was an impressive facade with Grecian pillars, a huge wrought-iron gate and wide gravel driveway. Samira shut the car door, shot at it with her key remote and hurried over the road.

"Car*mel!*" she cried, placing the stress on the last

syllable of my name instead of the first as she always did.

I never corrected her. I thought it made me sound exotic.

She took my hands in hers and squeezed tight. "How are you, my dear?"

"Good." I pointed up at the house. "Just doing a final bit of sorting before we exchange."

"I hear a young Pakistani family are moving in?"

"That's right. From Bradford. Two kids. He's a teacher and she works for the BBC in Media City."

Her eyes widened. "*Ooh!* Maybe she can introduce me to the stars of *Corrie*."

"*Corrie*'s on ITV, Samira."

She winked. "I know. Anyway, I've gone off it since Deirdre died."

She glanced up and down the street and sighed. "Did you know we were the first Asian family in Brantingham Road, Carmel?"

"I didn't, no."

"March 1969 we arrived. It was only English and Irish then. Most of the neighbours ignored us. Many made nasty comments. But not your mother. Not Tess. She always said hello and stopped to chat. She knew that we were both strangers in this land. She sensed we had more in common than what was different."

I swallowed. "That's really nice to know, Samira."

I'd always been bemused by Tess's friendship with Samira and I often wondered what they talked about. Samira was a retired GP and Radio 4 listener with a season ticket at the Royal Exchange Theatre and Tess was an eccentric part-time cleaner who liked Irish showband music, knitting and gardening.

As if reading my thoughts, Samira said, "Your mother and I would sit and talk for hours. She used to tell me all about her life in Ireland before she came here and I used to tell her all about mine in Pakistan."

"Really?"

I was piqued, envious almost. Tess rarely spoke to us about her childhood. All Mikey and I knew was that her parents died before we were born and she had an older brother who'd moved to London. She said he was a good-for-nothing who'd ended up in a shelter in Kilburn. They were estranged and she clammed up whenever I asked about him. Whenever we went to Ireland on holiday we stayed with Dad's family. I don't ever remember visiting the village where she was raised.

Samira sighed. "Your mother made me laugh but she also made me cry." She paused then searched my face. "So cruel to have her son taken from her like that."

I stared down at the weeds that were coming up through the paving stones, my lips trembling. I knew the tears would come if she said his name. Mikey was everywhere: kicking a football against the side wall, blaring the Stone Roses from his bedroom window and painting "I LOVE PARIS ANGELS", his favourite band, in huge blue letters on the porch wall for the entire world to see.

I quickly changed the subject and waved at the yellow "Vote Labour Vote Kahn" signs in every second garden. "Adeel is doing well. I saw him on BBC North the other week. You must be really proud of him."

She rolled her eyes and folded her arms across her bosom. "Oh yes. He's a hotshot politician but who does he leave his kids with all the time? Naniji. I ask you, Carmel. Where is my bloody life?"

20

Adeel Kahn was a couple of years older than me. As a boy he was small and scrawny with National Health glasses bigger than his face and masses of determination. At eleven he won a scholarship to Manchester Grammar, one of the city's top fee-paying schools, and then he went to Oxford. After graduating he returned to Manchester, set up his own business then got involved in local politics. The NHS glasses had long gone, he'd beefed up and recently won a narrow victory to become Labour MP for Withington.

We both jumped at the blare of a car horn. His youngest was leaping up and down in the front seat of the Galaxy.

Samira waved a fist and shrieked something in Punjabi. "Better go. I'm off to Pakistan tonight for six weeks and I've still got so much packing to do." She put her arms around me and hugged me hard. "Don't be a stranger, Carmel. Come visit."

I watched her hurry across the road, a silver sari drifting like a cloud under her navy M&S blazer. Then, with a heavy heart, I turned and walked up the path to the front door.

Chapter 4

I stepped into the hallway and picked up the post from the mat. I listened for her voice. It was like trying to remember a song when I only had the first few notes. When nothing came, the tragedy of it hit me. My mother's voice was gone from me forever.

I opened the venetian blinds in the downstairs rooms. Strips of light flooded through the slats and dust motes danced on the shabby pieces of furniture: a cheap plywood coffee table, a saggy floral sofa, a scratched dining set dating back to the seventies. Imprints of her lingered everywhere – a yellowing smoke cloud on the ceiling above her armchair, a crescent-shaped coffee stain on the kitchen worktop, a cushion with an impression of her tiny backside. Cold seeped through the walls as I walked around emptying drawers and filling binbags with the leftovers of her life: half-empty pill packets, old cigarette boxes and the unused nail-varnish bottles and lipsticks she used to pilfer from Boots Chemists. In the kitchen I found an entire drawer of *Ireland's Own* magazines and at the back of another a bunch of articles from the Irish newspapers. She had a wicked habit of tearing them out of the copies in the reading room in Chorlton Library. She'd been told off a number of times and banned twice but they always let her back in.

I pulled a pile of her knitting from under the sofa cushions. As it unravelled in my hands, I could see her in front of me in the armchair as clear as day. A manic episode could keep her up all night knitting. Sometimes it was jumpers for Mikey and me but often it was baby clothes, cardigans or jumpers with matching booties in pastel colours. I'd find a pile stacked neatly on the armchair the next morning. She'd take them to the New Mothers group in the Methodist Church Hall and hand them out.

Margaret, the kindly lady with large hands who ran the group, took me by the elbow at the funeral. "Your mother was a lovely kind woman," she said. "The new mothers loved her baby clothes. Nobody knits like that anymore. We used to call her 'The Baby Lady'. She loved to hold the new-borns and sing to them. It made her very happy."

There were baking all-nighters, too. A mountain of soda bread would appear on the kitchen table the next morning and I'd have to clean up the surrounding snowstorm before going to school.

Upstairs, I paused on the landing outside her bedroom. I'd found her lying at the foot of the bed the previous November on a morning of near-tropical rain. I'd rung and rung but she wasn't answering the phone. I knew something was wrong. She rarely left the house since Mikey's death six months before.

I entered, tightening the grip on my binbag. Most of her clothes and belongings had gone to the Heart Foundation shop so there was very little left in the room: a scattering of cheap pearls from a broken necklace, an empty bottle of Yardley's Lavender perfume and a gnarled Maeve Binchy novel. I picked up the bottle, closed my eyes and sprayed, longing for her smell one last time. But it was empty. First her voice and now her smell had gone from me.

Under the bed I found an old picture that used to hang on the far wall. It was a still from her favourite film, *The Quiet Man* starring John Wayne and Maureen O'Hara. In the top right-hand corner, the glass was cracked. As I stared down at it, guilt grabbed me by the shoulders, forced me to sit down on the bed and remember.

"I hate you. You are not my mother."

She was sitting on the stool in front of the dressing-table mirror, frenetically brushing out her blonde locks. The table was piled high with jars of Nivea and perfumes and lipsticks, heated rollers and hairnets. Philomena Begley was singing "Blanket on the Ground" on the cassette player on the bedside table and Mikey had fallen asleep in his clothes on Dad's side of the bed. It had been a hell of a day.

"None of my friends will ever speak to me again after what you did!" I hissed, stepping towards her. My ten-year-old hand grabbed the hairbrush and managed to wrestle it from her. I hurled it against the wall. It struck the picture which fell inches from Mikey's face. The murderous look on her

face was enough to propel me downstairs and out of the front door into the evening drizzle. I knew I'd be in for a belting later but a thousand lashes would never compare to the humiliation I knew I'd suffer at school the next day.

I'd noticed the signs the previous evening: the agitation, the talking and smoking at twice her normal speed. She'd circled a date on the kitchen calendar in red pen and kept doing it again and again. Dad had only been gone six months and I assumed it was something to do with him, maybe an anniversary of some kind. I plucked up the courage to ask and her face crumpled. She burst into tears, pushed me to one side and left the room. Later that evening I found her in the back yard on her hands and knees surrounded by suds and a bucket. She was scrubbing at the concrete with a wire brush, mumbling to herself.

I lay awake that night, worry gnawing at my insides. I knew something bad was about to happen. My world had changed since Dad died. It was full of danger and unpredictability now that he was no longer there. There was no one to shield me and Mikey from Tess's episodes and mood swings. But at least the next day was Sunday and I wouldn't have to get my brother to school when it all kicked off.

I woke late to the sound of the front door slamming. Out of my bedroom window I could see her sweeping down the street, dragging Mikey behind her. He was in his Sunday suit complete with dickie bow and waistcoat, his unruly mop plastered to his head. She was wearing a royal-blue skirt suit that hugged her slender figure, with yellow heels and a matching Monaco-style headscarf that trailed in the breeze. She looked like something out of *Vogue* and she lit up the dank Manchester street. An elderly couple walking their dog stopped and stared as she wafted past like a whiff of expensive perfume. Even though I knew she was up to no good, I was bursting with pride for my beautiful mother.

At about midday I returned from the shop to find a police car parked outside the house. Impulse told me to turn and run but I put the key in the lock. Holding my breath, I entered the living room.

Mikey was playing with his Evel Knievel toys in front of the fire and Tess was sitting on the sofa next to a roly-poly policeman. Strands of her hair were unpinned and her lipstick was smudged. The policeman looked like the TV detective Frank Cannon. He had a receding hairline, a hedge moustache and was scribbling something in his notebook. When I walked in, Tess inched away from him.

He put down his pencil and stared, a pink tongue resting on his lower lip.

He struggled to his feet. "What have we here, then? Another looker, just like her mam."

Still staring at me, he put his notebook in his jacket pocket and fastened the silver buttons over his enormous belly that protruded like an extra limb. He moved towards me and slowly lifted his hand to stroke my cheek. Tess leapt to her feet and I ran to her. She grabbed Mikey and I could feel the gallop of her heartbeat as she pressed us both to her chest. Frank walked slowly towards us then stopped. Raising a log-like arm, he sent everything flying off the mantelpiece: the Croagh Patrick snow globe, the clay ashtray I'd made in pottery class and the framed photo of Dad that the three of us kissed every night before bed.

"*Murdering Paddy bastards!*" he said, picking up his helmet and waddling out of the door.

I was too scared to ask Tess what she'd done or who she'd killed. But I found out soon enough when Eileen O'Dowd arrived on our doorstep that evening. Eileen was a popular girl in my class and one of the few other Irish girls at Oakwood High. Most went to the nearby convent school. Eileen's Omagh-born mother had recently done the unthinkable and left her alcoholic good for-nothing Irish Catholic husband for an English atheist called Jethro whose baby she was carrying. Eileen had been telling us for weeks about her baby brother Carl's upcoming naming ceremony at the Railway Club. She'd been boring us senseless about the buffet, her new outfit and how her mum and Jethro were going to duet to a Cat Stevens song. She explained that the ceremony was a non-religious event on account of Jethroe not believing in God and her mum turning into a hippy.

That night she stood in the lashing rain on our doorstep with a face of thunder and her arms folded across her chest. I took in the soaking wet rims at the bottom of her new pink jumpsuit, the glittery eyelashes and the strawberry-blonde hair that the rain had flattened against her face.

"I've come round to tell you I can't be friends with you anymore, Carmel Lynch, cos of what your mam did today," she said.

I swallowed. "OK, Eileen." My legs weakened and I tried to close the door but she put a wedged heel in the way.

"You have no idea, have you?"

I shook my head.

She glared at me. "Well, I'll tell you, will I? Your nutcase of a mother ruined our Carl's special day good and proper. She turned up at his naming ceremony at the club with your brat of a brother and shouted all the way during

27

it. She called us all heathens, she said our Carl would spend his life in limbo and she called him the B word more than once." She wagged her finger. "And I don't mean *bloody* either. Uncle Tony had to get the police and they dragged her away kicking and screaming."

My chin fell on to my chest and I wanted the world to swallow me up. I tried to close the door again but Eileen was enjoying watching me squirm too much to move her foot.

"And I wouldn't mind but you lot don't even go to the Catholic school or to Mass. Who does your mam think she is? My mam says she should be locked up."

After a few more insults she turned on her heel and walked away.

"Bye-bye, Carmel!" She raised her hand in a wave. "Nice knowing you."

"*She's not well!*" I shouted weakly after her but my words were swallowed up in the battering rain.

I went back inside, went into the living room and turned off the TV. I'd been watching an extended news programme about the Brighton bombing and how they'd nearly killed Mrs Thatcher. But now all I could think about was tomorrow and school. I was going to have to leave. How could I ever face any of my friends again? I could hear Tess moving around in her bedroom. Something inside me snapped and that was when I headed upstairs in a fury. The Brighton bombing wasn't the only atrocity committed by an Irish person that day.

I stood up from the bed, put the *Quiet Man* picture into the binbag and looked around my mother's bedroom one last time. When Mikey and I were growing up Tess's mental-health issues were shrouded in mystery and shame. Friends and family spoke about her manic episodes in hushed tones, telling us she was "bad with her nerves'" or "a bit delicate". It was only later in my teens that I learned that the pill bottles piled up in the bathroom cabinet weren't to ease her arthritis as she claimed, but to contain her dark depression, mood swings and debilitating anxiety.

That morning, when I found her at the foot of the bed, rain was hammering on the windowpane like an impatient God wanting to enter. I didn't know then that she'd suffered a massive stroke. My first instinct was to look around the room for empty pill bottles. She'd tried to end her life more than once before. After a lifetime of mental torment and now that Mikey had gone, I'd have understood if she'd wanted to do it again.

As I knelt beside her and closed her eyes, the rain suddenly stopped. And in the silence that followed I told her I loved her and that she was finally at peace.

Chapter 5

As I was about to leave the house, I returned to the living room and stuck a Post-it note on the old radiogram, reminding the house clearance people to drop it off at my house. I ran my fingers along the dusty mahogany lid. I'd persuaded Tess not to get rid of it. I wanted to restore it. Joe and I had a selection of vinyl and we'd actually use it. But, more importantly, it was once Dad's pride and joy and the only thing I had left of his.

Like too many Irishmen in those times in Britain, he died in a tragic accident on a building site. On a day of torrential rain in Salford, he jumped down from his digger to inspect the edge of a deep trench where pipes were being laid. He then lost his footing on the treacherously slippery ground and slid into the pit. An avalanche of mud, copper piping and concrete followed. As the blood was draining from his body I was at Priory Road primary, colouring in a picture I'd drawn of the four of us. I was looking forward to showing it to him when he got in from work. In it we were on holiday in Ireland in front of my grandmother's house. It was the last one I'd ever draw of us all of together.

My memories of him were fading but now and again I'd get flashbacks. He'd be hunched over the radiogram listening to Radio Athlone in the evenings or to the Gaelic football after Mass on Sunday. Michael O'Hare's banshee-like football commentaries would be filling the room and Dad would be raising a fist in the air whenever his beloved Mayo team scored. The Irish showband and country-and-western records he stored in the radiogram were the soundtrack of my early childhood: Big Tom and the Mainliners, Frank Mcaffrey, the Miami Showband. Sometimes when he and Tess got in after a dance at the Irish Club, I'd creep out of bed, sit on the bottom of the stairs and listen to the shuffle of waltzing feet behind the closed door.

I glanced down at my watch. Five to one. I was meeting Joe at the Infirmary at two thirty for my scan appointment. I was starting to fret and imagine the worst outcomes. I grabbed the binbags and was about to head out the living-room door when a song that Dad used to play a lot came into my head. I started to whistle the tune to myself. "The Men Behind the Wire" was an old song about internment and the raids by British soldiers during the Troubles. He used to play it on a loop and always on low volume in case the neighbours heard. I knew all the words. He'd bounce me on his knee and laugh as we sang along together, and he made me solemnly promise never to sing it at school.

I always assumed Tess had given away all of Dad's old records when I bought her a CD player. But I hadn't actually checked inside the radiogram. So I turned back and opened the lid. By the side of the turntable there was a storage space and I was delighted to find a pile of about twenty forty-fives still there. I picked some up and sifted through them: Margo's "If I Could See the World Through the Eyes of a Child", Big Tom's "Old Love Letters" – "Take Me Home to Mayo" – the song we played at Dad's graveside, Tess's favourite "My Son" by Brendan Shine as well as a selection of Jim Reeves and Johnny Cash. As I went to pick some more up I saw a brown envelope sticking out of the bottom of the pile. I tugged at it. It was fat and torn. I put the records back, sat down in Tess's armchair and shook the contents on to my lap. Old bills, Mass cards and yellowing insurance policies fell out.

I found the letter inside an old birthday card.

Dad's handwriting was beautiful. His words fell across the page like sloping rain. Black ink had faded to lilac and the blue of the Basildon Bond paper was blanched but I could read everything clearly.

Whalley Range
Manchester
3rd September 1960

My dearest Tess,

I hope you are keeping as well as can be expected in the circumstances. I lie awake every night wondering how you are.

Kathleen Slevin is a great girl to get the letters in and out, isn't she? The ganger man on my new job in Salford is from

Bohola. He knows the Slevins and says they are a decent family. It comforts me to know you have an ally in there.

Do you remember Pádraig Flynn from the dances in Ballinrobe? Tall fella with a lazy eye? He's on the Salford job too. One of the men he lodges with told me he was asking questions about us. I may have to have a word in his ear. Sometimes it feels like there are too many Mayo people in this part of Manchester. It's like I never moved away at all. I'm starting to wonder if we might be better off in London or Birmingham.

Not much has happened here since I last wrote. It seems to rain even more than back home. Earlier today I was watching yer man in his yard across the way – a big old beast with a knotted handkerchief over his baldy head. He breeds pigeons in a cage and coos and talks to them like a lover. Can you imagine! And the English say we are odd! I've half a mind to go over and ask if he could train one of them to fly between here and Tuam with our letters. Then Kathleen Slevin wouldn't risk losing her job and I could wake on a cold morning with one of them outside my window, your sweet words attached to its foot. That'd make me an awful happy man.

Overtime is plenty at the moment, though I'm hammered in subs. Every penny is going into the tin for our new life together. I stay out of the pub except for the odd pint at the Irish Association Club in Chorlton of a Saturday. I can't wait to take you there. There's dancing every weekend.

I have an eye on a house for us not far from here. I took a walk over there on Saturday morning. It's in a decent area and you can walk to the shops in Chorlton. I met a fella from Dublin, O'Grady, when I was looking. He lives across the road and his wife is a Corkwoman and a nurse at the hospital.

Anyway, my love, I must leave you now. My new roommate is coming up the stairs. He's a Roscommon lad, nice enough but he snores like a prize pig.

Try not to be too afraid of what is to come. Your confinement will soon be over. Then we can start our new life together.

I think of you every minute of every day.

All my love

Seán

xxx

I looked at the date and frowned. September 1960. Tess told us she and Dad met on the boat from Dublin to Holyhead in 1962. I was sure of it. But, according to the letter, Dad was already settled here and he was waiting for her to join him. So, what was she doing in Tuam, a town in north County Galway miles from her birthplace in 1960? I read the letter again, this time slowly. When I'd finished I sat upright and inhaled sharply.

Your confinement will be over.

Confinement. The word rose up off the page and slapped me in the face. How could I have missed it? *Confinement.* Meaning imprisonment, detention or detainment. But also a euphemism for pregnancy.

I grabbed the arm of the chair. "*Jesus.*"

A car horn beeped outside and I glanced out of the window. A crow was skimming through the cherry blossom, a slither of black slicing through the pink.

I searched frantically for more letters, opening every envelope and scrutinising every bit of paper but I found nothing.

My phone buzzed. It was Joe.

Where are you?

I looked at my watch. *Christ.* I only had half an hour to get into town, park and get to my appointment. I'd been so engrossed I'd lost track of time. I texted back immediately.

34

On my way.

I stuffed everything back into the envelope and slipped it into my bag along with some of the old records. Dazed, I gathered the binbags, locked the front door behind me and threw the rubbish into the bins. I hurried to my car. As I was about to open the door I looked back at the house. The clouds opened and a momentary sliver of sun cast a long shadow over the roof. It looked different, the way the face of an old friend looks different if they do something unexpected or out of character.

That morning, I'd been hoping make peace with my troubled childhood. To move on and to find closure. But now everything had been flung wide open. Had Tess and Dad really had another child out of wedlock fourteen years before I was born? Had they really kept it secret from me and Mikey for all those years?

In my excitement I put my hand on my phone to ring my brother and tell him. Then I remembered.

My heart dropped with the speed of a falling lift. I couldn't share my news with Mikey. I couldn't tell him anything ever again.

Chapter 6

My brother entered the world with the same drama he left it. He ripped out of Tess onto the lime-green lino in our kitchen in Brantingham Road on St Patrick's Day 1980. I was six and Dad had just left for work. Tess was kneeling in front of me attaching a hedge of shamrock to my school jumper, my head already a flotilla of green, white and gold ribbons.

She held me at arm's length to admire her handiwork. "Now then," she said.

As she stood up she gave a low moan. Water was cascading between her legs. She grabbed hold of the table to steady herself and knocked the remaining shamrock onto the floor. My fell mouth open and I watched the precious plant that had come all the way from Mayo float in the pool at her feet like lilies on a pond. With no explanation I was ordered across the road to fetch Mary O'Grady from Number 42.

Rose was a staff nurse at Manchester Royal Infirmary. Everything about her was wide and bountiful, her hips, her smile, her generosity of spirit. Yet she was married to the most curmudgeonly man ever to leave Ireland. Thin, unsmiling and monosyllabic, Tommy O'Grady spent most of his time in the pub or the betting office while Mary slaved away at the hospital then reared their five children at home. She was a loyal friend to Tess, one of the few in the Irish community who didn't shun her when her mental-health problems took their toll. In the weeks after Dad died, when Tess's depressive episodes pinned her to her bed, Rose came round every morning to check that Mikey and I were fed, dressed and in school. She put food in the cupboard, checked we did our homework and during Tess's spells on the psychiatric ward she took us in. She and Tess were in and out of each other's houses for fifty years until her death from breast cancer in 2010.

By the time I got back from Number 42 with Rose, Tess was on all fours roaring and shouting.

Rose ran the *Souvenir of Knock* tea towel under the tap and dabbed her forehead.

"What a wonderful day for a child to come into the world," she said breezily. "If it's a boy, you'll have to call him Paddy."

"*Shut your fucking hole, Rose!*" Tess banged a fist on the lino. "*I'll do no such thing! I may as well put a ball and chain around his leg!*"

Rose laughed then I looked away in horror as she knelt down behind Tess and lifted up the back of her housecoat.

37

"Not long at all," she said with a worried expression.

Tess let out another roar that sent me scuttling into the hallway in terror. Rose yelled at me to go back over the road and tell Conor, her eldest, to take me to school.

Walking to school with Conor O'Grady was only slightly less terrifying than watching my mother give birth. Fifteen and sullen with a jet-black widow's peak, deep-set eyes and a collection of Motorhead T-shirts, Conor had a slanty way of looking at you that sent a shudder down my young spine. A decade later at his sister's eighteenth birthday party, he asked me for a dance. He was home on leave from the army. His head was shaven, making the widow's peak more scarily prominent, but he looked impressive in his uniform so I said yes. He told me he and his father weren't speaking at the time. Tommy, a fervent Republican whose grandfather had fought in the 1916 Easter Rising, was appalled at his son's decision to join the British Army. But, to be fair to Conor, Thatcher's Britain in the eighties was hardly bursting with career opportunities so it was probably a choice between the army or the dole. Anyway, Conor shuffled me round the dance floor at Chorlton Irish like he was shifting a wardrobe then plied me with Pernod and Black. Later on, we ended up outside in the ginnel by the car park where he yanked up my skirt, grabbed my knickers and stuck his fingers inside me, calling me all manner of filthy names. I bit and kicked and managed to get away. I was ashamed and blamed myself afterwards. I never told a soul apart from Karen. Conor was later posted to Belfast where he lost both legs in an IRA ambush. Tommy wept for days at the cruel irony of his son's fate and Conor ended up living back with his parents in Brantingham Road. I saw him now and again on his mobility scooter with a huge St George's flag flying off the back. He was morbidly obese with a long grey ZZ Top beard. Conor O'Grady was obviously not right in the head from very early on. But I never imagined he'd end up on the front page of the *Manchester Evening News* doing the terrible thing he did. I was just glad his lovely mother wasn't around to witness it.

Mikey was an enormous baby with hamster cheeks and white-blonde curls. He fed off Tess like a suckling pig. As the years went by, friends and family said his reckless nature was at the root of some of her mental-health issues. He sucked her dry and worsened her condition, they said. But I knew otherwise. Mikey was her reason for getting up every day. She loved him feverishly and shamelessly and he could do no wrong in her eyes. And yet I can't remember ever resenting their closeness. I adored my brother. It was impossible not to.

Mikey was a risktaker and a cheeky chappie with an irresistible smile. Throughout his childhood he leapt off roofs, fell out of trees, performed Evel Knievel stunts on his bike and did all kinds of risky stuff that landed him in the children's A&E at the Infirmary on a regular basis. The staff were constantly amazed that he avoided serious injury. Sporting injuries followed in his teens. He was good at all sports and a keen City fan. But it was on the rugby field he shone. With his ham-shank thighs and shoulders the width of a van, he dodged his opponents on the field with the same skill he dodged danger off it. He won a sporting scholarship to St Bede's, a Catholic fee-paying school in Whalley Range, while I languished in mediocrity at Oakwood High, the local comprehensive. Oakwood was a non-denominational school as was Priory Road, our primary. Tess avoided the local Catholic schools which was unusual for an Irish family at that time. But she made the exception for St Bede's as she knew Mikey desperately wanted to go there.

He flourished and, despite his working-class background, became the golden boy at the school due to his sporting talents and roguish charm. But, by the time he got to sixth form, Tess and I sensed he was moving away from us. Semi-pro by then, he'd started to frequent the posh wine bars of Altringham and Hale with his wealthy peers. He spoke a lot about his goals and ambitions at that time. He wanted to go to London University and study something sports-related. But his big dream for as long as I could remember was to put on the white jersey and play for England.

One filthy winter morning in 1998, the three of us were having breakfast in the kitchen at Brantingham Road. Tess was standing by the sink in a pink housecoat and curlers, a bunch of letters in one hand, cigarette in the other. Mikey was wolfing down Weetabix from a mixing bowl at the table, his long hair hanging down the sides of his handsome face like dog-ears. He rolled his eyes and tutted as I put the Pogues' "Thousands Are Sailing" on the CD player for the hundredth time.

I danced around the kitchen, toast in hand. "Pure genius," I said. Shane McGowan was a poet who spoke volumes to me about what it meant to be Irish in England. I adored him.

"Genius, my arse." Mikey lifted his spoon and a slither of milk missed his mouth, landing on his Oasis T-shirt.

Tess stubbed her cigarette out in the sink and handed Mikey a letter. "I think you've been waiting for this."

40

Snatching it from her hand, he ripped it open, read it then leapt to his feet.

"*Yes! Fucking yes!*" He lifted Tess into the air and twirled her round the room.

I took it from him. "Bloody hell, Mikey! You did it!"

I was awestruck. At barely eighteen he'd been chosen to play for the England Under-21's.

Tess was flushed and smiling when he put her back down. "Well done, son," she said, smoothing down her housecoat, "But wouldn't you ever try for the green jersey and play at Lansdown Road?"

The euphoria drained from Mikey's face. She could do that sometimes, slice into your happiness without really meaning to.

He shrugged. "Yeah, Mam. I'll play for Ireland. Of course I will."

"But why wouldn't you? Your blood, your history, everything that makes you run around that field is Irish."

We both stared at her, open-mouthed, taken aback by the authority and clarity with which she'd spoken. The moments like that when she stepped out from behind the mist of her illness were rare and precious and made me pine for the mother she could have been.

"Not me, Mam." He snatched his parka from the back of his chair. "I'm English. I'll play for England thank you very much. And anyway, I don't see you worshipping at the shrine of the old country much. You haven't been back for years."

After he'd gone Tess lit another cigarette and stared out of the window at the rain hammering on the shed roof. I went over and put my arm around her.

"Take no notice of him, Mam. I'll take you back to

41

Ireland if you want. We could visit your village. I don't remember ever going when we were kids."

I felt her stiffen then she patted my hand.

"You're a good girl, Carmel."

I caught up with Mikey on the street a few minutes later. Rain was still heaving down and gusts of wind pushed me along the pavement, leaves skittered underfoot.

"Hey, tosser!" I punched him on the arm. "What was all that about? You were vile to Tess back there."

He frowned and dug his hands into his pockets as I hurried to keep up with his long strides.

"You take her to Ireland then," he said. "You're always going on about what a great place it is."

"I would if I had any money. Anyway, she's got a point. You could play for Ireland. Look at the Irish football team. Half of them are second-generation Irish."

"What the *fuck*?"

He stopped and stared at me like I was an alien or, at the very least, a foreigner.

I put my hands on my hips. "Look, Mikey, I hate to break this to you but you're half Irish."

"I'm no Tony Cascarino. I'm English. I'm no Plastic Paddy."

"Don't say that."

"But I am. I was born here."

"I meant don't say 'Plastic Paddy'. You know I hate that expression. You sound just like Sheila McEvaddy."

Sheila was a cousin on Dad's side from Mayo who had stayed with us for a few months. Fresh out of Trinity College Dublin, she had a trainee solicitor's job in town, wore Chanel perfume, Calvin Klein jeans and had notions. She spent most of her stay with us perched on the edge of the couch, looking like there was a bad smell in the room.

One night after much beer at a ceilidh in Chorlton Irish Club, she announced, "I don't think I've ever seen so many Plastic Paddies in one place in my entire life."

My jaw dropped and I folded my arms across my chest. I was gobsmacked she would say such a thing. "And what's that supposed to mean?"

She looked taken aback. "Well. People pretending to be Irish when they're not."

"You mean second-generation Irish celebrating their culture? Excuse me, Sheila. The parents of a lot of people in this room may have left Ireland but it doesn't mean their children can't identify as Irish if they want to."

"I suppose so." She shifted uncomfortably in her seat, looked at the ground and shortly afterwards made a quick exit to the bathroom.

I'd read somewhere that it wasn't the English who coined the term "Plastic Paddy". It was the middle-class Irish, the brain-drain like Sheila who came over in the eighties. Apparently, they did it to distance themselves from the working-class wave of emigrants like Tess and Dad who settled in the fifties and sixties. Of course, English people used the phrase to slag anyone who felt anything other than English. But in both cases the message was the same: "If you're second generation you can't be Irish so you must be English." And that is a sentiment I never really understood.

Following years of identity confusion, I settled on an in-between place. It was like balancing on a seesaw. I could tip either way and dip into both cultures. I championed the Manchester rave scene of the late eighties but felt the pain in every Christie Moore song. I went to the St Patrick's Day parade in town every year but got more excited about Guy Fawkes Night. I read more Irish writers than English but did my degree dissertation on Shakespeare. As the child of immigrants, I felt lucky. The in-between place I inhabited was rich and varied. I had choices. I could embrace one, both, or neither of the cultures in which I was raised.

"OK – the last thing I want is to sound like Sheila McEvaddy!" Mikey said with a laugh, his handsome face buried in the fur rim of his parka.

My brother had chosen to identify as English. And it would have made no difference to Tess if he'd chosen to identify with a sect in Outer Mongolia. She would have idolised him just the same.

We turned round at the sound of shouting. Tommy Carroll, Mikey's old friend from Priory Road Primary, squealed to a halt on his bike a few yards ahead of us. Mikey ran over and deftly manoeuvred his bulk up onto the handlebars. Shaking my head, I watched them zigzag down the road for a hundred yards or so. Then a white Ford Escort appeared out of nowhere doing at least forty. It was heading straight for them and I covered my face with my hands and bit my lip. A horn blared and tyres screeched.

A few seconds later I peeped through my fingers to see the pair of them disappearing around the corner into Egerton Road, hollering and laughing.

"*You stupid English bastard, Mikey Lynch!*" I yelled, my heart swelling with love.

But the luck of the English that had followed my brother since he was a boy was soon about to run out.

Chapter 7

Fierce winds weaved themselves around the city and rain needled the windscreen. I was late. If I didn't make it to the appointment it would be weeks, possibly months before I got another. A traffic diversion in Whalley Range added to my woes and I took the long route via Fallowfield and Rusholme. I put Classic FM on the radio for some relaxing tunes but instead got a news report about migrants in the Calais jungle breaking through security fences and heading for the Channel Tunnel. David Cameron was saying that all economic migrants posing as asylum seekers would be caught and detained and sent back. When had Britain suddenly become so unkind towards immigrants? I thought about Tess and Dad setting off for the boat to Holyhead. We were a far more welcoming place back then.

I pictured Dad writing the letter after a long shift on the building site, his damp work clothes spread out like a scarecrow in front of a coal fire in the room he shared with the Roscommon boy. He was barely twenty. He'd not long been transplanted from the rural landscape of Mayo with its craggy mountainous backdrop and lush green fields to a strange and grey industrial city. Though surrounded by his own in Manchester, he must have felt pain and longing after leaving his friends and family and landscape behind. Or maybe not. Maybe all he felt was excitement at the new life he was about to encounter and a sense of freedom. I wished he was around to ask. I could sense his love for Tess in every line of the letter and his hopes and dreams for their future together. It was a love that never waned, even at the most difficult times when she wasn't well. He was her rock and her stability and his untimely death swept the ground from beneath her feet. Her already fragile mental health deteriorated quickly after he died and the shock of the blow left us all floundering. I tried to recall the details in the letter and form some kind of timeline and narrative about what happened.

Tess would have been barely sixteen in September 1960. At a guess she was about seven months pregnant and detained in some kind of Mother and Baby home or maybe one of the notorious Magdalene Laundries, in a town called Tuam. I shuddered. I knew that Catholic Ireland of that era wasn't kind to girls and women who fell pregnant outside marriage. I'd seen documentaries and read about the laundries and the Mother and Baby homes run by nuns. Women and young girls were hidden away and forced to give their babies up for adoption. Viewed as sinners and a stain on society, they endured prison-like regimes and were used as slave labour during their pregnancies and beyond, doing unpaid laundry, needlework and lacemaking for up to twelve hours a day. Punishments I read about included shaven heads, bread-and-water diets and beatings.

Some of the homes weren't just for unmarried mothers either. Women and girls who'd committed petty crimes or girls whose families had too many mouths to feed often ended up there. I remember Eileen O'Dowd from school once telling me her nan had been locked up for two years in a home in Dublin for stealing a chocolate bar from the local shop when she was ten. The women inside often had very little contact with the outside world, which would account for Tess and Dad's letters being smuggled in and out.

I shook my head. Had Tess really been in a place like that? Poor, damaged Tess. Had she and Dad really given up their firstborn for adoption? But they were loving, devoted parents to me and Mikey. They were starting a new life in Manchester and leaving Catholic Ireland behind. Why put Tess through the anguish of having the baby in the home then giving it up to the nuns? Why not run away and keep the child? It didn't add up. Or perhaps their baby simply hadn't made it.

The signs were scattered throughout my childhood. Things were starting to come back to me. All those nights Tess sat up knitting baby clothes. Was she knitting for the baby she had given up for adoption? Was she making it warm clothes because she felt she'd left it out in the cold? The way she always kept us at arm's length from the Catholic Church. There were no pictures of the Sacred Heart or the Virgin over our fireplace. With the exception

47

of Mikey and St Bede's, we never attended the local
Catholic schools like all the other Irish families. We never
went to Mass either. I thought back to the day of the
O'Dowd baby's naming ceremony. Thirty years on, it was
etched in my memory like a scar. Tess went there to plead
with Eileen's parents to baptise the baby. She was obsessed
with the fact he was a "bastard". In her poor splintered
mind was it because she'd given birth to a "bastard" child
herself? There was no knowing the damage that her
experience in one of those homes could have done to her
mental health. Then there was her intense, almost obsessive
love for Mikey. Was her firstborn a boy and she saw Mikey
as a replacement? It would explain so much.

I suddenly gripped the steering wheel as I remembered
what Samira Khan had said that morning. "*So cruel to have
her son taken from her like that.*" She'd given me an intense,
searching look when she'd said it. I'd thought she was
talking about Mikey but now instinct told me she was
referring to the baby Tess gave away. I desperately needed to
talk to Samira but she'd left for Pakistan and wouldn't be
back for weeks. Tess's face came to me as it so often did: the
creamy skin, the careful hair, the Mona Lisa smile. She'd
always had an air of mystery about her, like she was holding
something back. I'd attributed her secrecy to her troubled
mind but now it was all starting to make sense.

I arrived at the cardiology department fifteen minutes
late and feeling flustered. After registering at the reception,
I hurried along the long corridor to the waiting room.
The sky outside the large windows was slate-grey but
everything else in the room was a shade of NHS blue: the
turquoise walls, the royal-blue chairs, the powder-blue
table. I needn't have worried about being late. There was

only one other patient waiting. Joe was sitting by the water cooler engrossed in a copy of the *Guardian*. He'd taken the afternoon off work and cycled over from his office at Manchester Science Park to be with me.

I sat down next to him, my chair creaking in the silence. "Sorry. The traffic was horrendous."

He looked over the top of his paper then carried on reading. My stomach was churning at the thought of the scan and what it might reveal. I rubbed my sweaty palms down the leg of my jeans and sighed audibly.

Joe put a hand on my knee. "It'll be fine," he said.

He took off his reading glasses, folded his paper and slipped them both into his man bag on the floor next to his cycling helmet. He looked good. His face was tanned from long cycle rides in the recent spell of good weather, intensifying the blue of his eyes. His salt-and-pepper hair was newly cropped and lightened by the sun. A snappy dresser, he was wearing the Pretty Green khaki jacket I'd bought him for Christmas with jeans and red Adidas trainers. Though craggier now, his round face still had the boyish look I'd fallen in love with when I was twenty-one. He'd aged well. If it wasn't for his grey hair, he could have passed for thirty.

I glanced up at the clock. My mouth felt dry so I got up and poured myself a cup of water from the cooler. I'd had echocardiograms before but they never got any easier. I always asked Joe to come with me. Calm and pragmatic, he quashed my irrational "what if's" with science and stats. We had our ups and downs like any other couple, but at times like this when I was at my most anxious he was like a large oak that I ran to for shelter.

On the drive to the hospital, I'd made the decision not

to tell him about the letter just yet. He'd only tell me to leave well alone and not get involved. Don't get yourself worked up, he'd say. You're still grieving for Tess and Mikey, you don't need any more emotional turmoil. But what he'd really mean was that *he* didn't need any more emotional turmoil. And I couldn't blame him for thinking that way. Life with Mikey and Tess had been one long episode of *Jeremy Kyle*, especially during Mikey's addiction years. Joe had put up with so much drama and now all he probably wanted was a bit of peace. Another reason I didn't want to tell him was because I felt strangely protective of Tess's secret. She was about to be exposed and I needed to find out all the facts before I was prepared to do that. Part of me felt hurt that she'd told Samira Kahn and not Mikey or me. I could understand why. The guilt and shame back then must have been overwhelming and it's often easier to talk to strangers about your darkest secrets than loved ones. But I couldn't help feeling sad and betrayed that she'd never confided in me. She and I had become closer in her later years. Or so I'd thought.

Apart from the shuffle of nurses' shoes along the corridor now and again, the cardiology department was very quiet. The other patient was engrossed in his phone. He was sitting under a poster of a smiling heart holding up a plate of fruit and vegetables. He looked like he hadn't seen an apple or a carrot in a while though. Rolls of fat hung over the sides of his chair like the drop of a tablecloth and his beautiful grey-blue eyes were hidden in folds of flesh and his ballooning cheeks. His breathing was heavy, his body odour pungent. I feared for him and I wanted to warn him. Stop killing yourself, I wanted to say. Your heart is far too precious.

Familial Hypertrophic Cardiomyopathy. I half expected to see the words illuminated on the neon sign opposite, the way they were illuminated in my mind after the coroner's report into Mikey's death. HCM, as it is commonly known, was the heart condition that had killed my brother. HCM this, HCM that. In the weeks and months after his death I became so obsessed with the details, I almost forgot to grieve for him.

"It's genetic," I explained to friends and family when they asked. "Some carriers have no symptoms at all and it never surfaces and other people have mild symptoms. But at its worst it can suddenly cause the heart muscles to thicken to the point where it stops the flow of blood from the heart. And that's what happened to Mikey."

HCM was an autosomal dominant condition which meant children of a carrier had a fifty-per-cent chance of having the gene. I had no symptoms and it looked like I was OK but any children I had would have a 50/50 chance of getting it. Tess was distraught to discover she had passed it on. Her symptoms went unnoticed. For years she had palpitations and breathlessness which we put it down to her twenty-a-day Silk Cut habit and the medication she was taking. She had a fear of going to the doctor's, probably the result of the harsh way she had been treated for her mental-health issues. I was overwhelmed with guilt when we found out she was a sufferer. If she'd been checked out, they might have discovered she had the gene and Mikey could still be alive.

His body stayed with the coroner for three weeks before we brought him home. Though he'd have hated it, Tess insisted on a traditional Irish wake. She sat and slept next to his open coffin for twenty-four hours. After the funeral she slept in his old room, rarely venturing out, eating very little and wandering around the house talking to him. She kept saying it was her fault, that God was punishing her, that she should never have had children. In her mind she'd killed the thing she loved most in the world and there was no persuading her otherwise.

"I hate these ultrasounds," I said. "All that prodding and they keep you in for ages."

Joe turned his face to the window and stared out at the leaves skittering across the courtyard in the wind. I'd been thinking about that other waiting room and that other scan and I wondered if he had too. It seemed like a lifetime ago now. I got pregnant a year into our relationship. I didn't know until I was almost three months gone and I was surprised and disconcerted when Joe said we should keep it. I started bleeding a few days later and he cried in the hospital corridor after the scan showed no heartbeat. I stood next to him awkwardly, not quite knowing what to do. I was relieved. I was twenty-two and I didn't even know if I wanted kids. At thirty-nine I was even more unsure, especially after what had happened to Mikey. Any child of ours could inherit HCM.

A door swung open and a stout nurse appeared with a clipboard. Squinting behind John Lennon glasses, she called out the other patient's name. I watched him shuffle down the corridor. He might be OK. After all, Mikey's heart had held up throughout the addiction years. But then, when he'd finally got rid of his demons, HCM came along and mowed him down.

Five minutes later I lay in the examination room, a young sonographer rubbing gel on my chest. As she pushed the probe down and moved it around, my heart pulsated inside a black-and-white triangle on the screen like a dancer on stage in a spotlight. Its beat echoed around the room. I thought about that tiny heart beating inside Tess more than fifty years ago. Could it really be true? Had she and Dad really handed their baby over to strangers?

"Try and relax." The sonographer frowned and probed some more.

I shifted around on the bed. "Everything OK?" It all seemed to be taking much longer than usual.

"Keep still and take deep breaths."

She had an Eastern European accent and drawn-on eyebrows that gave her a permanent look of surprise. Not a great look for a sonographer.

After a few more minutes she took the probe away, handed me a paper towel to clean myself and told me to get dressed.

"Everything looks fine. Full results in post in couple of weeks."

My dancing heart did a backflip. I was well. I was healthy. Tension and relief drained from me into a pool on the floor. I hopped off the examination table, wiped myself down and hummed to myself as I got dressed. But then, as I made my way back to the waiting room, guilt crept up behind me and threw itself over me like a dark cloak. My mood went from elation to deep sadness. I'd survived but Mikey hadn't. The odds were 50/50 and he'd drawn the short straw in the gene pool.

In the waiting room Joe picked up his bag and cycling helmet and looked at me expectantly. "Everything OK?" he asked.

I nodded and we walked along the corridor in silence. I was healthy, I told myself. I had every reason to be happy and Mikey and Tess would have been looking down on me and smiling. Yet the darkness pressed down on me like a boulder.

Joe took my hand. "Let's eat out later to celebrate the good news."

I pulled it away. "Mikey's dead. He got the bad genes and I didn't. What the fuck is there to celebrate?"

Chapter 8

Mikey's debut for England took place on a sweltering hot Saturday on June 6th 1999. It was a day I'll never forget. For all the wrong reasons.

The match was at Twickenham against France. Afterwards he'd arranged to spend the night in High Wycombe at the family home of his school pal, Julian Hammond. Julian was a boarder at St Bede's. Gawky and foppish, he was a little in love with Mikey. His barrister parents were away for the weekend at the family's second home in France and Julian's older brother Toby was in charge of the boys that night. Toby was a rugby fanatic who was keen to be seen in the company of the country's most promising fly half.

Mikey rang after the match from the train on the way to High Wycombe. He was using Toby's mobile phone but it was hard to hear what he was saying because of the roaring and singing in the background. I could tell he was already drunk.

"*This phone is proper mint*," he yelled. "*I want one.*"

"What about the match? How did you get on?"

"*Man of the Match. I scored twice.*"

Pandemonium broke out in the background and the line went dead. I ran into the garden to tell Tess. She was on her knees doing some weeding. When I told her, she held her face up to the sun and a wide smile spread across her face.

Toby Hammond was a city trader. At twenty-four, he had a flat in Battersea, a Porsche Carrera and a six-figure salary, a lot of which he snorted up his nose.

After drinking vodka and champagne all afternoon, Toby gave Mikey his first taste of cocaine then took him for a drive around the dark Buckinghamshire lanes in the Porsche. Losing control on a bend on an unlit lane, he wrapped the car around a tree. Toby escaped with a few minor cuts and bruises, a month in rehab and a fine for drink-driving that barely touched his bank balance.

The cost to Mikey was immeasurable. Three broken ribs, concussion and severe ligament damage to his right leg. When he woke up in hospital the next day the doctor told him he'd probably never play professional rugby again.

In the months and years that followed, my brother changed beyond recognition. The happy-go-lucky escape artist I knew and loved was left behind by that tree in that Buckinghamshire lane. His rugby dreams snatched away, he became despondent and indifferent to life. He left St Bede's without sitting his exams and lost the place he'd secured at London University. Throughout his twenties he limped from job to job on building sites, drank heavily and then abused drugs during the noughties. He became a small-time dealer in the Manchester clubs, narrowly escaping custodial sentences on several occasions. His relationships with women were destructive and always had drink and drugs at their core. Whenever he was drunk or high, he'd tell people that the drag in his leg was the result of a bad tackle when he played rugby for England.

Julian Hammond followed his brother Toby into a career in the city. When Mikey died he sent a letter of condolence on headed paper with a Kensington address. Julian wrote effusively about Mikey being a loyal friend, a legendary sportsman and a superb drinking buddy.

I wrote "*Fuck you and fuck your brother*" in red ink over it then returned it to sender.

At the time of his death Mikey had finally overcome his demons. Things were on the way up. He'd been sober for three years and had a flourishing personal-trainer business. Innovative surgery had repaired his leg and rid him of his limp, he was playing rugby again locally and he and his beautiful partner Maria were trying for a baby. When I asked him to join me on the BUPA 10k, he jumped at the chance.

"Let's do it for MIND, the mental health charity," he said. "Let's do it for Tess."

On the day of the race, blustery winds and heavy rain swept over the Atlantic and Ireland and landed in Manchester town centre just before the start. It was like the winds had come to claim Mikey, to whip him up and steal him away. By afternoon they'd gone, leaving behind an eerily silent city and a hole in my heart.

We set off in the morning from Deansgate under a

charcoal sky. Rain stoned down on our exposed limbs and faces and gusts buffeted us into other runners. But we buoyed each other along the way. We passed a DJ stand playing "Things Can Only Get Better" and crowds cheered us on from the pavement. I grinned at Mikey who was running slightly ahead of me. The wind had blown his hair to one side and I noticed he had a bald spot. For the first time it occurred to me that my kid brother was getting old. As we approached the 5K mark at Old Trafford, I started to flag. We passed White City Retail Park and I lengthened my strides to keep up with him. Then, as we turned towards the stadium near the row of shops and takeaways, he spurted forwards into a gap between runners. Flinging both arms into the air he started to sing. "*We love you, City, we do – we love you, City, we do!*"

A few of us joined in and whooped. I raised my arms in the air. As I did so I looked upwards and gasped. Above the roof of one of the takeaways was a murmuration of starlings, rolling and unfurling like a grey ghost against the dark sky. The incredible sight took away what little breath I had left. I looked round for Mikey, pointing skywards and shouting excitedly. And that's when I saw him stagger and fall.

I elbowed my way through the current of runners to get to him. Some circumvented him with outstretched arms, others hurdled over him. A space had cleared by the time I got there and he was clutching his chest and writhing like a bad break-dancer among the discarded water bottles and litter. The sight of his bloodless face sent a slither of cold through my core. I crumpled to my knees, blocking out most of what happened next. Only fleeting images remain: the shoulders of the young doctor in a Christie's Hospital vest rising and falling as he attempted resuscitation, the blue lights of an ambulance dancing in a puddle and the long eyelashes of the paramedic when she lowered her eyes and told me he'd gone.

"*No!*" I pleaded and grabbed her arm. "*No. It's not true. He can't be dead. He's only thirty-four.*"

A foil blanket rolled by in the wind and wrapped itself around my feet like a silver shroud.

"What am I going to tell Tess?" I heard myself say then I felt a stone fall from my heart.

Chapter 9

I sank back into the sofa in the kitchen extension, laptop on my knees, waiting for the internet to download. I picked up my glass of Riesling and sipped. The wine hit the back of my throat, chilled and fruity. It had been one hell of a day.

Joe had gone out. After I said I didn't want to celebrate the scan results he got the hump and we exchanged words in the hospital car park. He said he was only trying to cheer me up and called me a doom-and-gloom merchant.

He yanked the lock off his bike and shook his head. "You used to be such a laugh."

"So did you." I clutched my car keys tight. "Until you became one of the dull-as-fuck Lycra lads."

He hopped on his bike and rode off in anger, narrowly

missing a bollard on his way out.

When I got in, he'd left a note saying he was going out for a drink with a crowd from the cycling club. The other day he'd mentioned that one of them had recently become a dad and they were planning a pub crawl to wet the baby's head.

Dusk was falling. Despite the squally weather earlier, there were signs of spring in the garden. I could just about make out the milky-white snowdrops by the apple tree and a bunch of flame-coloured tulips had appeared in the flower bed. I'd also spotted a swallow on the telegraph wire earlier and the daffodils Karen had helped me plant the previous year were in full bloom.

I hadn't heard from her since my visit that morning after the fundraiser. Though I was reluctant to tell Joe about Dad's letter, I was desperate to tell her. Not that long ago I'd have simply turned up on her doorstep waving the letter in the air like an excited child. She'd have pulled me through the door and we'd have examined every word for hours over glasses of wine. She'd never tell me to leave well alone like Joe would. But something held me back from sharing my news with her. Fear of her indifference, mainly. I was scared she would feign interest and I'd come away feeling I was wasting her time. It saddened me to think that after all our years of friendship things should come to this.

I clicked my nails impatiently on my wineglass. Despite Joe working in IT we had the world's slowest internet connection. I finished the last of my wine then headed to the fridge for more. Our gigantic American fridge that Joe had insisted on buying was half the size of the galley kitchen in our last house in Old Trafford. I closed the door of the fridge and surveyed the room. The glass-box kitchen extension, the sprawling Habitat corner sofa, granite worktop and underfloor heating. I constantly had to pinch myself. Did I, Carmel Doherty, who was raised with no central heating and a pay-as-you-go meter, really live here? In a three-storey town house with a loft conversion and wine cellar on one of the most desirable roads in Chorlton?

Our last house in Cranley Road in Old Trafford was a two-up two-down new build. It had damp, paper-thin walls and noisy Geordie bikers for neighbours. Alan and Shelley were large and hirsute with matching dragon tattoos. They were pleasant enough but they revved their Harley Davidsons at all hours and had lots of loud theatrical sex. Times were tough for me and Joe back then. He'd not long been made redundant from his IT job with a banking firm after the 2008 crash. Interest rates were rocketing so I had to teach evenings and days at three different colleges for a low hourly wage to pay the mortgage. Joe hated being at home and got very down about it all. But the one good thing about living in Old Trafford was Karen. She was a five-minute walk away and came round a lot. I got to spend time with my gorgeous goddaughter but not enough to make me want kids of my own. Karen's positivity was a ray of sunshine back then. I don't know what I'd have done without her. Then one June morning in 2009 when Joe got a phone call from his dad in London and everything changed.

For half a century Joe's parents, Peggy and Paddy, lived a quiet existence in an unremarkable street in Greenwich. Peggy was a retired midwife who busied herself making pottery in her shed and working with

South London Irish Community Care. Paddy was a large florid-faced and gently spoken man with a mischievous sense of humour and his own building firm. They visited us regularly and we visited them. I loved them dearly. They were simply a joy to be around.

It was a sunny June afternoon when Peggy got off the bus in Greenwich High Road after visiting her friend Marjorie in Lewisham hospital. As she stepped out into the road, she was hit by a speeding car driven by teenage joy riders. She died of serious head wounds the next day. A month later Paddy died of a massive cardiac arrest. Many attributed it to a broken heart, such was his devotion to Peggy. A few months later Joe and I scattered their ashes in Skibbereen in County Cork, where they used to go courting before they came to England. Joe sat on a nearby rock and wept for a long time, one of the few times in our marriage I'd ever seen him cry.

Peggy and Paddy bought their Edwardian terrace in 1972. Paddy built upwards and backwards, hoping to fill it with children. But they were blessed with just one. A year after they died, it sold for just over a million. Joe was hammered for inheritance tax but there was still enough left for us to leave Cranley Close and buy our dream home in Chorlton outright. I couldn't believe it was happening. I'd never had any money in my life. Shortly after we moved in, Joe got a job as project manager with a small IT firm based in the Science Park in town. It meant a lot of travelling but we couldn't complain. A year after that I was offered a permanent position at the university for three days a week. Overnight we'd gone from struggling to keep a roof over our heads to enjoying a very comfortable existence.

As I made my way back to the sofa I raised my glass to Paddy and Peggy, to their kind hearts and wonderful attitude to life. I still missed them and would have gladly given up the house and everything in it to see them walk through the door one more time.

I sat back down and picked up my laptop. Connection at last. Taking a deep breath, I googled the words **Mother and Baby Home** and **Tuam**, the name of the town in Galway where Tess was staying when Dad wrote the letter. The first result that came up was a Wikipedia page. I read the first few lines. There was indeed a home operating in the town in the early sixties. It was run by an order of nuns called the Bon Secours. I was about to click on the page but I was distracted by the second search result showing underneath. I sat upright.

It was a headline from an Irish broadsheet dated June 2014 that said:

Mass Grave of up to 800 Dead Babies Exposed in Mother and Baby Home County Galway

Chapter 10

I clicked on the article, my hand trembling slightly.

The building in Tuam operated as a home for unmarried mothers and their babies from 1921 until 1961. It was run by the Catholic Bon Secours order of nuns. Babies born there were adopted or fostered or stayed in the home until they came of age to be sent out to local industrial schools, themselves recently the centre of many abuse scandals. The mothers were made to stay on in the home to breastfeed and to work after the birth in order to pay for the services the nuns had provided. All the mothers lived separately from their babies.

In 1975 two boys playing in the grounds of the

home discovered a number of tiny skeletons in a concrete pit. The local community at the time said the find probably dated back to the times of the Great Famine and the area was sealed up. Later, a nearby family made a small grotto at the site and tended it as if it were a grave.

In 2012, a local historian looking into the history of the building came across the story of the boys and the bones. Suspicious, she started to research the number of deaths in the home. She traced the death records of almost eight hundred babies and toddlers who had died there during its sixty-year existence. The historian then looked for graves and burial records in the burial sites in the town and the surrounding areas but found only two official graves relating to children who died in the home. The questions now being asked are these: Where are the others? Are the children buried in a mass unmarked grave at the spot where the boys had been playing? If not, then where are they?

Other disturbing facts about the home have emerged. It seems the death rate was more than five times the national average and one in four of all children who lived there died before the age of five. Many died from malnutrition which was most odd as the local council were paying the nuns a considerable sum to house the children. Others died of infectious diseases such as TB and measles. Rumours have also been circulating for some time about children being adopted illegally in the US and the UK.

The spokesperson for the Bon Secours Order had

no comment to make and said that all death and burial records are currently held by the local health board in Galway.

★★★

I put the laptop to one side and sat perfectly still, trying to process what I'd just read. Had that actually happened? Had the nuns really done that? Discarded hundreds of babies' bodies in a mass grave without giving them a burial? I leant forward and pressed my hands over my stomach. I felt nauseous. It was almost like I'd witnessed the depraved acts myself. I sat like that for a while then I went back online and read another five articles in quick succession, all from the Irish press, all saying similar things.

"*Oh my God,*" I kept saying over and over. All other words seemed to lodge in my throat. Why hadn't I heard about any of this before? Admittedly, I didn't read the papers every single day but this was a major story that broke over a year ago. Why hadn't I read about it in the British press? I put my palms on my cheek. My neck and face were burning. I needed air. Wrapping myself in a throw from the sofa, I picked up my glass and headed into the garden.

The air was fresh, cleansed by the wind and rain of earlier and slightly chilly. I walked over to the small rockery under our bird table. Lifting one of the rocks I took out the small plastic bag I kept hidden there. Then I sat on the patio steps, pulled the throw tight around me and rolled myself a joint. Joe disapproved of me smoking. He probably thought I was killing the few remaining eggs left in my ovaries. He used to partake of the odd joint himself but gave up when he started his health kick. I didn't want to give up. I was too fond of the lull it gave me whenever I felt anxious, that lovely calm that fell over me and mollified my jittery thoughts and pounding heart.

I waited until Susie next door had finished smashing bottles into her wheelie bin then I lit up.

Veiny blue smoke snaked into the night sky. At the bottom of the garden, finger-like shadows from the apple tree fell across the lawn. There was a bald patch of grass near the flowerbeds where the previous owners had a trampoline, and the grass was taking ages to grow back. I wondered if grass ever grew over the unmarked grave in Tuam. Did the sun ever warm it? Did snowdrops or daffodils ever bloom there in the spring?

I churned over what I'd just read: one in four children dying before the age of five, many from malnutrition despite the state paying the nuns good money to keep them, women and girls working throughout their pregnancies and beyond, then forced to sign away any future contact with their child, rumours of illegal adoptions to the US and UK.

Then there were the survivors' stories. One woman recalled daily beatings by the nuns, the ache of hunger pangs and seeing the other children's extended bellies. A man remembered lines of urine-soaked mattresses propped against a dormitory wall. Another said that some of the children spoke to each other in their own made-up language, such was their isolation from the outside world. Then the final insult. After all that suffering in their short lives, the children were denied dignity in death and their bodies were cast in the ground like pieces of rotten fruit without even a headstone or a simple cross to mark their existence. I shook my head and exhaled. After the paedophile scandals and the Magdalene Laundries I thought nothing more could shock me about the Catholic Church. How wrong I was.

After I'd finished my joint, I went back inside and filled my wineglass once more. I took a photo of Tess from the bookshelf and lay down on the sofa with it. It was one of my favourites. Karen had had framed it in onyx and silver and given it to me on the day of the funeral. I held it up to the faint lamplight.

Tess was holding me shortly after I was born. Even though she was thirty at the time she looked about eighteen. She was a slip of a thing in a blue shift dress with a white collar. Her blonde hair was curled at the ends and pulled back in an Alice band and she looked more like a schoolgirl with her baby sister than a mother with her child. I looked closely at her face. I'd always thought she looked happy in the picture but now I saw that only her mouth was smiling. Her eyes were wide and scared, like a rabbit caught in headlights. She'd waited fourteen years after the birth of her firstborn to have me and then another six to have Mikey. I knew she'd had a spell in hospital after I was born and I now wondered if my arrival had triggered bad memories of her time in the Mother and Baby home. I still couldn't understand why she and dad didn't simply get married after the birth – surely the nuns would have allowed that? Instead, they put the baby up for adoption, started a new life and tried to forget all about it. But the memories returned to haunt her like a weed bursting through a cracked paving stone. And I strongly suspected that burying her secret made Tess mentally ill.

I'd once seen a TV programme about women who'd been forced to give their babies up for adoption in a Mother and Baby home. Every single one said they thought about their child every day of their lives. One called hers her "ghost child". It was now clear to me that Tess also had a ghost child – one who had haunted my childhood, who had been in the kitchen the day Mikey ripped out of her belly, in our bedrooms every night when she tucked us in and on the doorstep every morning when she waved us off to school – and was also hovering in the porch on the day the picture was taken.

I looked out of the window at the plate-moon hanging high in the sky and an image came to me. Another moon, the outline of mountains and two silhouettes on a hilltop in the dead of night. The caretaker from the home and a nun passing him a small bundle. I closed my eyes and swallowed. Is that what happened to Tess's baby? Was its tiny body, now a mass of bones, lying in the mass grave in Tuam with all those others? It was a possibility. Yet thousands of babies had passed through the Tuam home in the years it had been open. Statistically it was far more likely my sibling had been adopted.

My initial feelings of shock and disgust were turning to anger. Tess was sixteen when she went into the home. No more than a child. I had no doubt she suffered terribly at the hands of the nuns. How could any of those women and girls escape a hell hole like that without mental scars? Her mental health issues had to be related to the time she spent in that home. I was sure of it.

I looked at the picture again, kissed her face and whispered, "I'm going to find your baby, Tess, I promise you."

I held it tightly to my chest. I was determined to find out what had happened to my sibling and to Tess. Someone was going to pay for what they'd done to my mother.

Chapter 11

"Why the hell didn't you wake me?"

Startled, I looked up from my laptop. Joe was standing in the kitchen doorway pulling on his high-viz jacket. He looked dishevelled, unshaven and cross.

"Sorry, I didn't notice the time. I've been up for ages but I've been engrossed in something."

I'd dozed off on the sofa in the kitchen, clutching Tess's photograph, the night before. Then not long afterwards I'd been woken by the sound of Joe clattering through the front door. He stumbled into the kitchen and headed straight for the sink. He had his back to me and didn't see me in the dim lamplight. I lay still without making a sound. I was stoned and drunk and didn't want another argument. For once though, Joe was in a worse state than me. He wasn't much of a drinker. He usually managed to stop after a couple and behave himself, unlike me. But it must have been a hell of a pub crawl that night. I watched, trying not to laugh, as he swayed and grabbed the edge of the worktop and tried to hold himself up. He started making ominous choking sounds like he was about to barf over the spice rack. He was all over the place and downed glass after glass of water. Then to my amazement he started to cry.

"*Shit!*" he said, slamming his palm hard on the worktop. "*Shit, shit, shit!*"

I was taken aback. He never cried.

Then, as if suddenly reminding himself that Joe Doherty simply didn't do that sort of thing, he straightened up like a soldier standing to attention, wiped his face with the back of his hand and staggered upstairs to bed.

I tightened the belt of my dressing gown. It was a bright morning. Corn-coloured sunshine flooded the room and birds chirped through an open window. I'd been up since six scouring the internet for information about the Tuam home.

I scrutinised Joe's face. His eyes were puffy and surrounded by dark shadows. He'd pretended to be asleep when I slipped into bed the night before.

"How was your evening?" I asked.

"Fine."

"You were wrecked when you came in. I was on the sofa in the extension but you didn't see me. You were hilarious."

He frowned and tugged at the zip of his jacket. "I may have had a few pints too many."

I laughed. "You could hardly stand up."

He leant back and folded his arms over his chest. "So

how was your evening getting stoned and drunk on your own again?"

His sharp tone felt like a slap across the face and I flinched.

"You stank when you came to bed. You do know the neighbours can smell it through the window when you smoke in the garden, don't you?"

"I may have had a joint and a few glasses of wine too many."

He shook his head and pointed at the empty bottle of Riesling by the recycling bin. "You had a *bottle* of wine and *fuck knows* how many joints too many."

"Yesterday was a hell of a day. I might tell you about it some time."

"Isn't *every* day a hell of day for you though, Carmel? Can you actually remember when you last had an evening without a drink or a spliff?"

I shifted in my chair, under attack. "No, but something tells me you can."

He narrowed his eyes. "You're not the only person in the world to lose loved ones, you know."

I stared down at the keyboard, willing him to leave. I wasn't in the mood for any of this. But he did have a point. My drinking and smoking were constant and, I feared, becoming medicinal.

"You coped much better with your grief than I did."

He snorted then bent down and tucked his trousers into his socks.

"Or at least you seemed to."

He straightened up. "How the hell would you know? You were always too pissed or stoned or wrapped up in yourself to ask."

My mouth opened but no words came out. What the hell was wrong with him? Yesterday at the hospital he was husband of the year but now he was acting like he hated me.

He picked his cycling helmet up from the worktop and as he turned to leave it hit me. This wasn't about my drinking and smoking at all.

I sat up. "They were all talking about babies last night, weren't they?"

He turned around slowly and nodded. "I was the only one there without kids. I want to be a dad, Carmel. You're forty in a few months. We don't have much time left."

I shut the laptop lid and sighed. "I'm scared, Joe. There are so many things that could go wrong. It's not like the gene pool on my side is great, is it? There's a very good chance any child of ours could inherit HMC."

He stepped towards me. "I've been reading up on it. They're developing new tests that can check if a foetus has it early on."

I shrugged and folded my arms. "OK. So imagine I got pregnant and I did one of those tests and it came back positive. Then we'd have to decide whether or not to have an abortion. How difficult would that be? HMC killed Mikey when he was thirty-four. Tess lived all her life with it. A child of ours might live to be eighty so how could we go ahead with an abortion?" I put my elbows on the table and rubbed at my temples. "And then there's Tess."

"What about Tess?"

I swallowed. "A child of ours could inherit what she had. Her mental instability."

He shook his head wearily. "Let's face it, Carmel. You just don't want kids."

"You had a happy normal childhood, Joe. That's why you're so sure you want kids. You had two healthy parents who were in a good marriage and you never had to worry about money. Tess did her best for me and Mikey but growing up was tough after Dad died. What I experienced as a child isn't something I want to replicate. And, unfortunately, we do replicate the past." I sighed. "I suppose what I'm trying to say is that I'm just not sure I'd make a good mother."

He came over, knelt beside me and took my hands in his. "You'd make a brilliant mother, I know you would."

I shook my head. "No, I wouldn't. I'd be anxious and overprotective and scared all the time. That's not good for any child."

I slipped my hands from his, placed them on his shoulders and looked directly into his eyes. "I have to be honest with you, Joe. I just don't know if I have it in me."

Chapter 12

I met Joe Doherty on a day cratered in the minds of most Mancunians. It was Saturday, the 16th of June, 1996. The day the IRA bombed our city.

The skies were cobalt blue and cloudless when Tess and I caught the early bus into town that morning. We were on a mission to find an outfit for her for a wedding. Rose O'Grady's eldest Sinéad was getting married the following Saturday at St John's Church in Chorlton, followed by a reception at Chorlton Irish. Tess, Mikey and I had all been invited.

That weekend the city had been infected by a serious case of football fever. The Euros were in full swing, England versus Scotland was being shown in the pubs that afternoon and Russia versus Germany was being played at Old Trafford the following day. The hangover of the football hooliganism of the eighties still lingered and when we got into town just after nine a large police presence hovered everywhere. Vans blocked side streets and officers in short sleeve shirts and helmets stood on corners, radios at the ready. A group of German fans got on the bus at Deansgate and a couple of England shirts at the back splayed their arms like wings and started to hum the *Dambusters* tune.

Tess shook her head. "Gobshites," she said and I laughed.

We got off at the Arndale bus station and headed across the road for Marks and Spencer's and the reduced rail. We soon found the perfect outfit, a fuchsia trouser suit and white satin blouse. With her slender figure and ash-blonde hair piled high, Tess received a lot of admiring glances in the changing room. She was in great form that day. She didn't get invited many places and she was excited about the wedding. I watched, enchanted, as she charmed the shop assistants, making them laugh. On days like that when the mist of her illness lifted, she filled the world with colour and light. It was a joy to see but at the same time it pained me because it gave a glimpse of how different life might have been if she was like that all the time.

We left the store via the Corporation Street exit at about ten. The streets were humming with shoppers taking advantage of the good weather. Father's Day gifts filled shop windows. I felt a yank on my heart. Eighteen years on, I still missed Dad desperately. When we stepped outside, Tess said she wanted to go to Kendals on Deansgate for some lipstick to match her outfit. So off we went. Neither of us remembered seeing the white van parked on the double yellow lines on the corner of Cannon Street. Or the flashing lights or the parking ticket slapped on the windscreen. It was only later that evening as we watched the news unfold on TV that we realised we'd walked right past the bomb itself.

We'd been in Kendals for about twenty minutes when a burly security guard with dreadlocks and a gold front tooth started telling everyone to evacuate. His face had an expression of mild annoyance, like someone had interrupted him when he was on his break. Tess had wandered off and I looked around, unable to see her anywhere. I walked up and down the aisles of the make-up department in the mist of perfume and women in white frocks, some of whom were also heading for the exit. I wasn't unduly worried but then I heard someone say something about a bomb being defused in the Arndale and I started to panic. I ran up and down shouting out Tess's name with the security guard at my heels yelling at me to leave. Eventually I found her at the front of the store by the revolving doors. She was chatting to a man of about my age in a khaki shirt and jeans.

I glared at her. "Thanks," I said. "She's mine."

Tess tutted and patted the stranger's arm. "She's terrible for wandering off, so she is."

I gritted my teeth and grabbed her elbow. The three of us squeezed into the revolving doors, the last to leave the store.

The man gave me a coy smile. "She was getting worried. My parents are Irish too. From Cork."

He had a soft London accent and he sounded a bit Marc Bolan. In the confined space I could smell apple-scented aftershave and mints. I looked closely at his reflection in the glass door. A round face with boyish features, all spaced pleasantly apart, startling blue eyes and a steady gaze. His face was slightly tattered, suggesting a lot of late nights, which I liked, and he had a sturdy frame. But he was at least two inches shorter than me. For a woman of five feet ten those inches mattered. I'd only ever dated one man shorter than me and it was uncomfortable, like wearing the wrong-sized shoes.

The three of us were spat out into sunshine and chaos. Policemen with sweat pouring down their faces were shouting and waving the crowds away from the Arndale. Cars and buses were turning round and retreating and a group of teenage girls in crop tops and shorts with Walkmans were linking arms and running down the middle of the road.

"I'm Joe Doherty, by the way," he said as we joined the flow of people.

I linked arms with Tess. "Carmel Lynch and this is Tess."

He walked alongside us on the edge of the pavement, his body turned slightly as if shielding us.

"I was never in Cork." Tess's voice was high-pitched and nervous. She gripped my arm, her eyes darting around.

Strangers exchanged worried looks, others fixed their eyes on the ground. We quickened our pace. I caught Joe Doherty looking at me. He smiled shyly and seemed nonplussed by what was going on around us. Behind him on the other side of the street I saw a young bride running down the pavement holding her wedding dress off the ground. Her groom and a young bridesmaid were running along either side of her.

I pointed and Joe Doherty turned and looked.

"Cold feet?" He smiled as a mounted policeman trotted past, waving and telling us to get a move on.

I opened my mouth to reply but the words never came out. An unearthly roar reared up behind us, the force of the blast raising the three of us off the ground. Joe and I stumbled forward and managed to steady ourselves but Tess flopped onto the pavement like a rag doll. In the seconds that followed the world was cloaked in silence, broken only by the sound of falling glass. Shop windows shattered everywhere and crystal rain came teeming down. A horse whinnied somewhere then the shrieking of sirens, car alarms and screams all followed.

I felt a ringing in my ears and I was shaking. Joe picked Tess up. A large shard had lodged itself in her forehead. She was shaking too, her breathing shallow and blood was streaming down her face. He carried her down the street and I ran alongside holding her hand. The police who were preparing for hooligans earlier were now everywhere, frantically leading us away from the blast. We later learned they'd been warned about a second bomb. I saw one officer was leaning over a pregnant woman looking like he was having a panic attack but trying to hide it. We stopped for breath after about a hundred yards or so. Joe and I turned round. A mushroom of white smoke covered the dazzling blue sky and bits of paper floated over the Manchester skyline like dying doves. We locked eyes and love raised its head from the ashes of destruction and hatred.

We continued along Deansgate and I witnessed small acts of kindness on every street corner: a homeless man cradling an old man's bleeding head in the doorway of the Sawyers Arms, two young England fans carrying a buggy with a baby in it for a struggling mother, a group of taxi drivers in turbans turning their black cabs into makeshift ambulances. Dust clogged the air and carrier bags of shopping and Father's Day gifts were abandoned everywhere. On the corner of John Dalton Street one of the taxi drivers spotted Tess and shouted out that he was going to the Infirmary. Dazed, the three of us got in. Two bloodied Russian fans sat opposite. One was moaning and holding his gashed leg under his knee with both hands.

"I was buying socks," said Joe, staring straight ahead, "I forgot to bring a spare pair. I was supposed to meet Jan and Stefan. They're over from the Dusseldorf office. We were going to watch the Scotland game together." He shook his head. "I've no idea where they are."

I realised he was in shock and put my hand on his. The young Russian let out another moan and Tess grabbed my arm. "What about Mikey?"

As the taxi pulled away, I saw a battalion of Marks and Spencer's staff, dust-covered middle-aged women in navy, marching down the road followed by a line of shoppers. Further on, I gasped at the sight of bodies scattered in the road, all slim females, one with her white dress ripped off.

"Mannequins," Joe said. "Blown out of shop windows."

At the Infirmary we were treated by a pretty young nurse from Mayo. Aiofe Kelly had alabaster skin and tar-coloured curls and as she took down a box of dressings from the medical cabinet, I could see she was crying. I went over and put my arm around her.

"Sorry." She wiped her eye with the back of her hand then nodded at the gap in the cubicle curtain where an older nurse was standing with a clipboard. "The charge nurse sent me over to your ma. 'She's one of yours,' she says to me. 'Your lot did this so you can treat her.'" Aiofe sniffed. "I've worked with that woman for ten years."

We knew immediately it was the IRA. In my university years I'd read up on all the Irish history I'd never been taught at school. I read about De Valera, Collins and Markievicz, names I'd never heard in any of my history lessons. For a while after I was angry about all the British atrocities heaped on the Irish in the past. I sang rebel songs in lock-ins in Levenshulme, learned the names of all the hunger strikers and developed a crush on Martin McGuinness that I kept to myself. My relationship with Irish nationalism had its ups and downs over the years but that day, as I watched the walking wounded flood into the hospital waiting room and wiped blood from my Irish mother's face, all I felt was rage.

Joe queued at the hospital phone box and called his parents and the Old Trafford hotel where his work colleagues were staying. They'd been on their way into town in a taxi when the driver was alerted about the bomb over the radio car and the taxi turned back. I asked him to ring the house to see if Mikey was there but there was no answer.

Joe accompanied us back to Brantingham Road in a taxi and the three of us watched the news unfold on TV. I stared in disbelief at the images of our city centre in tatters. Over two hundred injured but no fatalities due to the efficiency of the police evacuation. Tess chain-smoked in her armchair and every five minutes she asked where Mikey was. I had no idea. He was sixteen and probably hanging out with his friends or some girl. He'd said nothing that morning about going into town. She got more and more agitated and paced up and down in front of the gas fire, spots of blood seeping through her bandaged head.

She wrung her hands. "How can I ever open my mouth in the shops in Chorlton again?" she said. "I feel ashamed to be Irish."

I put my arms around her. "Don't be daft, Mam. Half of Manchester is Irish."

Deep down I felt ashamed too, though. And I was going to have to end it with Martin McGuinness.

Joe joined me in the kitchen where I was making a brew and some cheese-and-ham sandwiches. I was struggling with a jar of chutney. As he took it from me, our fingers touched, and a current passing through me.

He opened the jar effortlessly and handed it back. "Is Tess OK?" he asked.

I looked down and sliced open a packet of ham. "She gets bad with her nerves sometimes."

He asked no further questions and we buttered bread rolls together in silence, the sun warming our faces through the window.

Mikey sauntered through the front door just after six.

I ran into the hall. "Why didn't you ring? Tess has been going out of her mind with worry."

He was at that age when he thought of nobody but himself and I felt like slapping him.

When he walked into the living room Tess burst into tears and flung her arms around him.

He looked at her bandaged head. "What happened to you?" he asked.

When she finally let go of him, we told him about the

bomb. He said he'd been at his friend's house on the PlayStation all day and hadn't heard a thing. Shortly afterwards Tess went upstarts for a lie-down and the three of us sat in the kitchen drinking beer.

Mikey gulped his down and frowned at Joe. "Who are you?" he asked, as if he'd only just registered his presence.

Joe laughed. Those were the days when Mikey was a loveable cheeky teenager. He had yet to turn into the drug-and-drink-addled yob that would give us both so much grief and heartache in the years to come.

"So that's my messed-up family," I said to Joe when Mikey left us and went upstairs to his room.

He slugged back his beer and smiled. "I think they're great." He moved to the chair next to me, his face suddenly grave. "There's something I need to tell you, Carmel."

I swallowed. "Go on."

"Tess was shoplifting in Kendals. I saw her put three lipsticks in her bag." His face broke into a grin.

I threw my head back and laughed. "She'd better have got one for me!"

"Well, I was about to ask her to get me some socks but they started evacuating."

We laughed long and hard, the tension of the day loosening and falling off us like a suit of tight-fitting clothes. Then we locked eyes for a second time. I'd forgotten all about the missing inches. In my eyes Joe Doherty was ten feet tall.

He fiddled with the ring on his can of beer and asked me if I was seeing anyone.

I shook my head and as he leant in to kiss me a siren wailed in the distance.

Chapter 13

The following week I started my search for my sibling in earnest. I knew there'd be no point contacting the order of nuns who ran the home. The Bon Secours sisters were publicly denying all knowledge of a mass grave. They said that all documents from the home had been returned to Galway County Council after the home's closure. This came as no surprise. When the Magdalene Laundries and paedophile scandals surfaced, the Catholic Church pulled up its drawbridges and operated a similar vow of silence. I had to look elsewhere.

So I emailed TUSLA, the family agency in Ireland which held the birth, death and adoption certificates of all the former residents of the home. I sent on Tess and Dad's details and an approximate date of birth for my sibling.

After that I wrote to the local historian who was in possession of the death certificates of all the children who'd died in the home. Statistically, the chances of my sibling being among them were very slim but I needed to know. My gut instinct told me Tess's baby had been adopted. The thought that I had a brother or sister out there in the world, a doctor in Dublin, a labourer in London or a hairdresser in New York, sent a river of excitement coursing through my veins. Losing Dad, Mikey and Tess had left me feeling disconnected, like a great chasm had formed between me and my past. The idea that I might have another sibling, possibly the sister I'd never had, filled me with hope. My third plan of action was to track down Kathleen Slevin, the young maid in the home who'd smuggled out Tess and Dad's letters. Hopefully she was still alive. She be in her late seventies or early eighties by now if she was.

Like a detective in TV crime drama, my project consumed me. I was constantly thinking about possibilities and looking for my next lead. I found it hard to concentrate at work. I started leaving my phone on during lectures in case I got a call from Ireland. One time, when an Irish number came up on my screen I rushed out of the room in a fit of excitement. On my way I tripped over my bag, to the hilarity of my second-year students. I was disappointed to hear my Aunt Julia's voice on the other end of the line. It was the only time I'd been less than delighted to speak to her. Fortunately, Tallulah Phillips wasn't in the lecture hall at the time. She'd probably have told her mother about my fall and Bryonie might have asked her if I'd been drinking or made another comment about university lecturers and their inappropriate behaviour. Luckily though, I was getting no vibes from Tallulah to indicate that Bryonie had told her anything about what happened at the Irish club that night. It looked like I'd been overanxious and, as was often the case. I'd been fretting about nothing at all.

On Thursday night I took myself off to a spa hotel in Cheshire with some vouchers Joe had bought me for Christmas. We'd stayed at Crewe Hall for our tenth anniversary, a stunning listed building that dated back to the seventeenth century. We'd walked around the landscaped gardens hand in hand, taken a dip in the pool and dined well. We were penniless and living in Cranley Road then, so a night away was a real treat. I'd asked Karen to join me this time but she'd already committed to a leaving do in Chorlton for a friend from work. Joe was out with friends so he couldn't come. I was happy to go on my own, but I spent very little time in the spa. I ended up staying in my room all evening with room service for company, engrossed in yet more research on the Mother and Baby homes. Then I stayed up into the early hours reading an excellent book about the illegal adoptions that took place in homes all over Ireland.

The next morning I was standing in the grand hall at reception waiting to check out when I got a phone call from Ireland on my mobile. It was a major breakthrough and I couldn't believe my luck.

I was desperate to tell someone. I didn't want to tell Joe. Things were still frosty between us after our discussion about having kids and I knew the story about Tess's baby would spark off more arguments. I was going to wait for the right time to tell him. Mary was at a conference in Milan so I couldn't talk to her. Deep down, the only person I really wanted to tell was Karen. She'd known Tess most of her life. So I swallowed my pride and texted her.

I have big news. Fancy meeting up for lunch tomorrow?

I was surprised when she texted back straight away.

Great. Got something to tell you too.

I suggested the café in Central Library in town. It wasn't far from her clinic and the library had recently had a spectacular refurbishment. I'd taken some students there recently and I wanted to show her.

A curtain of drizzle was falling from an ashen-coloured sky as I stepped off the tram in St Peter's Square. Central Library is Manchester's Pantheon. It has white Corinthian columns, a two-storey portico and a dome façade. It stands out like a flying saucer above the red-brick industrial and gothic architecture that dominates the rest of the city. The recent refurbishment had transformed it. They'd created a new three-hundred-seater reading room, a gaming area with Xboxes and PlayStations and a children's section in the basement based on *The Secret Garden*, one of my favourite childhood books. The dark stairwells and gloomy corridors that I remembered from my student days had been replaced by light and airy open spaces. Like a dried-fruit cake with its filling scooped out and replaced with sponge.

I hurried towards the entrance steps past the small homeless camp that had sprung up outside. Tents and anti-austerity banners filled the passageway between the library and the gothic town hall next door. A frazzled woman with henna-pink hair and an Irish accent asked me for money. I immediately examined her face. I'd quickly developed a habit of scrutinising tall gangly types with fair hair who vaguely resembled Mikey or me. Or anyone with an Irish accent born around 1960. I'd even followed a couple of candidates down the street for further inspection before telling myself to cop on.

And yet my sibling could easily be living on the streets. Maybe he or she hadn't been adopted into a good family as I hoped, instead staying in the home and sent to one of the industrial schools and been scarred by neglect and abuse. The streets were teeming with damaged souls raised in institutions who'd never adjusted to normal life afterwards.

I rummaged in my purse for some change, handed the woman a two-pound coin and made my way up the steps.

Karen was sitting at the far end of the café on a grey retro sofa below a sepia image of marching suffragettes. Elegant in skinny jeans, a teal silk scarf and tan knee-length boots, she was talking intensely into her phone. She didn't see me approach and, when she did, she ended the conversation abruptly. Looking flustered, she slipped the phone into the pocket of the camel coat beside her. I suspected Simon Whelan was on the end of that line. I felt like shaking her. How could she still be involved with him after everything that had gone on? But I hugged her instead. Our friendship was already strained. The last thing I wanted was to get into an argument about her love life.

We joined the queue at the food counter and picked up trays. I put a Diet Coke and halloumi salad on mine and she opted for a thick green smoothie and goat's cheese panini.

She looked around. "Love the make-over. So light and spacious."

She paid for both meals, waving away the tenner I held out to her. "My treat," she said, unaware of the smooth-skinned Eastern European behind the till giving her the eye.

We sat back down on the sofa where we'd left our coats.

It was lunchtime and the café was busy. Behind us a table of Chinese students were giggling and eating Lancashire Hot Pot and opposite an elderly couple in pastel-coloured rain-jackets were looking down at an iPad.

I ripped the plastic off my salad. "How's my gorgeous goddaughter doing these days?" I asked.

Karen shifted in her seat. "She got an email last week about her place on the Erasmus programme."

"Really?" I dug my fork into a chunk of halloumi. "Already?"

"She's off to Rome in September."

"Rome. *Wow.*"

Karen rolled her eyes and stirred her coffee. "Her dad's pissed off because she's chosen Italy and not Portugal or Brazil. He wanted her to improve her Portuguese."

"I didn't realise she saw much of Marco."

She frowned and raised her goat's cheese panini to her lips. "She sees more of him since she went to uni. He doesn't live far from Sheffield now."

We chatted a bit more about Alexia and we ate. Karen seemed ill at ease. She took a few more bites of her panini then left it and her eyes kept darting around the café, unable to hold mine. She was usually such a cool customer and it was unlike her to be agitated. She'd always been good for me that way. Her calm confidence was a balm to my angsty nature and tendency to overthink things. She helped me talk things through and put things into perspective. I poured some of my Diet Coke into a glass and we reminisced for a while about the Old Trafford days when Alexia was a little girl.

"Joe's probably going to bugger off soon if we don't have a baby," I said suddenly.

She looked taken aback. "Don't be daft. Joe will never leave you."

"He might."

She shook her head dismissively. "Anyway, didn't you say you had some news in your text?"

I sat up straight and fanned myself. "You won't believe it."

"Try me."

I took Dad's letter out of my bag, handed it to her, then everything gushed out of me like water from a cracked pipe. I told her how Tess had given her baby away, how it had affected her afterwards and how I was determined to find my sibling. She sat up straight and adopted her therapist's pose, legs crossed and hands resting on her knees with her head slightly bowed. She listened carefully, shaking her head now and again, a pained expression flickering across her face. When I finally stopped for breath, I could see she was genuinely affected by what I'd told her and I loved her for it.

She sipped her coffee then her face suddenly screwed up like she was looking closely at something. "Remember the time you brought Tess to the hospital when Alexia was born?"

I nodded. "Vaguely."

"You left the room at one point and Tess asked if she could hold her. When I put Alexia in her arms she started crying."

"Really?"

"I asked her if she was OK but it was like she didn't hear me. She kept stroking and kissing Alexia's head then she started singing to her. It was like she was somewhere else. I probably forgot to tell you about it. Those first few days are such a whirlwind with a new-born."

I closed my eyes. "I keep going over and over about how she scared she must have felt in that home. She was only sixteen when she gave birth. She must have been terrified. Even though I've never given birth myself I can imagine the horror."

Karen shook her head slowly and sighed. "They're so tiny and defenceless. All you want to do is hold them close and protect them forever. Her pain must have been unbearable."

"Whatever anyone says, she and all those other women had no choice when they gave up their babies. They were forced adoptions. They were made to sign their babies away under duress because the sight of a single mother on the loose was too much for Catholic Ireland at that time to bear. Their families, the Church, the State, they all wanted them to disappear. They were seen as a stain on society and they were made invisible."

Karen put her coffee on the table. "I had a client once who was forced to give her baby away in a Mother and Baby home. She was young and never told anyone. Afterwards she almost drank herself to death. She couldn't cope with the barbaric treatment she received in the home at the time of the birth and the fact that her baby was gone. I just can't imagine Tess's pain. No wonder she was unwell."

I fought back tears. "And all those years afterwards wondering where her baby ended up. Was it adopted? Did it end up happy in a good family? Or did it make it out of the home alive at all? The not knowing must have weighed on her."

Karen leant forward and put a hand over mine. Then she sat back and frowned. "But why do you think Tess and your dad didn't just run away when Tess got pregnant? Why give the baby up? They had two more kids together."

I poured the rest of my Diet Coke into my glass and drank. "I know. I can't get my head around that either. Maybe it was the shame they'd have brought on the families they left behind. It's hard to grasp the hold the Church had in small towns and villages in Ireland then. Having a daughter up the duff out of wedlock was a catastrophe."

"Not only in Ireland, Carmel. Mum's parents in Glasgow refused to speak to her for two years when she told them she was keeping her black baby and not marrying my dad."

I sat up. "God, yes. I forgot about Dee."

An image of Karen's mum came to me. She was in the front room of their council flat in Hillingdon Road curled up in a battered armchair. She was drunk. Her arms were swaying above her head and she was urging us to listen to the words of Dylan's "Desolation Row" which was playing on the turntable. Dee wore multi-coloured maxi dresses and chokers years after they'd gone out of fashion, drank neat vodka and took shit from no one.

A shadow of sadness fell over Karen's face and I leant over and squeezed her arm. "Dee had her demons but she also had guts," I said.

She batted her hand in the air as if squatting a fly. "If you say so." Her face brightened, a wide smile spread from ear to ear and she rubbed her hands together. "Bloody hell, Carmel. You could have another brother or sister out there in the world. How amazing is that?"

Her phone rang. Rolling her eyes and letting out a heavy sigh, she fished it out of her coat pocket. She looked down at the screen and blushed. "Sorry, hon. I've really got to get this. I'll be back in a bit."

I watched her head out of the café with the phone to her ear. Simon again. Why couldn't she just come clean and tell me she was seeing him again? Or was it the married Dan from the fundraiser night after all? I picked up the plastic coffee spoon and snapped it.

Before Karen mangled him, Simon Whelan was a stable individual with a happy family life. He was a leading psychiatrist at the mental health clinic where they both worked with a GP wife, teenage twin boys, a Cheshire farmhouse and a holiday home on the Algarve. Six months into the affair, he abandoned it all to move into Victoria Road with her and Alexia.

I met him a couple of times. He was her type, older and married, but not particularly attractive. Short and squat, he had an untidy mop of grey-white hair, watery blue eyes and a slight squint. But after a few hours in his company, I could see the attraction. He didn't say much but what he did say was worth hearing. He was witty, highly informed yet very unassuming. But as soon as I spotted the devoted way his eyes followed Karen around the room, I knew the relationship was doomed. True to form she dumped him a year later. She never went into the details of what exactly happened but Simon had a breakdown and he lost his job. His wife eventually had him back, a broken man by all accounts. She'd sold the house in the meantime and downsized to a flat in Didsbury. His boys took it badly, turning up at Karen's house and threatening her and Alexia a number of times.

We only ever talked about what happened once at her place. I was sitting at the kitchen table and she was sitting on the floor in the corner next to Springer Bell's bed. He'd just had a minor operation on his leg and she was fussing over him. She seemed removed, almost dismissive of the turmoil her affair with Simon had caused and more concerned about the welfare of her dog. Karen had a tornado effect on men. She sped through their lives leaving chaos and destruction behind. I'd seen it all before. I'd listened to the ins and outs of her turbulent love life for years without judgement or criticism. But that day I spoke up.

Eying her sternly, I tapped my fingers on the table. "Have you no remorse at all? That poor bloke lost his mind. His career's gone and his family have lost their home."

She looked taken aback. "I didn't force Simon to leave his family."

"So you take no blame at all for what happened?"

She fed Springer a biscuit. "No, Carmel, I don't. Simon wasn't a victim. He made his own choices. It simply didn't work out."

I shook my head. "You are so fucked up."

She threw me a murderous look. "Just listen to you with your perfect marriage!"

Then she tightened her arms around Springer and we never spoke about Simon Whelan again.

Karen's issues with men obviously had something to do with her dad Hassan's abandonment of her and Dee before she was born. Dee's dodgy lifestyle can't have helped either. Karen tracked Hassan down shortly after Alexia was born. He'd moved to Nigeria. Curious to meet his only grandchild, he paid for them both to fly out and stay in his luxury beachside villa in Lagos. Karen lasted three days. She moved to a hotel where she rang me, livid, ranting on about his entourage of women and shady business dealings. She never said as much but I guessed he was some kind of pimp. She showed me a photo of him on her return. He was a mountain of a man and was leaning against an E-type Jag, surrounded by palm trees and blue skies. Dressed in a white suit and lilac open-necked shirt, he had her smile.

She scowled down at the picture. "My gangster daddy," she said. "Was it any wonder my mother took to drink?"

The male role models in Karen's life had certainly let her down but I suspected her inability to commit lay elsewhere. In her eyes, unrequited love seemed the only true kind. She was an addiction counsellor with a dependency of her own. She was addicted to men she couldn't have.

While I was waiting for Karen to return, I got out my phone and checked my Ryanair app for flights to Knock. I hugged myself at the thought of a trip to Mayo and the recent developments. As they said in the crime dramas, I now had a solid lead to go on.

When Karen arrived back she looked flushed and distracted.

I scrutinised her face. "Everything OK?"

She nodded and looked away. She'd barely sat down when I reached into my bag and thrust a sheet of paper at her. It was one of the articles I'd photocopied about the mass grave in the Tuam home.

"Have a read of that," I said, sitting back and crossing my legs.

Frowning, she looked down at the article, her face twisting and contorting as she read.

"Sweet Jesus," she said when she'd finished. She handed it back, holding it between finger and thumb like it was contaminated. "So Tess definitely had her baby there?"

"I'm pretty sure of it. According to Dad's letter she would have given birth to the baby in late 1960 and it was the only Mother and Baby Home in the area. It closed down in 1961."

"Please tell me she never knew about any of this."

"Hard to know. There wasn't much about it in the news here at that time. Most of the reports came later on after she died."

She scratched her jaw. "Let me get this right. So pregnant girls and women were put into the homes and forced to give their babies up for adoption. The government paid the nuns money to look after the kids that weren't adopted. But the nuns kept the money and neglected and starved them and then when they died they threw their bodies into a mass grave of some sort without a proper burial."

"Well, they haven't actually found many remains as yet. But the historian who did the research has found the death certificates of the seven hundred and ninety-six children who died in the home between 1920 and 1961. She didn't find any graves anywhere to match that number. I mean, think about it. Where else would those children be buried? Their mothers had moved on. Their grandparents would hardly bury them in the family plot, would they? Grandchildren or not, they were considered bastards and outcasts. There is no record of them in any local cemeteries either."

She shook her head. "Unbelievable. Almost eight hundred bodies."

"The Irish government are talking about doing some kind of commission. Maybe they'll excavate. Who knows?"

She looked over at the table opposite where a mother

was feeding her toddler in a highchair.

"Those nuns and priests must have truly believed those babies were lesser human beings because they were born out of wedlock. Babies like me and Alexia."

I nodded. "The Church and the State, which really amounted to the same thing, wanted to present this image of pure Catholic Ireland to the rest of the world. Fallen women had no place in that world and had to be hidden away and punished. You know how they referred to the women? 'First offenders' if they got pregnant once and 'recurring offenders' if it happened again. In the eyes of the State and the Church they were criminals who needed to be locked up. Though, of course, it was the families themselves who put them in the homes."

"Unbelievable."

"And Tuam probably isn't the only Mother and Baby Home with a mass grave. It looks like there are others all over Ireland."

She winced then leant forward and lowered her voice. "So what are the chances . . . that Tess's baby is buried there?"

"Most of the deaths occurred in the thirties and forties when there was a lot of poverty. It's far more likely Tess's baby was adopted, probably illegally."

"Why illegally?"

"In a word – money. Legal adoption was introduced in Ireland in 1952 but thousands of illegal adoptions involving wealthy Americans took place before and after. Families who had failed vetting in the US or wanted a child and didn't want to hang around, simply went to Ireland. The whole process was a well-oiled adoption machine. Interested couples gave sizeable donations to Catholic charities elsewhere. The Church covered their tracks and made sure the donations couldn't be traced back to the Mother and Baby Homes."

"So a form of trafficking, then."

"Exactly. Jane Russell, the Hollywood actress, did it. It caused a huge media storm in the UK at the time."

She glanced down at her watch. "Sorry, hon, this is so fascinating, but I really have to get back to work. So what next? What's your plan of action?

"I've contacted the Irish family agency to try and get hold of any birth or adoption certificates and I've written to the historian to see if Tess's baby is on the list of children buried in the mass grave. But I haven't heard anything back." My face broke into a grin. "Then yesterday I had a breakthrough."

Her eyes widened. "Go on."

"Remember the girl in the letter called Kathleen Slevin who smuggled Dad and Tess's letters." I clasped my hands together. "Well, I've only gone and found her."

"You haven't."

"I bloody well have. It was amazingly easy. In the letter Dad mentioned she was from Bohola, a small village not far from his home place. Slevin isn't a very common surname in Mayo so I looked in the Irish Yellow Pages and found a couple of entries in Bohola. The very first one I rang was Kathleen's nephew. He gave me the number of Margaret, Kathleen's daughter. I rang her and explained why I wanted to talk to her mother. She was lovely and Kathleen was actually in the house with her at the time."

"No way!"

"So Margaret went and spoke to Kathleen then she rang me back ten minutes later. Margaret said Kathleen wasn't great on the phone so she wouldn't put her on but that Kathleen remembered Tess well from her days in the home. She said she'd be happy to meet up the next time I was in Mayo."

Karen grinned. "You've already booked a flight, haven't you?"

I nodded. "Next week. I'm going to stay with Julia. Kathleen's in her eighties now so she might not remember much but I'll give it a go."

She clutched her fists to her chest and cocked her head to one side. "Oh Carmel, I'm so very excited for you." Her phone rang again. "For God's sake!" She took it from her pocket, frowned down at the screen again but this time she didn't answer it.

"You sure everything's OK?" I asked.

She cleared her throat. "It's the buyer of the house again."

I drew my head back. "Buyer? So you've sold the house? Oh my God, that's fantastic news! You've been wanting to move for forever. You said in your text that you had news and I've been going on and on about myself all this time. I'm so sorry. So have you found somewhere else?"

She caught my eye briefly then looked away. "Kind of. I'm moving to Rome with Alexia."

Chapter 14

I met Karen for the first time when we were eleven years old. She stood, sullen-faced, in the classroom doorway in Oakwood High. Mrs Burns gestured sternly at her to take the empty desk next to mine. I'd clocked her in the playground on her first day, one of the few mixed-race girls in year seven, the only girl taller than me. She'd recently moved down from Scotland and joined the school mid-term. Two weeks in, she'd been moved out of her class into mine after almost being expelled.

Slowly, she made her way down the rows of desks, head held high, eyes focussed on the back wall. Two fat bunches of golden curls tied with red ribbons stuck out from behind her ears and an embroidered green bag threaded with silver swung from her shoulder. When she sat down next to me, I could see she was fighting back tears. Her blue eyes shone like jewels against her dark skin. Throughout the lesson she rubbed at the red marks on her right palm when she thought no one was looking.

As we gathered our things after the bell rang, I said I liked her Wham pencil case.

"Andrew's my favourite," I added nervously.

"No way!" She had a throaty Scottish voice that sounded a bit dangerous. "George is my dream ticket." Her face brightened. "My Auntie Joyce is getting me and Mum tickets to see them live in London next month."

I wasn't sure what a dream ticket was but I skipped home that day repeating the words in her accent, rolling the 'r' in a 'dream' around my tongue the way she did.

We quickly became friends. I hung around with a couple of girls but I'd never had a best friend. I never invited anyone home as I was scared of them finding out about Tess not being well.

I was over the moon when Karen invited me to Hillingdon Road for tea a couple of weeks later. Her mum Dee was out. Karen made Findus Crispy Pancakes followed by Angel Delight and we listened to, "I'm Your Man," in her bedroom. A huge CND wall-hanging covered the window where curtains should have been, dreamcatchers dangled above her bed and incense candles burned on the dressing table. I thought it was the coolest room ever. Picking at a loose thread on the patchwork quilt, I tentatively asked Karen if being caned had hurt.

She shook her head. "Not as much as Julie Kawalski's stitches."

I put my hand over my mouth, trying not to laugh. "Julie defo won't be calling you names again, that's for sure."

Julie Kawalski was in Karen's former class. She had targeted Karen with racist taunts from the day she walked through the school gates. Pudgy and lank-haired, Julie lived on the Nell Lane Estate with her fat parents, a rake of skinhead brothers and a litter of pit bulls. One day at break she called Karen one name too many and Karen snapped. Catching hold of Julie by a pigtail, she slammed her into the school railing. Julie caught her head on an iron spike and had to be taken to the Infirmary by the deputy head to have five stitches. The next day Julie's dad, two brothers and one of the pit bulls turned up at the school baying for Karen's blood. She was moved out of Julie's class and caned, the last girl ever to receive corporal punishment in the school. Years on, she still maintained it made her feel like Ruth Ellis.

She once told me the episode was life-changing. Karen was born in Manchester, not Scotland. But when she was a toddler, Dee had fallen on hard times and left Manchester to return to the tiny village outside Glasgow where she was raised. After their initial shock and horror at having a mixed-raced grandchild, her grandparents doted on Karen. They were both teachers in the local secondary school and well respected and Karen suffered surprisingly little racist abuse growing up in the village. During that time she'd had no contact with her dad or any relatives from Nigeria so she said she didn't really identify as black. It was only when she was targeted by Julie Kawalski that she started looking in the mirror and asking questions about her identity. She said everything changed after that.

Karen and I had things in common and we bonded quickly. We were both outsiders and the children of immigrants. We were waifs and strays, jetsam bobbing around the streets of South Manchester with no stable home life. Tess was struggling to cope with Dad's death and spent a lot of time in bed, crushed by depression. The few cleaning jobs she had were long gone and we got by on benefits cheques. Karen's home life wasn't much better. Dee was rapidly descending into alcoholism. No matter how bad Tess was feeling, at the end of the day she always managed to put a meal on the table for the three of us. But at Hillingdon Road the fridge was always empty. After school Karen would often have to go in search of Dee for money for food. She was usually in the Spread Eagle or the Royal Oak in Chorlton. If her luck was in, the pair of us would count out the pennies then skip to the Chinese chippy for chips and scrapings with curry sauce and cans of Iron Bru. We shared everything we had, which was never much. Any money I got from relatives in Ireland went on sweets and copies of *Smash Hits* magazine from Etchells newsagents for both of us.

At fifteen we were clubbing. With our wages from our Saturday jobs at the Kellogg's factory we made our own clothes: taffeta tutus and silk bodices from the cut-off basket in Leon's fabrics in Chorlton. We shopped for cheap accessories in Affleck's Palace in town, we backcombed our hair and saved up for twelve-hole Doc Martens boots. Some of the clubs used to let us in for nothing because the bouncers said we looked good on the dance floor. They called us "Ebony and Ivory" and "Chocolate and Cream". I once asked her if we should go in if they were calling us names like that, but she said she didn't give a toss as long as we got to dance the night away for free.

I often stayed over at Hillingdon Road after our clubbing nights. Tess never let me stay out that late, but Dee was usually trashed and never noticed what time we got in. Karen had a lock on the inside of her bedroom door. When I asked her why, she said it had been there when they moved in. But something happened one night to make me think otherwise.

Desperate for a pee, I woke up in the early hours. As I made my way across the landing to the bathroom, I bumped into a man coming out of Dee's room. Burly and ginger, he was fastening his belt. He looked familiar and he took one look at me then scarpered downstairs like a startled guinea pig. The room to Dee's room was open. She was sitting on her bed. A red kimono fell from her bony shoulders revealing tiny breasts, stockings and suspenders. She was putting bank notes into a small black purse.

The next morning Karen and I were lying in bed, hungover. I told her I dreamt I saw Julie Kawalski's dad on her landing.

"Oh him," she laughed. "He's a regular."

She scrutinised my face for a reaction but I looked away. I didn't want to show her how shocked I was. Neither of us ever mentioned the episode again. Six months later and four days after Karen's sixteenth birthday, Dee died of chronic liver failure.

We spent the next two years in each other's pockets. Karen had a proper grown-up life. She got a nine-to-five job at the Council Housing Department and stayed on in Hillingdon Road. She coped with her grief by keeping busy. The pair of us redecorated the place from top to bottom, scouring south Manchester for second-hand bits of furniture and painting her bedroom black. We had parties most weekends and brought boys back. Only now and again did she speak about Dee but not talking about stuff was normal at the time. I don't think I ever spoke about the pain of losing Dad. In my eyes Karen was the strong silent type. Then one day I found some counselling leaflets in a kitchen drawer. When I asked her if she was seeing someone, she snatched them off me and told me to mind my own business.

When I went to Manchester Poly we pulled away from each other. I was living at home with Tess and Mikey and swotting, and she was reading *Spare Rib*, getting involved in women's groups, attending every anti-apartheid march going and sleeping with both men and women. She despised a lot of my student friends. She asked why they were in the Socialist Workers Party and living in "poverty" in the Crescents in Hulme while Mummy and Daddy were sending them fat cheques from the Home Counties. I invited her along to some student parties but she got into so many arguments I stopped. One day she told me I was turning into a middle-class twat and I told her she was bitter and jealous. Our friendship cooled for a while after that but we still kept in touch. Later on, when she was a working single mother in her thirties, she got a first-class degree in psychology. She was studying for her Master's when we were both living in Old Trafford and that was when our friendship got fully back on track. It was like the intervening years had never happened and we saw each other all the time.

But now, without a word of warning, she was leaving the country.

The café was starting to get very busy.

I picked my jacket up from the sofa. "Rome. Wow, Karen. That's huge news."

"I got a private buyer for the house." She slipped her

106

phone into her bag. "I applied for voluntary redundancy at work and they got back to me a few weeks ago." She smiled weakly. "At least I won't have to listen to those bloody trains at the bottom of the garden anymore."

I stood up. "So you're going with Alexia in September?"

She winced then stood up too. "Actually I'm off in a few weeks. I've got a place on a training course to teach English as a Foreign Language at a college over there. Then Alexia and I are going to explore Italy for a bit before she starts uni."

An awkward silence hung in the air as we walked out of the café into the corridor. One of the library staff was having words with someone from the homeless camp and they were blocking the exit.

As we waited to pass, I shook my head and turned to her. "What the hell, Karen? We've been friends for nearly thirty years. Why the fait accompli? Why didn't you mention anything before?"

She reddened. "I suppose I didn't want you to persuade me otherwise."

"That's bullshit and you know it. You don't give a toss what I think about anything anymore."

"That's not true. You'll always matter to me, Carmel."

"Look me in the eye and be totally honest with me. Are you back with Simon Whelan? Are you running away to Italy with him?"

"What?" She stepped back, blinking rapidly. "No. Of course not." She gave a nervous laugh. "Why would you think that?"

I examined her face then shrugged. "Dunno. All the secrecy, I suppose."

"I'm not running away with anyone. I simply want a

change of scene. I've been trying to sell the house for years and I've never lived abroad." She gestured around the library. "My life's getting a long overdue make-over and new beginning like this place."

I started to walk away and she hurried after me.

"Rome's only a two-hour flight away," she said, her voice trembling. "We can always Skype and you can come out and visit."

When I turned round, I was shocked to see tears in her eyes. Like Joe, she rarely cried.

She stepped forward, pulled me towards her in a hug and I let her. "I'm so very sorry for the way I've treated you. You so deserve to find your sibling." She pulled away and wiped her eyes with the back of her hand. "Please be careful though, won't you? Don't build this unknown person up too much in your head. You might be disappointed like I was with my dad. Promise?"

"I promise."

We walked across the square to the tram stop and said goodbye under a swollen mass of pewter clouds. A few minutes later as the tram trundled away, I watched her stride across St Peter's Square and disappear down the passageway between the library and the town hall. It would be over a year before we spoke or saw each other again.

Chapter 15

I picked up the copy of the *Manchester Evening News* from the mat and headed into the kitchen. I looked at the wall clock. Three-quarters of an hour before the taxi was due. It was a bank holiday so the flight to Knock would be busy. A burst of adrenalin rushed through me. I was both excited and nervous about my trip and the possibilities it might unearth. I was also looking forward to being back in Mayo. I hadn't been back since Tess passed away. I couldn't wait to wake up to those breath-taking views of Clew Bay from the spare room in my Aunt Julia's house.

I slipped my passport, Ryanair ticket and car-hire documents into my new travel wallet. I ran my fingers over the soft red leather. Joe had given it to me when he got back from a business trip to Madrid a few days previously.

We spent a perfect evening together. We ordered a seafood curry takeaway from Coriander, our favourite Indian, and opened the oaked Rioja he'd brought back. We ate and drank by candlelight and snuggled up to a film. He apologised for being an arse recently, told me he loved me and didn't mention the baby issue. We had sex on the sofa. Good, bonding sex that made me feel cocooned and safe again.

Then the previous night he'd flown at me again for no apparent reason. I was packing for my trip in the bedroom and he was changing out of his work suit. I noticed he'd lost weight. His once fleshy torso had hollowed out and his arms seemed skinnier. His face looked gaunt too, as if he was ailing for something.

I still hadn't found the right moment to tell him about Tess's baby and the real reason I was going to Mayo. We'd both been busy. He'd been in Madrid and I'd been at a conference in Bristol. But I'd decided I was going to tell him everything over dinner that evening.

Karen was on my mind a lot and so I told him about her leaving.

Joe didn't seem particularly interested. He acted like it was something in my world that didn't concern him.

"I still can't believe she never told me," I said, reaching into my wardrobe for a couple of thick jumpers, "Not even about selling the house."

"You're not her keeper!" he snapped, looking on in disapproval as I squashed the sweaters into my holdall. A regular traveller, he meticulously folded and rolled to fit everything into a cabin-luggage-sized case. It really got on my nerves. "Why do you have to be so negative? Why can't you be happy for her?"

"I am happy for her. I just don't like the way she did it without saying anything, that's all. We've been friends for years. She should have told me."

"Sounds to me like you're jealous," he said, throwing his shirt in the laundry basket and zipping up his track-suit top.

"*What?*"

"Well, I am," he said. "Starting a new life in a new country and leaving this shithole behind. Who wouldn't be?"

"What the hell is wrong with you?" I yelled, picking up a pair of jeans and throwing them after him as he left the room.

The front door slammed shortly afterwards. I sat on the bed with my head in my hands, bewildered. What the fuck?

Joe and I had been together for almost twenty years and, though we had our ups and downs, he'd never been as cruel as he had been in those past months. I was started to feel scared and paranoid. Yes, he annoyed the hell out of me sometimes, but I loved him. I didn't know what I'd do if he were to leave me as well as all the others

The forecast for the west of Ireland was clear skies and sun. For once I was looking forward to the plane landing at Knock airport without being buffeted by fierce Atlantic winds and brutal rain. I had a busy three-day itinerary. After I'd picked up the hire car I was going to drive to Tuam to visit the site of the Mother and Baby home. After that I was going to Westport to Aunt Julia's.

Julia was Dad's youngest sister. We were close. We spoke on the phone and Skyped regularly, and I visited a couple of times a year. I hadn't yet told her the reason for my visit. I had no idea if she knew anything about Tess and Dad and the baby. In 1960, when it all happened, she was living in America. It was too big and emotional to tell her by phone. I wanted to sit down with her in the Chesterfield chairs in front of the open fire, glass of red in hand and talk it through. I'd arranged to meet Kathleen Slevin at a hotel near her home in Bohola the following day.

I made myself a coffee and had turned on the radio when the doorbell rang. A shaven-headed lad in a blue boiler suit stood on the doorstep looking at me expectantly. Tess's radiogram stood on the path and an orange house clearance van nudged over the hedge behind him.

"Oh yes, thank you," I said. "Could you just leave it in the hall for now, thanks."

I'd received a text from the house-clearance people telling me about today's delivery but in my rush to get ready for my trip I'd forgotten all about it.

I stepped back and opened the door wide as the boy picked the radiogram up and carried it into the hall. Rattling noises came from its belly, like something might have broken inside. Before I could complain he had scarpered out of the door. Shaking my head in annoyance, I went back into the kitchen and sat down with the *Manchester Evening News* and my coffee. From the hallway, the radiogram reproached me, like a frail old lady who'd been removed from her home of fifty years and put into care. I felt like stroking her sleek wooden lid and apologising.

As I looked down at the front page of the paper, a familiar face stared back at me. It took a few moments for me to realise who it was. I could just about make Conor O'Grady out under the unkempt mop of grey-white hair, bushy beard and three chins. I read the headline and gasped.

ARMY VETERAN ATTACKS
LOCAL POLITICIAN

Kahn was outside his mother's house in Brantingham Road, Chorlton when he was approached by his neighbour on a mobility scooter. A passerby, who witnessed the scene, said she heard O'Grady shout, 'Go back to where you came from!" as he produced a knife from under his jacket. He proceeded to stab the Labour MP for Withington three times. Kahn escaped with minor wounds to his arm and abdomen.

O'Grady, a former soldier who lost both legs while serving in Northern Ireland in the 1980s, was described by neighbours as a bit of a loner who kept himself to himself.

I looked down at Conor's glassy eyes staring back at me. I clenched the edges of the paper and took a few deep breaths. I was back in the Irish Club car park again: the stench and heat of his breath, his grabbing hands and his gruff voice calling me a slag over and over. Rose O'Grady would be turning in her in grave and his poor father Tommy would never be able to hold his head up in Brantingham Road again. Not to mention Samira. She'd probably had to come back from Pakistan. Conor had never been right in the head. But this? Stabbing Adeel

Kahn and telling him to go back to where he came from? What the hell? Adeel was born and bred in Manchester just like he was. They'd grown up together in the street and played together as kids. I shook my head. UKIP, the anti-immigration party was gaining support from nutters like Conor O'Grady every day and people were taking its leader Farage seriously. When did all the hate kick in? Conor O'Grady and Adeel Kahn were both the children of immigrants, for Christ's sake. The world was going bonkers.

Ten minutes before the taxi got here. I checked my documents one more time then went into the hallway to get my coat. Stopping by the radiogram, I lifted the lid to see what damage was done and if it was still worth repairing. I knelt down. Two corners of the metal turntable that were slightly loose before had come apart. As I lifted up the arm of the needle the whole thing came off. A small white folded-up envelope slipped out from underneath. I picked it up and dusted it off then I took it into the kitchen, placed it on the table and sat staring at it for a while. The sun warmed the back of my neck and my heart pounded as I opened it. Inside were two newspaper cuttings from the Irish press.

One was one of the first reports of the discovery of the mass grave in Tuam. The other was a published list of the names of the seven hundred and ninety-six babies who'd died there.

Chapter 16

As the plane started to descend, the elderly woman sitting next to me held out a boiled sweet in her mottled hand.

"They say it's good to chew when you're landing," she said in a pure Mayo accent.

I wondered what her story was. Did she leave Ireland when she was a girl and was returning to visit family who stayed behind? Or had her children left and she'd just spent a holiday tuning herself into the unfamiliar music of her grandchildren's English accents? I took the sweet and thanked her. I felt guilty. Throughout the flight I'd avoided her attempts at conversation and turned back to my book even though I couldn't concentrate on it. She had such a kindly face. I knew if we got talking I'd have to tell her everything – how all my dreams and hopes had been dashed that morning and how my despair was quickly turning to rage. As the plane descended I looked out of the window at picture-box Ireland: the scattered white houses, smooth strips of road and lush green fields. I gripped the arm of my seat, anger coursing through my veins. Babies were buried in unmarked graves in fields all over the country and my brother was among them.

The list of dead children had been published in a national Irish newspaper. I'd missed it in my search but Tess hadn't. Seven hundred and ninety-six names, dates of birth, age and cause of death, all in chronological birth order from 1920 to 1961. Many died of flu, whooping cough and gastroenteritis. Others suffered from epilepsy, fits and convulsions and others died of respiratory illnesses. There were twins, Anthony and Mary, described as "congenital idiots" – probably with Down Syndrome, I guessed – who died at two and three months from bronchitis. The youngest baby, Haigh, died at ten minutes because he was premature. The oldest, Mary Connolly, died when she was seven after an outbreak of measles. One word "marasmus" recurred again and again. The dictionary definition was "undernourishment causing a child's weight to be significantly low for their age". Three children died in 1960. Donal Dempsey, my brother, was one of them. Dempsey – Tess's name. His date of birth was listed as 29/11/1960, his age of death 5 months and the cause of his death was unexplained heart failure. Tess had underlined his name in black ink and beside it she'd written,

"*Rest with the angels, my beautiful boy.*"

I let out an involuntary cry when I saw it. I imagined her discovering it in the reading room at Chorlton Library where she went to read the Irish papers. I saw her tearing it from the newspaper, her hand shaking as she slipped it into the pocket of her shopping trolley. She probably sat alone in her armchair by the gas fire reading it over and over. So much unbearable pain after spending a lifetime thinking he'd been adopted and was living a good life in America or somewhere else. She had given birth to a healthy baby so why would she think otherwise? I looked back at the cause of death again. Unexplained heart failure. Had she made the connection with Familial Hypertrophic Cardiomyopathy as I had? She'd already passed the faulty gene on to Mikey and blamed herself for his death. So after seeing this, did she think she'd killed her firstborn as well? I checked the date on the newspaper. Tess died three weeks after it was published. Had the shock of the discovery killed her?

"Welcome to Ireland," the cabin crew said as we taxied into the airport. *Céad míle fáilte. A hundred thousand welcomes.*

Rain splattered the windowpane as the plane ground to a halt. It looked like the forecast had been wrong. I wasn't going to get blue skies and sunshine after all.

117

Chapter 17

Dusk was falling by the time I got to the site of the Mother and Baby Home. The sky over Tuam was a swollen mass of bruised grey-blue clouds edged with yellow.

It wasn't at all what I'd imagined. The building itself had been demolished in 1972 but I'd still pictured the site in a rural isolated spot. Instead, I found it in the middle of a modern housing estate, overlooked on all sides. To get there I had to walk through a small playground. It was empty apart from a shaven-headed boy of about ten. The boy was hanging upside down on the climbing frame, his bike abandoned nearby. When I stopped and looked around, he swung back onto his feet. He pointed in the direction of a small iron gate with a white wooden cross on it.

"*The dead babies is over there, missus!*" he shouted, then

he hitched up his shorts, hopped on his bike and rode off.

A gentle drizzle was falling and I put up the hood of my waterproof and walked towards the gate. A lawn the size of a large garden was enclosed by a tall grey stone wall. In the far corner a woman stood under a red-and-white striped golfing umbrella in front of a small grotto. I went through the gate and walked across the lawn, conscious of every footstep in the dampening soil and what lay underneath. As I approached I saw a statue of the Virgin standing in a glass case. The blue of her dress glowed in the darkening air and her arms were outstretched. She was surrounded by lilac blossom, and bunches of other flowers, cards and soft toys were piled on the stony grass.

Despite being surrounded by houses, there was a stillness about the place, a silence only interrupted now and again by the rush of a passing car or the cawk of a crow. As I approached the woman turned and looked at me from under her umbrella. A string of Celtic stone rosary beads hung from her wrist. She smiled then closed her eyes again and went back to her prayers.

I reached into my bag and took out the bunch of lilies I'd bought at a Centra store on the way. The woman moved to one side as I leant over and placed them at the foot of the statue. On the card I'd written: *'For our beloved brother and son Donal, All our love, Mummy, Daddy, Mikey and Carmel.*

Donal. At least he had a name and sex now. But Tess's maiden name – Dempsey. If Tess and Dad had kept him, he'd have been a Lynch. Donal Lynch. One of us.

Not one for prayers, I stood up and glanced around. The damp lawn glistened in the fading light. I wondered where his body might be. Would I ever know? All I wanted was to take back what was left of him to

Manchester and lay him to rest with Tess and Dad and Mikey where he belonged. How could that happen, though? Even if they excavated the site and used DNA techniques, would they really be able to identify the remains of eight hundred children after all this time?

I stared at the statue of the Virgin with her welcoming, outstretched arms. The irony of it was not lost on me. An icon of *virginity* and *motherhood* watching over this grave. I dug my hands into my pockets and read the notes attached to the flowers:

God bless the angels.

May the Lord look over you.

I pray for your souls.

I had a sudden urge to pick up a stone and hurl it at the glass case.

"*Lord have mercy*," mumbled the woman, kissing her rosary beads and slipping them into her pocket.

"He didn't though, did he?" I said.

"Pardon me?" she said in an American accent.

"Your Lord. He didn't have mercy. Not on any of the children here, anyway."

She lowered her eyes. She was sixtyish with a creamy complexion and faint freckles. She wore expensive Gore-Tex and spotless white trainers and I imagined her preening a garden behind a white picket fence in a tidy suburb in Ohio, smiling and waving to passersby and telling them to "Have a nice day".

An awkward silence ensued. We both watched as a young chaffinch landed on one of the teddy bears scattered at the Virgin's feet. It hopped for a while then took flight, the white flash of its wings disappearing into the grey mist of rain.

"I get your anger," she said after a while. "I lost faith in the Church a long time ago and I haven't been to Mass in years. But I never lost my faith in God. Praying and forgiveness are very important to me."

"So you can forgive this?" I snapped.

Sadness fell over her face and I immediately regretted my outburst.

"I'm sorry." I felt myself well up. "I found out today that my brother's buried here. I'd only just discovered he existed and I was hoping to trace him."

She turned and placed a hand on my shoulder.

"I'm so sorry," she said and I broke down at her touch.

To my embarrassment, minutes later I found myself sobbing and holding on to her hand, finding solace in the comfort of a stranger.

"Sorry," I said when I finally pulled away.

"Not at all." She handed me a pack of tissues from her bag. "I'm Louisa. Louisa Schulter."

I wiped my eyes and blew my nose.

"Carmel Doherty."

"You're English?"

"My parents were from Mayo but I was born in Manchester."

"We have a Manchester in Boston too. I really am so very sorry for your loss."

I sighed. "My mother got pregnant by my dad when she was fifteen. She never told me or my brother anything about the baby. Shortly before she died she got hold of the list of children who died here and discovered he was on it. He was called Donal."

"They never told her he'd passed?"

I shook my head. "I think she assumed he'd been adopted."

Louisa Schulter frowned down at the rain firing on to the muddy lawn and tucked a stand of hair under her hood. "That's terrible. When I eventually found my birth mother she told me she hoped and prayed every day of her life that I'd gone to a good family and had a happy life."

"Oh. So you were in the home here? You're a survivor?" I reddened, mortified at the way I'd spoken to her.

"Not here. I was born in the Bessborough home in Cork in 1952. When I was six months old I was taken to Boston to live with my adoptive parents."

"So that's why you're here now?"

She nodded. The rain was starting to come down heavily and she moved her umbrella over my head.

"I guess I wanted to come here and pay my respects to the ones who didn't make it. I don't really think of myself as a survivor though. I'm one of the lucky ones. I can't remember anything about my time in Bessborough and I ended up in a loving home in Boston."

"Were you legally adopted, if you don't mind me asking?"

"Yes, I was legally adopted. But when I was searching for my mother I came across a number of people who weren't. It was tough for them. I remember one woman finding out when she was fifty-seven years old. Her adoptive parents died without telling her – then one day she heard it from an elderly aunt during a family argument. And because it was done illegally her adoptive parents were named on her birth certificate, not her natural parents. So when she started searching for her birth mother she had no information to go on."

"So what happened?"

"She lost hope in the end and gave up."

I shook my head. "Imagine waking up one day and discovering that. You'd feel like your life had been one a big lie."

"I know. I count myself lucky. I met my birth mother."

She looked down at the ground.

"Do you mind me asking what happened?" I asked tentatively.

She shook her head. "Not at all. My adoption was easy. Dad was serving in the armed forces in the UK at the time and he popped over to Dublin to fill out all the papers. He collected me from Cork the next day." She laughed. "Like collecting a parcel. I was ten when I found out. Mom and Dad sat me down after Mass one Sunday and told me. I'd always had this feeling I was different, though. Not because I felt unloved or unwanted. My family were Italian. Mom, Dad and Elena my sister were dark-haired and olive-skinned and I mean – just look at me." She pulled her hood down to reveal a thick head of strawberry-blonde curls. "I always looked like Annie from the musical." She smiled. "We had a lot in common, Annie and me. I could never put my finger on it, but it felt like I didn't belong. When Mom and Dad told me, it was a relief."

"But you had a good childhood?"

"The best. When he left the forces Dad started his own printing business and Mom worked part-time as a third-grade teacher. We had vacations by the ocean, a college fund, a nice home in a good area. My parents treated my sister and me exactly the same too."

"So you think being adopted was a good thing?"

"In some ways, yes. I mean there was so much poverty here back then. People were emigrating in droves and everyone, the Church, the politicians, they all truly believed children like me would have a better life in America."

"Everyone except the birth mothers. Most of those women wanted to keep their babies. I'm pretty sure my mum did. They were forced adoptions."

"Most. But the way I see it, I was lucky. I could have ended up abused in an industrial school or washing priests' underwear for forty years in a Magdalene Laundry."

I laughed. I was warming to Louisa Schulter and I was sorry I'd misjudged her.

"What was it like, finding your birth mother?"

An unmistakable flicker of sadness crossed her face.

"Sorry," I said, touching her arm. "I'm asking too many questions."

"Not at all. I understand. It's all new to you." She looked out past the wall into the distance. "It took me ten long years but I finally found her in 1983. It was so goddamn hard. The adoption agency, the Boston charity who vetted the families, the nuns at Bessborough, the Irish Department of Foreign Affairs, they all shut the door in my face so many times they put my nose out of joint."

"Let me guess. They all told you it was to protect the privacy of the birth mother?"

She nodded. "I've heard it's easier now. It was actually with the help of a nun from Cork that I found Eileen, my birth mother. Sister Mary Teresa was a beautiful person and she did so much for the poor communities in Boston. She died in a home for the clergy last year. It was a sad place, full of nuns and priests who'd dedicated their entire lives to the Church. Most were good people but in their final years they had to watch the scandals unfold – we had a huge paedophile problem in Boston – everything they believed

124

in was up for scrutiny. Mary Teresa said it was like watching your house burn down slowly in front of your eyes."

Louisa looked down at her watch.

"Sorry. Am I keeping you?" I said. I didn't want her to go. I had so many more questions to ask.

"I'd love to stay but my husband is waiting in the car park by the church."

We started to walk back across the lawn. The rain was letting let up and Louisa put the umbrella down.

"Just one more thing before you go, Louisa. Can I ask about your mother's story?"

"Sure. Like your mom, she was just a girl when she had me. She and my father were childhood sweethearts. He was banished to England and Eileen never saw him again. He died a few years before I traced her. After my birth, Eileen had me then she moved to Dublin and married a man who became successful in business. She had four more children but she never told them or her husband about me. She said the scandal would destroy her family and his career. So we met in secret, in cafés and restaurants in Dublin every summer when I came on vacation. I also called her once a month. It was her dying wish that I never told any of her family. I've always respected her wishes." She smiled and trailed the tip of the umbrella into the soil. "I stalk them on Facebook sometimes though."

"God."

"I understood why she was scared of anyone finding out about her past. She'd done well for herself. She'd dragged herself up from her life as a farm girl and she had a beautiful home in Howth and a perfect family. I certainly wasn't about to ruin any of it for her."

"Did you like her?"

She wrinkled her nose.

"Not really."

I laughed.

"She was kinda cold and steely. She rarely showed emotion and shrank from physical contact. That was tough. All I dreamt about since I was ten years old was hugging my birth mom. She always maintained she did the right thing giving me up. Said it was hard but she could see no way round it."

"So sad."

"But least we got closure. Not like your poor mom. Now that's sad."

Before she left, I hugged Louisa and thanked her. She gave me her contact details, saying she'd be happy to talk anytime.

I watched her walk away then I stood at the gate for a while. Staring down at the damp black soil and silver grass, I said goodbye to my brother. I told him how sorry I was for what had happened to him and how his family loved him. I looked up at the lighted upstairs window of one of the houses that overlooked the site. A child was climbing up the ladder of a bunk bed, his mother standing nearby. She turned and said something to him then she stepped towards the window and pulled the curtains shut.

"Goodnight, sweet Donal," I said, a lump congealing in my throat.

Chapter 18

I woke the next day to the sound of gulls circling outside my window and waves crashing on the rocks below.

I slid out of bed, the pain of my discovery pressing down on me. I had already lost one brother, now hope had died and I'd lost another. The more I thought about it, the more convinced I was that the shock of finding out her baby had died in the home might have killed Tess. Being forced to give him up, spending her life never knowing what happened to him then finding out he'd suffered neglect and abuse in his short life. Only the strongest of hearts could survive that. Why had she never told me any of it? The thought that she'd suffered alone was unbearable. It stabbed my own heart over and over.

Julia had left me a key under the mat the day before.

She was in Belfast at the christening of one of the grandchildren and was due back late afternoon. I sat on the bed and glanced over at the window. I knew there was one thing that might lift my mood. So I got up, opened the curtains and took in the view.

Julia's stone farmhouse was nestled in the shadow of Croagh Patrick with the Nephin Mountains curving in the distance. It rested on the bend of a winding road overlooking Clew Bay. The sea below was dotted with small islands. Legend had it there were three hundred and sixty-five – one for every day of the year. John Lennon owned one. The rains of yesterday had cleansed the landscape. It was bright and breezy and white puffs of cloud slid across an azure sky. The islands looked like emeralds scattered on turquoise silk. I stood for some time and took in the glorious colours. Maybe there was a God after all.

Julia's was the only old house on the road. All the others were newly built mansions with glass box extensions, extravagant pillars and gravelled drives. Most were empty holiday homes owned by Americans or Germans and many were up for sale. Julia longed for families to move into the road again to bring life back to the community. A cyclist passed on the road below. It was the perfect day for a bike ride and I knew exactly where I was going to go. If I got a move on, I'd be back before Julia returned in the afternoon.

After a hurried breakfast of coffee and a few slices of Julia's delicious soda bread, I drove to the seaside town of Mulranny. There I picked up a bike from a man with a van and set off for Achill Island on the Greenway Trail, a disused railway line transformed into a cycle path that hugged the coastal roads.

128

I visited Achill every time I came to Mayo, alone or with Joe. Cycling on the Greenway was heaven for him. We usually came by ferry from England so he could bring his own bike. The island evoked happy childhood memories for me. Dad loved it. The first time I recall going there it was just the two of us. Tess was heavily pregnant with Mikey and she stayed behind at Granny's house.

Before we left, Dad spread a map of Mayo out on the cold stone floor and pointed to a piece of land attached to the coast only by a narrow bridge. It looked like the spout of a teapot.

"That's where we're going." he said, tracing his finger across the vast blue of the Atlantic. "Next stop America."

I looked down in awe.

"But Daddy, that's the edge of the world," I said.

He laughed and kissed the top of my head. "So mind you don't fall off."

Later, on the white sands of Keel beach, I refused to go near the water, scared I might just do that. Hiding behind his legs, I looked out for the Statue of Liberty on the horizon.

I cycled on, slapped around by a fierce headwind. There were few other cyclists or walkers on the path. Olive peatland swept down from the mountains, the rough earth patched with purple heather and chalk-white rocks. The light on the island had a clean quality that polished the colours of the landscape, adding sheen and lustre. When we visited in the seventies and eighties, the island was desolate, the residue of mass emigration everywhere: tumbledown cottages, clapped-out old cars and barely a shop or a hotel in sight. Then the boom brought glass-fronted holiday homes with solar panels, fish restaurants with Michelin stars and surfing schools.

It was almost two when I crossed the swing bridge then cycled some more until I came to Keel village. The sun was high in the sky and the heat dropped over my shoulders like a warm coat.

I leaned my bike against the wall of a small shop and headed inside to get a drink and a sandwich. As I pushed the door open, I stopped and did a double take at the man standing in the queue by the till. He was bending down talking to a tousled-haired boy of about ten or eleven by his side. His hair was loose and falling down over his face so I couldn't be sure if it was him at first. Then he straightened up and tucked his hair behind his ear. Yes, it was Dan, the bloke I'd met at the fundraiser in the Irish Club. I froze, suddenly mortified at the memory of that night, remembering my drunken state and how he'd had to help Joe get me down the steps and into a taxi. My anxiety got the better of me and I hurried out of the door to the far end of the street where I hid behind an orange camper van.

He came out a few minutes later and sauntered towards a silver Mondeo with the boy. I watched from behind the van. As the boy climbed into the back of the car, Dan took the ice cream, licking it and teasing as the boy tried to grab it back. Then a woman appeared at the passenger side in a loose yellow raincoat, dark curly hair billowing across her face. She was beautiful and, as she opened the car door and lowered herself into the seat, I could see she was heavily pregnant. The sun was high in the sky above their heads, the sea sparkling in the distance. They looked like such a happy family. How could I have suspected anything might happened between him and Karen?

I waited until the Mondeo had driven off before I emerged. He was pretty old to be an expectant father. His wife looked younger but still in her late thirties. They looked so idyllic. Maybe it wasn't too late for me and Joe after all.

I headed back into the shop. What were the chances of meeting him again, here on Achill Island, at the edge of the world? Then I remembered he'd said his wife was from Achill and it was half term in England so they were probably visiting family.

After buying lunch I cycled down to the beach. I was cursing myself for being such a wimp and running off and hiding like that. I thought he might have been embarrassed to see me because he was actually flirting with Karen that night and he might not want to be reminded of it. But the real reason I ran off was because I'd made an idiot of myself and he might remember. Why was I always so anxious about everything? Why couldn't I have behaved like a normal person, put on a mask, said hello and feign normality? Why did I have to run and hide? I hated the way my anxiety got the better of me. Sometimes it pinned me down and I was powerless to break free.

I parked my bike, sat on the beach wall and tucked into my salmon and cream-cheese sandwich. Wind rippled through the rivulets of sand like a thousand snakes. Surfers dipped and curled themselves over the high waves and a red kayak appeared, the tide carrying it out further.

I watched the waves ebb and fall and I thought of all the victims like Tess that shame had put on a boat and sent away from these shores. When I was doing my initial searches for my sibling online, I had come across lots of survivors' groups across the world that had been going for years; older Irish men and women who'd been gathering in draughty community halls in Ireland, the UK and the US to talk about the traumas they'd suffered at the hands of the Church and State. Women incarcerated in Magdalene Laundries and Mother and Baby homes, grown men abused by clergy in industrial schools and church sacristies, adults illegally adopted who were trying to trace birth parents. It struck me how the diaspora was home to so many wounded souls. In their shoes I'd have fled Ireland too. I'd have tried to erase my past and make a new life elsewhere just like Tess did. I was both devastated and enraged to learn that my baby brother had died. But, at the same time, I could see that something was happening out there. The tide was now turning. Survivors were unearthing their secrets and opening up about what had happened to them. Their stories were spilling out onto the shores all over Ireland and I was rooting for every single one of them. I just wished Tess could have done the same and told me hers.

Chapter 19

Julia eyed me as I poured myself another glass of Chianti. It was our second bottle and I'd drunk most of the first. I relaxed into the battered Chesterfield in her front room. It had large windows and spectacular views over the bay. I stretched my legs and rubbed my stomach, bloated from the delicious Thai green curry and cheesecake she'd made for dinner.

The room was happily chaotic and smelled of dog. Once vivid yellow walls were faded, floor-to-ceiling shelves overflowed with books, photographs and CDs and a Singer sewing machine sat in the corner swathed in fabric. The warm morning had turned into a cold evening and Julia had made a small fire. She leant towards it, coaxing the coals with a poker. The heat was intense but rest of the house, with its high ceilings and cold tiled floors, was permanently draughty. Mattie had stayed on in Belfast to perform at a corporate event after the family christening so I had Julia all to myself. I asked her to put on one of his CDs. His lovely voice filled the room with "O Mio Babbino Caro" so it was like he wasn't absent at all.

My favourite aunt was the youngest of Dad's four sisters and the wild child of the family. The oldest, Moira, worked in finance and lived respectably with her family in Dublin. Twins Nancy and Irene were both nurses who'd settled in Cleveland, Ohio. Julia, also a nurse, had joined them when she was eighteen. After a short stay she'd upped and left Cleveland, hitch-hiked the length and breadth of the States, and settled in a hippy commune in California. There she met and married Tony Shapiro, a chisel-jawed draft-dodger from Brooklyn with red-leather cowboy boots and a Charles Bronson moustache. A honeymoon photo that Julia sent to Dad had pride of place on my living-room wall. She and Tony are in the Nevada desert standing in front of turquoise camper van painted with sunflowers. She looks like Ali McGraw in *Love Story*, with waist-length dark hair, razor-sharp cheekbones and tiny denim shorts. The marriage lasted only five years because of Tony's philandering ways. Granny got cancer not long afterwards. Grandad had died a few years earlier so Julia reluctantly returned to Westport to nurse her. She decided she liked being back in Ireland a lot more than she'd expected and stayed. She carved out a dazzling career in women's health, campaigning on abortion and contraception issues at a time in Ireland when very few did. In her late thirties she stumbled across Mattie at a bridge evening. A bulky Belfast widower, he had six children and a beautiful tenor voice.

They lost a daughter, Maeve, to cot death early in the marriage. Julia's feisty spirit never quite recovered afterwards.

I loved my aunt dearly. After Dad died I spent three summers at the house in Clew Bay. She taught me to ride a horse, apply make-up, and follow a dress pattern. She took me to the seaweed baths in Enniscrone and she pierced my ears with a sterilised needle. When it was time to go home, I clung to her, dreading my return to Manchester's drab streets and Tess's black moods. I secretly wished Julia was my mother just as she probably wished I was Maeve, the daughter she'd lost.

Now she put the poker in its holder and sat back in her chair. I leant over and touched the silky sleeve of her blouse. It was mustard with an intricate pattern of tiny white butterflies and it looked perfect next to her snow-white bobbed hair.

"One of your own creations?" I asked.

She nodded and picked up her wineglass. "I got the fabric at a market in Rome when we were there a few months ago."

"It's gorgeous. My friend Karen's moving to Rome. You remember Karen, don't you?"

"Sure, how could I forget her?" she said with a weak smile. "Wasn't she the talk of the village here once?"

I winced. Karen had made quite an impression back then. Eighteen and backpacking around Ireland, we had dropped in on Julia for a couple of nights. After a raucous evening in Lydon's pub in the village with the local youth, we ended up at a party in the holiday home of the O'Connells, a wealthy Dublin family down the road. Mr and Mrs O'Connell were away and Karen spent the night in the marital bed with their eldest son. Luke was a toned and tousled med student at UCD who revved around the coastal roads on a Harley Davidson. The next day Karen hopped on the back of it and the pair of them took off to a festival in Kerry without telling anyone. Mrs O'Connell was livid, though. She arrived at Julia's house and paced up and down the kitchen with big, lacquered hair and shoulder-pads, crying and wailing about her innocent boy.

After she'd gone, Julia stood by the door with her hands on her hips.

"You'd think he'd been abducted by the fecking IRA," she said. "Innocent boy, my arse! The woman's a racist. She's hysterical because Karen is black." She turned to me and shook her head. "But she shouldn't have left you like that. You're supposed to be on holiday together. She's supposed to be your friend."

I shrugged. I wasn't concerned. I was used to Karen doing mad spur-of-the-moment things like that.

Mattie's CD finished and Julia went over to the sideboard and put Mary Black on. Flushed from the wine and the fire, she fanned her face as she sat down again.

"You'll miss Karen when she goes to Rome, so."

"We aren't really that close anymore."

"No?"

"She does her own thing these days."

"She always struck me as someone who did her own thing. I had the impression she only ever thought of number one."

I glared at the fire, taken aback. "She's not a bad person. She's just not that reliable."

"You were always very good to her, Carmel. Too good, if you ask me. You were like a puppy at her heel. I never understood why you were so in awe of her. I'm probably biased but you were always the nicer, kinder girl by far."

I felt my neck and cheeks flush. I'd never seen myself as subservient to Karen at all. I shrugged off Julia's comments. She didn't like Karen but then a lot of people didn't. I often wondered how much of it was racist. She was considered "difficult" because she questioned and challenged. Joe didn't like her when they first met either. He said she was uncompromising and controlling but they got along as the years went by.

Dev, Julia's grey pointer, trotted into the room and curled on the Indian rug at my feet. He was called after Eamonn de Valera. Not that Julia was a fan of De Valera's politics. Far from it. It was because of the aquiline nose and pinched expression.

"I'm not here to talk about Karen though, Julia," I said. "I want to ask you about something else."

I took a quick slug from my glass and cleared my throat.

"Did you know Tess had a baby before she had me?"

Julia swallowed and placed her own glass on the side table with a trembling hand.

"I did," she said in a whisper.

"And about the Mother and Baby home in Tuam and the mass grave?"

She nodded. "I wanted to tell you, Carmel. I really did. But your mother made me swear not to. How did you find out?"

"From an old letter Dad had sent her when she was in the home. I also found a list of the children buried in the mass grave. Tess had underlined the baby's name – Donal. I was gutted. I thought he'd been adopted. For a while I thought he was alive and well. I hoped I had another

137

sibling out there in the world somewhere."

She looked down at her feet. "I was the one who sent her the list."

"You?"

"She rang me after she read about the mass grave. She was in a bad way. She said she needed to know if her son had died in the home. I saw that the list had been published in a newspaper, so I sent it to her."

"God!"

"I thought she had a right to know, Carmel. I know what it feels like to lose a child and I'd want to know in her situation." Julia put a hand to her face like she was about to cry. "But then she died so soon afterwards. If I'd known the effect it would have on her I'd never have done it."

"Don't go there. You're not to blame." I leant over and put my hand on hers. "But there's one thing I can't get my head around. Why did Tess and Dad give the baby up? I just don't get it. They were devoted parents. Why didn't Tess just join Dad in Manchester, get married and keep the baby?"

"Because it wasn't his."

"*What?*"

"Tess and your father split up then Tess met someone else. That's when she fell pregnant. Seán wasn't the baby's father, Carmel."

Julia poured us both a brandy. The wind was whistling outside and the night sky was clear. I sat back in the Chesterfield and listened.

"Mammy wrote to me in America saying Seán had suddenly upped and left for England. I was living in Cleveland at the time with your Aunt Nancy. No one knew why he'd gone. He returned for a couple of weeks in the summer when Nancy was home on holiday with her boys. He and Nancy were always close growing up and Seán told her everything. He was eighteen, your mother only fifteen when they met at a dance. He was stone mad for her. Tess was beautiful until the day she died but at fifteen she was like a film star. She was a natural blonde and she had this child-like way about her that made men want to protect her. She was ditzy, a little like Marilyn Monroe. Anyways, after his long shift in the bacon factory your dad would bike fifteen miles just to sit with her on the wall outside her house for an hour. He spent every penny he had buying her gifts and taking her to the dances. Mammy told him he'd lost his head. Then one day, completely out of the blue, Tess told him she'd met someone else. Seán was broken-hearted. He found out it was a friend of Tess's brother. I forget the brother's name now."

"Tadhg. Tess rarely spoke about him. She told me once he'd ended up on the streets in London."

"I didn't know that. I just knew they were estranged. Anyway, the baby's father was called James – she never told me his surname. He was a Protestant from a wealthy Anglo-Irish family who lived in the big house outside the village. Apparently he was older than Tess and very good-looking. He used to swan around the village in a fancy blue sports car with the roof down. Poor Seán knew he could never compete with that so he left for Manchester. Then the next thing Seán got word that it was all off with James. So he wrote to Tess saying he couldn't forget her and asked her to join him in Manchester. She wrote back telling him she was pregnant and hiding it from her parents. She said she'd made the biggest mistake of her life choosing James over him but

139

now she had to face the consequences. The next thing her mother noticed she was putting on weight and confronted her. All hell broke loose. James said he had no intention of marrying her. The local priest got involved and he and the brother took Tess off to the Mother and Baby home in Tuam."

"God. Her own brother?"

"Tess told Seán he had notions. She said he was far more concerned about protecting the rich Protestant family than his own. Sure, you couldn't blame her for not having anything to do with him after that."

I uncrossed my legs, accidently kicking Dev who yelped beneath my foot. I leant over and patted his silky coat then sat back and exhaled loudly.

"Despite all that, Dad stuck by her. He really loved her, didn't he?"

"He was besotted. Mammy was livid when she found out they were getting married."

"And what happened to Tess's parents? They didn't die before we were born, like she told us, did they?"

Julia shook her head slowly. "They both lived well into their seventies. Nancy Corley, a nurse who worked beside me at the hospital in Westport was a neighbour of theirs. She told me when they passed away and I rang Tess and told her. But Tess never came home to either funeral."

"She never forgave them."

"No, she didn't."

I got up and stood in front of the fireplace, my hands behind my back, the fire warming the back of my legs. Julia sat forward on her chair and put her head in her hands.

"I know what it's like to lose one child, Carmel. But

your poor mother. To lose two sons. And to find out one of them had been neglected in that home and died and not had any kind of burial. It devastated her."

I knelt down beside her and stroked her thinning hair.

"None of it is your fault, Julia. The Church and State and Tess's own family are to blame for what happened to her, not you."

I stood up and picked up a photo from the mantelpiece. Dad, Mikey and me were standing in front of the whitewashed wall of Grandma's old house when I was six or seven. Dad was dapper in an orange floral wide collared shirt and bellbottom jeans. He was grinning down at Mikey in his arms and I was leaning into him, shyly, in a lemon summer dress.

"Dad was a very good man, wasn't he?" I said.

"One of the finest that ever walked in shoe leather," she replied, picking up the poker, leaning over and poking the fire again.

Chapter 20

Kathleen Slevin asked if we could sit outside so she could smoke, which she did heartily. The fine weather had held and it was a tepid afternoon with a pleasant breeze. The Breaffy House Hotel was just a few miles from Bohola, the village where Kathleen had lived alone since the death of her husband the previous year. Set in wooded grounds, the impressive Victorian grey-stone building boasted turrets and gargoyles. Once the ancestral home of an Anglo-Irish family, it was easy to imagine the tinkle of upper-class English accents, the flurry of a pheasant shoot and the yell of a hunt. Nowadays the place was known for its GAA training ground, its golf course and as a key wedding venue in Mayo.

"I missed the vaping boat." Kathleen lit her second

cigarette in five minutes then smiled, revealing a jaundiced set of teeth. She was hobbity, barely five feet tall, with small green eyes and dressed in a pale-blue summer dress that hung off her bony shoulders. She shook two packets of sugar into a large coffee cup that was almost the size of her face.

I had almost cancelled our meeting. There didn't seem much point. My baby brother was long dead and buried. Why would I want to torture myself further by learning about Tess's time in the home? It wasn't going to be good. But I changed my mind for two reasons. The first was meeting Louisa Schulz. She'd made me stop and think about the courage of all the survivors who were telling their stories and reliving the painful episodes of their past. Tess was also a survivor. I felt I owed it to her to find out exactly what happened in the home and tell her story too. I also wanted to find out more about the baby's father. Tess and Kathleen were friends in the home. I was hoping Tess had confided in her about James. Who was he? Was he still alive? Maybe she knew more about Tess's brother, Tadgh, too. I had to grab my chance to find out these things when I had it. Kathleen wasn't going to be around forever, especially if she carried on smoking at that rate.

"It all happened such a long time ago," I said to her. "I expect you don't remember much."

"Oh, I remember it all very well. I've often thought about your mother over the years and wondered how she was going on. I tried to contact her a couple of times after she left the home."

I sat up. "You did?"

"I wrote to your father's lodging address in Manchester

where he was staying when she was in the home. I knew he'd moved on but I hoped they might forward the letters on. I never heard anything back."

"I see." I stirred my latte. "Do you mind if we start from the beginning, Kathleen?"

"Sure we can," she said.

"So how come you were working in the home? I thought only nuns worked in those places."

"They were desperate for the extra help. I was sixteen when I was sent to work there. Our local priest, Father McGrath, knocked on the door of our house and asked my parents if I'd like to train as a nursery nurse in a maternity home near Galway. I was told I'd be looking after sick babies. My parents saw it as a great opportunity and an honour to be asked. I jumped at the chance. The alternative was the boat to Holyhead or the plane to America and I was awful shy and didn't want to emigrate."

I soon realised that Kathleen was a great talker and as sharp as a tack. I was so relieved I didn't have to prise information from her and poke and prod her memory, but I did have to keep her focussed on Tess's story. She had a tendency to digress.

"When I arrived I was shocked to see so many sick babies, all lined up in cots in the nursery. It didn't take me long to realise they weren't sick at all. I soon discovered it was a home for unmarried mothers. I was scandalised."

"Really?"

"We were very innocent about sex and that kind of thing in those days. I never knew such babies or places existed." She sucked on her cigarette with thin puckered lips. "It was awful hard. You'd get attached to the babies and then the next thing you knew they were gone."

144

"And the women?" I asked tentatively, "Were they treated very badly?"

"Do you want the truth, Carmel?"

I nodded.

"No better than cattle. Your mother and those other poor creatures were put to work doing laundry and cleaning the minute they arrived. No matter how far gone in their confinement. When the babies were born the mothers nursed them until they left but they were only allowed to spend a limited amount of time with them before the adoptive families came to take them away. The poorer mothers had to stay on to pay for their keep. But if the girls' families had any money, they could pay money for an early release."

"And Tess?"

"Your father paid up."

I sighed.

"The nuns told me not to talk to any of the mothers. They said they were fallen women and I was to keep away from them. Like they were infectious or something. It was the silence I found hardest of all. We were all Irishwomen. We love to talk so it was a form of torture. I worked from seven in the morning until eight at night scrubbing floors and offices as well as looking after the babies. But at least I was paid. Those poor girls got nothing but beatings and abuse."

I pushed an ashtray towards her to catch the mountain of ash about to fall from the end of her cigarette.

"They never did it in front of me, mind. I'd see the bruises the next morning when we arrived at work."

"So you didn't live in?"

She shook her head. "I lodged with an elderly couple

in the village. Mr and Mrs Kennedy. Pair of auld bastards. They only let me out to go to work at the home and to Mass. It was only afterwards I copped on why. The nuns didn't want me to mix with people in the village in case I told them what went on behind that big stone wall."

We both turned at the sound of laughter as two girls of about six or seven ran through the patio area in salmon-pink bridesmaids' dresses. The bar inside was filling with wedding guests. I watched as the smaller girl tripped over and the older one helped her up and gave her a hug.

I turned back to Kathleen.

"And the older kids?" I asked. "Did you have anything to do with them at all?"

She shook her head. "They were in a separate wing altogether. The nuns kept me well away. But I remember seeing them going to the school in the village in hobnailed boots."

"And the babies? How were they treated?"

She erupted in a coughing fit. When she'd finished she cleared her throat. It sounded like the thrum of an old engine starting up.

"Sorry about that," she said, sipping her coffee. "Where was I? The babies. We were told to feed and bathe and clothe the babies but there was no time for anything else. If they cried or were sick it was reported but it might be a while until they were seen to because there were so many of them. It was like conveyor belt. There was no time to hold or play with them and if one of them didn't take their bottle you were told to carry on feeding and bathing the next one. It all sounds so terrible now. But I just did as I was told. I was awful scared of making a mistake and harming one of them. The nuns would stand around

146

watching. Not doing any work, mind, just watching. They weren't all bad though. Some of the younger ones took pity on the mothers and let them sneak in and hold their babies once in a while. But I was terrified. You never questioned a nun those days. All I wanted was to please my parents so I went along with it."

"You were only a young girl too, Kathleen. I understand." I leant forwards and lowered my voice. "And Tess? How was she was treated in there?"

She swallowed.

"There were good nuns. Sister Martha was the nicest. She was a gentle soul who was kind to the girls. But there was one, Sister Pauline, who had it in for your mother good and proper. Tess was such a beautiful girl. She giggled a lot and reached out and touched you when she was talking to you. She couldn't help it, it was just the way she was, but the nuns saw her behaviour as indecent. They saw it as their duty to stamp it out. That was the way their twisted minds worked. Sister Pauline was a fat old sow from Cork. She tormented your mother. We used to call her She Devil."

Kathleen stared down into her coffee cup.

"She beat your mother. One time she shaved all her lovely hair off."

I fought back tears then put my hand over hers. "It's OK, Kathleen. I need to hear this."

"Those girls have haunted my dreams for most of my life, your mother especially. This is the first time I've spoken about any of it. I buried it in the back of my mind, like a stain. When you rang, I knew I had to tell you what happened in there. I had to talk about it to someone after all these years."

147

I gestured to the passing waitress and ordered another coffee for us both and a slice of chocolate fudge cake for Kathleen.

"Please, Kathleen, take your time," I said, when the waitress had gone.

"Your mother was six months pregnant when she arrived. She Devil would make her work in the evenings after the other girls had gone for tea. That's how we became friends. She Devil would feck off and feed her face and leave us to polish the floors. I was awful relieved to break the silence. Despite her terrible situation your mother was great craic. The pair of us used to slag the nuns big-time. We laughed a lot. She told me all about your father in Manchester and asked me to write to him for her. She told me what to say and I'd memorise it. Then I'd write it down at my digs in the evening and post the letter on my way to Mass. Your father wrote to me at the Kennedys' address. I let on I had a brother in England then I'd smuggle the letters in to your mother."

"I can't thank you enough for that, Kathleen. You took a huge risk."

"I did it because I thought your mother might lose her mind in there. The day after she gave birth, She Devil had her on her hands and knees scrubbing floors even though she'd torn badly. I never forgot the sight of her, bent double, crying out in pain, blood soaking through the back of her grey dress."

I inhaled sharply at the memory of Tess on her hands and knees in the back garden of Brantingham Road, manically scrubbing the path.

"She had mental health issues, for most of her life," I said.

"It doesn't surprise me after what they did to her in there."

"Do you think she was singled out because the father of her baby was a Protestant?"

"What?" Kathleen frowned. "But I thought the baby's father was Seán, your da."

"No. It was someone from an Anglo-Irish family in her village."

"Are you serious? Your mother made out it was your father." Kathleen turned her head and gazed over the sloping lawns and the golf course. "I suppose she was scared I'd turn against her too if she told me the truth."

The waitress arrived with our coffee and cake. Kathleen chewed on small mouthfuls and helped it down with sips of coffee. The sun was going in and the patio was getting busy with wedding guests. I pulled on my jacket I asked her if she was cold and wanted to go inside but she said she was fine and that her daughter Margaret was coming soon.

"Why did you leave the home?" I asked.

"Ma Kennedy opened one of your da's letters and I was done for."

"No way!"

"Oh yes. It wasn't long after your mother left. I was marched into Mother Superior's office. She Devil was standing next to the big desk with your da's loving words in her hands and Mother Superior sprang out from behind the desk and gave me a whack around the head. She was raging. She accused me of aiding and abetting a fallen woman and encouraging her to sin. I told her I'd leave there and then. But she said I was to stay on and work a month without pay as penance or she'd tell my

149

parents. She Devil was going to accompany me to Kennedys' to fetch my things then I was to live in the home for that last month."

"Good God!"

"She also said I was to keep away from post boxes." Kathleen laughed but her face clouded over quickly. "I'd seen older women working in the gardens. They'd been in there for decades. I was terrified and thought they were going to do that to me too. So when I was collecting my things from Kennedys' I stuffed my savings inside my bra and gave She Devil the slip on the road back. I dropped my suitcase on the side of the road and made a run for it over the fields. Her fat old legs couldn't catch me and I called her all the names under the sun. I walked for miles in the pitch black and hid in a cowshed for the night. I knew they'd be looking for me all over the town. So the next morning I stole a bike from the side of a house and cycled the thirty-five miles back to Castlebar."

I clasped my hands together and laughed. "What an amazing story, Kathleen."

"There's more. By the time I got home Father McGrath had already got to Mammy and Daddy. The nuns told him I'd compromised myself with a boy in the village near the home and said it would be best for everyone if I went back to avoid bringing shame on my family."

"You are fucking kidding me!"

"Those bitches lied and tried their best to get me back there because they were terrified I'd talk. But I was lucky. Mammy and Daddy didn't believe the lies and they showed Father McGrath the door when he returned. But even though I'd done nothing wrong I was sent to London to live with my aunt. I was away five years. I

150

trained to be a nurse at St Thomas'. That's where I met my Jimmy, a Breaffy man who was working as a porter. He was given the home place and we moved back with the kids. So it didn't turn out too badly for me in the end. We were married for fifty-three years and I've got six grandchildren."

"You are a marvel, Kathleen Slevin."

I glanced down at my watch. It was almost four thirty and she said her daughter was coming to collect her in ten minutes. I was driving straight to the airport for my six-thirty flight afterwards.

"My brother Donal . . . Tess's baby," I said. "Do you remember anything about him at all?

"Oh, he was a bonny baby and a good weight, a good weight. Lots of curly blonde hair. I remember him well the day they came for him."

I sat up. "Sorry?"

"The day the two fellas came for him in the fancy car. It was a few days after Tess left for Manchester."

I shook my head. "You must be mistaken. Tess's baby died in the home when he was five months old. His name was on the list of the dead children from the home."

Kathleen frowned. "There must be some mistake. I saw them take him away. Two fine-looking men, one dark and one blonde. I'd just arrived for my early shift. They often came for the babies early in the morning or late at night so the mothers couldn't see them taking them away. The two men took him to a fancy car and drove off. The dark man was driving, the blonde one holding the baby. I knew it was Tess's baby because of all the hair and the red cardigan your mother had knitted for him."

151

"Are you sure, Kathleen?"

"I am, of course."

"Can you remember anything about the car?"

"It was a blue sports car. The roof was down. I'd never seen the likes of it before. I remember thinking they were eejits for putting a baby in it with no bonnet on him. The poor mite would catch his death of cold."

Chapter 21

My grandparents' house in Mayo. A white fuzz of heat, blue
skies and the sound of crickets. Tess and Dad were waltzing
in front of the bungalow and Karen, Mikey and I were
running through the adjacent field. Karen and Mikey were
sprinting ahead. I yelled at them to stop and wait but they
ignored me, their heads dipping and disappearing into the
tall yellow grass. A sudden sharp pain. I stopped and looked
down. Blood was oozing from the ball of my foot. A white
bone that looked like a needle had pierced it. The grass
around me started to roll back like a carpet, revealing a layer
of black glistening soil that looked like tar. Piles of tiny
white bones were scattered at intervals and more appeared
as the grass rolled back further. I shouted for Tess and Dad
and Karen and Mikey but they'd all disappeared. All that

was left was the outline of the house on a shimmering horizon.

I woke up in a cold sweat with Joe leaning over me, a concerned look on his face. He said I'd been calling out in my sleep and flailing my arms. Joe went to the bathroom to get me a glass of cold water and I sat up and wiped my damp face with a pillow.

It was 5am, the morning after I arrived back from Mayo. Shafts of orange and yellow light filtered through the bedroom blinds. It looked like the world was on fire outside and the dawn chorus was alive.

When Joe returned I finally told him everything, about Dad's letter, the mass grave, finding the list of dead children and all the things that had happened in Mayo including what Julia had told me and Kathleen Slevin's sighting of the two men taking Donal out of the home. I told him I was now convinced my brother was alive and well somewhere out there in the world.

Propped up against pillows, Joe listened in silence. His face had remained expressionless and he hadn't interrupted once or asked any questions. It was like none of it came as a surprise. But life with Tess and Mikey had always been turbulent and eccentric so to Joe it was probably yet another chapter in the life of my fucked-up family.

When I'd finally finished, he cleared his throat and stared at the wardrobe door where stripes of morning light flickered like light sabres. He looked at me, the corners of his mouth turned down.

"And you never once thought of telling me any of this?" he asked quietly.

I inhaled sharply. "You've been away so I haven't seen you that much to tell you. And I was about to a couple of times but we always ended up having a barney." A milk van creaked on the road outside and I slumped back on the bed. "You've hardly been the easiest person to be around lately."

He pursed his lips and said nothing then he leant over and put his arm around me. "Sorry. Work's pretty stressful these days. Poor Tess," he said, kissing the top of my head. "And poor you, going through this on your own. So this Kathleen Slevin woman – what she said about the what men taking the baby away – you think it's reliable?"

"I can't think why she'd make it up. She seemed of sound mind to me."

"She could be confused. From what you said, she's getting on. We're talking sixty-odd years after the event here."

"I know. But something tells me she remembers everything about Tess's story because it affected her directly. She escaped from the home and ended up being sent to England because she helped Tess out. Then there's the blue sports car. As soon as Kathleen described it, I knew what she was saying had to be true. I rang Julia and said cars like that would definitely have been a rarity in rural Mayo at that time. I'm also pretty sure the blonde man with James was Tadgh Dempsey, Tess's brother."

"Do you really think he'd help steal his sister's baby and never tell her where he was?"

"For some reason he was desperate to please James' family. Plus he and Tess had fallen out. Tess never heard from him again as far as I know. She said he ended up living rough on the streets in London."

Joe scratched his chin. "But how did the nuns get away with it? If they faked your brother's death, surely they had to have a body to get a death certificate?"

"Or a doctor faked it. The more I've delved into all of this, the more I've come to the conclusion that the nuns couldn't have worked alone. Doctors, social workers, solicitors, politicians – they all had to have played a part in the illegal adoptions. There was an organised system at work. It was a well-oiled machine."

"A well-oiled adoption machine."

"Yes."

"James' family were very wealthy so I'm guessing they paid a lot of money to get Donal back. And Tess would never have known. Before she left the home, she'd have signed consent papers thinking that her baby was going to a good family in America. She'd never have imagined James would return to claim him."

"Christ. That's so fucked up."

Joe pulled me towards him and held me tight. I buried my head in the crook of his neck and he ran the tip of his forefinger along my arm. Then he turned my face to his and searched for my mouth. We kissed for a long time. When we pulled apart, I told him I'd stopped taking the pill. Something had shifted inside me when I was in Mayo. Visiting Julia again and hearing about Tess from Kathleen Slevin had made me feel connected to my family and to my past again. And seeing the bloke from the Irish Club looking so serene with his family in Achill, the place I was happiest as a child, had stirred something in me.

Joe looked at me startled, then his face lit up like a child on Christmas morning.

"Really?"

I nodded and smiled. "I thought about it a lot in Ireland. Let's go for it."

He grinned and started to unbutton my nightshirt. His tongue ran down my breastbone with every unfastening. Soon it was circling one nipple then another then his fingers slithered inside me, searching and teasing out the place only he knew existed. When he was inside me I pushed in rhythm with him, slowly at first then faster, reaching together. When he came his face exploded in pain and joy in the blaze of morning light and I was moved.

Chapter 22

In the week that followed I jump-started the search for my brother. I returned to my friend Google for help. Having no surname for James, the baby's father, I searched for the house outside Tess's village where his family had lived. It had been turned into a B&B and the current owners were English with no knowledge of an Anglo-Irish family ever living there. I'd need another trip to Mayo to talk to the locals to get the information I needed. A google search for Tadgh Dempsey also came to nothing. It didn't surprise me. If what Tess had said was true and he'd ended up on the streets, he wasn't exactly going to have much of a digital footprint.

The following Wednesday I was at home having breakfast when I received an email back from TUSLA, the government family agency in Galway that I'd written to way back at the start of my search. They more or less stated what I'd feared. As the sibling of a former resident in the Tuam Mother and Baby home, I wasn't legally entitled to access any records. I threw my phone on the sofa in annoyance and paced the room. It was a major setback. How the hell could family members ever find out what had happened to their relatives without access to records? I remembered what Louisa Schulz said about her search for her birth mother, how she'd had so many doors slammed in her face her nose was put out of joint. But she never gave up and neither would I. I'd fallen into a low despairing mood when I found Donal's name on that list of dead children but now hope had sent me high again. I was back on the emotional roller coaster, aware that the shock of the fall could be waiting around the corner, but as long as there was the tiniest glimpse of hope I would never stop the search for my brother.

I hadn't seen Joe all week. He'd been working in London. I wouldn't see him that evening either. I was off to a conference at the university in Liverpool on women in Shakespeare. Afterwards I'd arranged to meet Claire, an old friend from my Oakwood High days. Karen knew her too and I'd texted her to see if she wanted to come along but she said she was busy as usual. Claire had booked us a table at one of the best Italian restaurants on Lark Lane. I hadn't seen her for months. She was a social worker in the adoption services and lived in a rambling house in Aigburth with her lecturer husband, two cockapoos and three kids under ten. She was hard to pin down and any arrangements to see her had to be made months in advance. Claire's family were Irish and I was hoping to ask her about the illegal adoptions in the Mother and Baby homes and if she knew of any other possible routes I might try to find Donal. That aside, I was looking forward to her company and catching up.

But before that I needed to get some food in, so I headed out to the local deli for supplies. I used to shop in the Barbakan Deli with Tess when it was a small Polish grocery. Over the years I'd watched it transform into a Mancunian foodie heaven. Nowadays people travelled miles for its sour dough, German rye and ciabatta. They packed bags stuffed with Danish pastries, original Italian pasta, smoked hams, salamis and continental cheeses into the boots of their cars. The outdoor terrace had recently been revamped with new rattan furniture and it had become a popular venue for Chorlton parents after the school drop-off. I parked in the small Tesco car park on the opposite side of the road and headed over.

As usual it was busy with a queue snaking out of the door. I exited after a long wait with my steaming Americano, soda bread, pasta and cheese. As I crossed the terrace I spotted Bryonie Phillips at a far table with a group of friends. I hadn't seen anything of her since that night at the fundraiser. She was wearing Jackie O sunglasses and a flouncy yellow top that made her large breasts look like a pair of canary melons. She caught my eye and waved. I had a sudden flashback to the night of the fundraiser when I'd been so shamefully horribly drunk. God only knows what she was saying about me to her cronies. True to form, I panicked. I pretended I hadn't seen her. Hurrying down the steps onto the pavement, I took my phone from my pocket and started talking into it. Then as I was waiting to cross the road, I heard the unmistakable high-pitched screech of her laughter behind me, like chalk screeching on a blackboard. I froze. It was too loud and too forced to be natural. I was meant to hear it. I walked across, still in conversation with my imaginary friend, my heart pounding.

On the drive home I cursed myself yet again, powerless in the face of my debilitating anxiety. Why couldn't I slip on a mask and smile and say hello to Bryonie like any normal person might? Avoidance was supposed to be the worst strategy for anxiety-sufferers but I'd been doing it for so long now it had become second nature. When I got home I put Classic FM on the radio to calm myself as I got ready for work. I tried to fill my head with positive thoughts. The conference looked very promising and I was seeing Claire later. I started to feel better. I shut the front door behind me and headed down the path with a slight spring in my step. Little did I know that when I opened it again I'd be stepping into a very different life.

Chapter 23

As the taxi pulled up, Joe's black BMW was disappearing around the corner of the street in a silver mist of rain. I thought I saw the profile of someone in the passenger seat but I couldn't be sure because of the rain. A furious wind thrashed around the street and a woman passed me holding her umbrella in front of her face, with all her strength like she was rolling a stone up a hill. I paid the driver and ran into the house. I wondered where Joe was off to. A man of habit, he went to the cycling club every Thursday but it was vicious out there so it must have been cancelled.

After an enjoyable conference I'd gone for drinks with a couple of colleagues at a wine bar near the university. I was about to call a taxi and head over to Lark Lane to meet

Claire when she called. She was stranded in A&E with Sam, her sports-mad ten-year-old. It looked like he'd broken his arm and they weren't leaving the hospital any time soon. Deflated, I made my way to Lime Street and boarded the train for Manchester Piccadilly. I ordered a coffee from the trolley and gazed out of the window as the train trundled between grey Lancashire towns. Dusk was falling. Rain swept over the valleys and gently undulating hills, avocado and mint green in the fading light. I'd always thought of the Lancashire terrain as mellow and calming compared to the violent landscape of the west coast of Ireland. Both had a beauty of their own. Both were part of me in equal measure. Like two sides of a coin.

A harassed-looking mother on a nearby seat was trying to placate her crying toddler with a game on her phone. Sometimes I couldn't help resenting my friends' children when I saw how they sucked their mothers dry. Of course, I was sorry that Claire's boy had broken his arm but at the same time I felt hostile towards him for robbing me of an evening with her. From what I could see, children didn't drain their fathers in the same way. Fathers managed to maintain a sense of self but mothers were left with very little of their own. Something to think about if Joe and I ever did get pregnant.

I was exhausted and couldn't be bothered cooking so I helped myself to some of the brie and soda bread I'd bought from the Barbakan that morning. I looked around. The kitchen was spotless but I'd left it in a tip that morning. Now the worktop glistened, the floor had been scrubbed and even the tea towels were piled neatly by the sink. The only time Joe cleaned like that was after an argument or when he'd done something that upset me. It was our standing joke, how doing housework was his unspoken way of apologising. I poured myself a glass of red and smiled. I wondered what he'd done for me to deserve all this.

I took my food and wine into the front room. I was looking forward to catching up on more Irish history and watching the next episode of *Rebellion* on Netflix, a show about the Easter Rising. I spent at least five minutes searching for the TV remote and had started cursing and was about to kick the coffee table when I finally located it under a sofa cushion. As I picked it up, I felt something hard and metallic against my fingers. I pulled it out. It was a bracelet, slim and gold with the two ends shaped in the form of a snake's head with tiny emeralds for eyes. Karen's bracelet, the one I'd admired that day at her house after the fundraiser, the one I'd suspected was a gift from Simon Whelan. I sat down, frowning and trying to remember. I was sure she'd told me that day it was new. To my knowledge she'd never been here to the house since then. I sat down. My chest tightened and my thoughts quickened. We'd texted days before when I invited her to come along and meet up with Claire. She knew I wouldn't be at home tonight. I stared down at the bracelet for some time, clenching my fist around it and turning it over in my hand.

I paced up and down the kitchen and glugged my wine.

"*No*," I said aloud. "*It can't be true.*"

Rain fired down on the windowpane and I waved my free hand in the air like I was warding off an invisible threat.

Karen definitely knew I wouldn't be home. The clean kitchen, the figure in the passenger seat of the car. I suddenly felt nauseous at the whiff of lemon disinfectant, a smell that would trigger memories of this day for years afterwards.

I stopped pacing and stared at the upturned coffee cups on the draining-board. I went over, picking them up one by one and inspected them for lipstick smudges. Then I yanked opened the dishwasher looking for wineglasses or plates, for some sign or evidence she'd been there. After that it was the bin's turn. I upturned it on to the shining floor then got on my knees and rummaged through the rubbish with my bare hands. I wasn't exactly sure what I was looking for. He was hardly likely to leave a used condom or the packaging from an M&S meal for two behind, but I was compelled to look just the same.

When I'd done I raced upstairs, pulled back the duvet cover in every bedroom, frantically running my hands along the sheets. On the landing I heard my phone buzz in the hall and almost fell down the stairs in my rush to get to it. My hand shaking, I yanked it out of my bag. It was a WhatsApp message.

Stuck drinking with clients after work. Back late. Enjoy your evening. X

I texted him back immediately.

What was Karen doing here today?

I sat on the stairs, trembling and waiting for him to text back. Nothing, but I knew he'd seen the message. I texted again.

Where the fuck are you? What's going on?

Again nothing, except the blue ticks at the side of my message telling me he'd seen it. I put my head in my hands and felt myself start to crumble. His silence told me it was true. I took a deep breath and sat up. I'd run away from difficult situations all my life but I couldn't run away from this one. I needed to know the truth and I needed to know now. If Joe wasn't going to tell me, Karen was. Summoning every sinew of strength I could find, I put on my jacket, grabbed my bag and headed out of the door.

It was almost ten. The sky was murderous and steely grey and a fierce wind had wrapped itself around the streets. I'd drunk too much to drive so I'd have to walk. Emboldened and enraged by the wine, I pulled my hood up and headed off towards High Lane. As I emerged onto Edge Lane, I decided to take a shortcut through Longford Park so I crossed over and headed up through the gates by the parkkeeper's lodge. I started to regret my decision immediately. I loved the park and had spent a lot of my life in it but recently it was getting a reputation for gang-related crime at night. There'd been a shooting not long ago and a man had hanged himself by the tennis courts a few weeks previously. Yet I ploughed on, quickening my pace and keeping to the wide treelined path as the wind roared around me. Willow branches hung overhead like widow's veils and tar-like puddles shone in the fields either side. I hurried past the playground and Pets Corner where Karen and I had spent so many happy mornings with Alexia when she was little. Then up by the Scout hut where the pair of us had smoked our first spliff with Kevin Cave and his cousin when we were fourteen. Then over the football field where we'd cheered on Alexia in her green-and-white club strip on Sunday mornings. Ahead of me the zip wire dangled like a noose against the night sky and I jumped at the hiss of a bat. I finally exited onto Kings Road not far from Morrissey's childhood home where we'd once entwined gladioli around the gate for his birthday.

I made my way over the Quadrant roundabout towards Old Trafford, exhausted and slightly delirious. My thoughts ran on ahead of me. How long had it been going on? Where? When? So that's why she'd distanced herself and excluded me from her plans to move to Italy. I knew she was seeing someone but I'd assumed it was Simon Whelan. She'd been overly emotional that day when we'd met in Central Library. I gasped as I recalled her parting words. "Sorry for *everything*," she'd said. Then there was Joe's recent "he loves me he loves me not" behaviour. But why was she going to live in Italy if they were in the middle of an affair? Unless he was planning on going with her?

I stopped for a moment, leant against a wall and bashed my fist against my forehead.

Betrayal. It was everywhere I looked. Though I could understand why she'd done it, Tess had betrayed me by keeping Donal's existence from me. She in turn had been betrayed by everyone, her family, the Irish State, the Church and all the others who worked the adoption machine. And now Joe and Karen had betrayed me.

My mother, my husband and my best friend. The people I loved and trusted most in the world had kept secrets from me for God knows how long. My whole life was starting to feel like one long extended lie. I finally made it to Karen's road. As I walked up the empty street, I'd never felt so lonely in all my life.

Chapter 24

I knew she'd already gone when I saw the front lawn. Old IKEA chairs, Alexia's battered desk and Springer Bell's tartan dog bed were scattered among black binbags. A framed poster stuck out of one. Last year's Liverpool Fleadh. We'd had the best time. Stoned and drunk, the pair of us had danced front of stage to Van the Man singing "Brown Eyed Girl" like we were eighteen again.

The rain had turned to a light drizzle as I knocked on the door. A middle-aged man with a ruddy face in a crumpled linen suit answered.

I shrugged off my hood. "I'm looking for Karen," I said.

He stroked his goatee. "Ah, I'm afraid you've just missed her. They left for Rome a couple of hours ago."

I stiffened.

"Sorry. By 'they' do you mean Karen and her daughter?"

He shook his head.

"No. Her daughter's already there. She was with a friend. Joe, I think he said his name was." He pulled a bunch of keys from his pocket and jangled them like a prize. "I'm the new owner. She left me a forwarding email address if you need it."

"I've got it but thanks anyway."

He gestured skywards as I turned to go.

"Lucky woman, escaping this weather, eh?" he said.

I gave him a weak smile then walked down the path and out into the street in a daze.

Lucky woman. Oh yes. That's exactly what Karen Obassi was. She'd got away with it yet again.

Once, I was babysitting Alexia. She was about eight or nine and I was teaching her to play badminton in the garden. At one point she got frustrated, whacked the ground with her racket and broke it. I gave her a lukewarm telling-off and we stopped the game.

"You should have followed through with a punishment," Karen said afterwards when I told her what had happened. "It's so important for children to face up to the consequences of their actions. It's how they learn not to repeat bad behaviour. At the end of the day it's what makes them decent adults."

Her words had stayed with me and, as I walked down her street in the drizzle, I thought about them again.

Karen the therapist sat in her chair every day telling vulnerable people to face up to their demons. Karen the tough parent insisted on following through with punishments and consequences. But when it came her own

169

life and relationships, things were very different. When had she ever once faced up to the ramifications of any of the emotional car-crashes she had caused? And there were many. I shook my head as I remembered the time Simon Whelan's teenage twins arrived on her doorstep looking for their father. She hid upstairs until they were gone. Then there was the episode in Julia's village when she'd absconded with Luke O'Connell to the festival. After she returned, Karen refused to enter Julia's house for fear of rebuke and she made me meet her down the road with all her belongings instead. And when the wives of the numerous married men she'd fucked over the years landed at her front door, she escaped out the back. Karen was a hit-and-run driver, pure and simple. She never stayed around to face the consequences of her actions. She lived her life with impunity.

Why oh why was I so naive? Why had I never thought she would do it to me too? But she had. I knew it. And now she'd escaped like a thief in the night with a chunk of my heart.

Ash-coloured clouds floated in a smouldering orange sky above the Manchester skyline as I walked away from the house. Then I heard the sound of a car pulling up on the other side of the road. I turned, narrowed my eyes and looked. I could just about make out Joe in his black BMW leaning over the passenger seat and opening the door. I clenched my fists. I wanted to carry on walking and never stop. But I did stop, a pathetic dripping statue on an Old Trafford pavement. I had too many questions that needed answers and my head would burst if I didn't get them. So I crossed the road.

Chapter 25

I got into the car.

Joe said nothing.

"I found her bracelet in the front room."

I closed my eyes, imagining I was driving at a hundred miles an hour and he was flying through the windscreen.

He stared out of the car window at the puddles of polished silver in the road ahead.

"How long has it been going on?"

He swallowed. In the dim streetlight his face looked pale and sunken, his neck blotchy.

"Once. It happened once."

"I don't believe you."

"It's true."

"When?"

"In April when you were at the Spa in Cheshire for the night. I was out drinking on Beech Road and I bumped into her in one of the bars. We were having a laugh, we were both very drunk and I asked her back to the house and it happened."

"In April?" My voice sounded small. "That recently?"

In the silence that followed a car swished past, spraying the pavement in front like a wave. Joe put his hands on the steering wheel then lowered his head onto his hands.

"I'm so very sorry, Carmel."

"So you fucked her one night out of the blue? Just like that? I don't believe you. You said you didn't even like her when you first met her."

He shook his head and sighed.

"I used to see her at the gym and we'd chat. Mainly about you. Sometimes we'd have a coffee. You were in bits about Mikey and Tess and we were both worried about you. I suppose we bonded."

"How lovely for you both. So that's why she cooled off our friendship. Because she was bonding with you."

"Let me finish. Nothing happened. We just talked. Then we bumped into each other that night and it just happened. We both regretted it immediately. It was just sex. You have to believe me."

I slammed my hand on the dashboard and his head flew up.

"*What about today?*" I yelled. "The new owner of the house just told me you took her to the fucking airport! Don't tell me nothing happened!"

"It didn't. I swear. We just talked. "

"And you expect me to believe that?"

"It's true. She texted and said she was leaving for Italy

172

today. She asked if she could come round. I hadn't seen her since that night. She was really upset and begging me never to tell you. She wanted to say goodbye but she couldn't face you."

I gave a high-pitched, brittle laugh. "I bet she couldn't."

"She cares about you, Carmel." His voice lowered. "We both do."

I laughed again.

"I offered to give her a lift to the airport. Nothing happened. I swear."

I looked at him, a vat of pure hatred boiling inside me. I badly wanted to tell him what had happened at the conference that time, to make him hurt like I was hurting.

"Where did you fuck her?"

He looked at me sharply. "Don't do this."

"I need to know."

He shook his head. "No, you don't."

I stuck my face inches from his.

"*Yes, I fucking do!*" I screamed.

"*In the front room!*" he yelled back, recoiling.

"What position?"

"For fuck's sake!"

"I need to know."

"Christ. I don't know. I was on top."

"Was it good?"

"Not particularly."

I dug my hands into the pockets of my jacket, tears streaming down my face. A man and woman were kissing goodbye on the doorstep of a house opposite. They lingered then he walked down the path and she blew him a kiss, laughing. I leaned my head against the window and drew a large question mark with my forefinger on the glass.

"Why?" I asked.

He leaned back and sighed. A fly was slowly making its way along the shoulder of his jacket then up his neck. If I had a knife I'd have sliced it in half, stabbing into his jugular.

"It was a moment of weakness. I swear it meant nothing. But I will say this. It's never been easy being married to you, Carmel. For years I was always at the bottom of your list of priorities. Everything was always about Tess and Mikey and their problems. Sometimes it felt like there were four of us in our marriage."

"Oh, come on! You can do better than that."

"It's true."

"So let me just recap for a minute. Tess was mentally ill and Mikey had a drug problem. They were vulnerable adults who needed me. I was a bad wife because I spent time with them, so you slept with my best friend?"

"That's not what I'm saying. I slept with Karen because I was weak. But I'm just trying to explain how I felt about you and your family. Yes, Mikey and Tess needed you. But a lot of the time they could have managed without you. In some ways you enabled them."

I put my head in my hands. "You have no fucking idea. You never got it, did you? You've never had to care for anyone in your life. Mammy and Daddy did everything for you. They threw money your way whenever you wanted it and acted on your every whim. Enable them? I was doing my best to keep my brother and mother alive. Someone had to."

"And the day of Dad's funeral?"

"Oh, here we go again!"

"You left me to grieve alone. I'd just lost Mum and instead of staying with me you fucked off back to

Manchester to watch your good-for-nothing brother get fined in court for drug possession. That's exactly how high up I was on your list of priorities."

I folded my arms across my chest.

"Tess was convinced he was going down and I thought she might do something stupid. I had to be there to stop her."

"That one day I needed you. But you couldn't give me that one day. You always put them first."

"So you slept with my best friend."

I yanked down the window, breathed in the damp night air then turned and looked him in the eye.

"Did you do it because I wouldn't give you a child?"

He shook his head and tutted.

"What the hell is it about her? Why do men want her so much when she treats you all like scum? Does she give twenty-four-hour blow jobs? Go on, tell me."

"I'm not doing this."

I pummelled his shoulder with my fist.

"*Yes, you are! You fucked my best friend. I deserve to know why.*"

He grabbed hold of my wrist and held me still, his eyes burning.

"If you want to know why she's attractive it's because she grabs life by the throat and lives it. Because she's not neurotic and not always worrying about the what-ifs. Because she doesn't overthink everything. Because she lives for the moment. Because she's fucking brave."

He let go of me and I fell back into the seat, feeling like I'd been shot.

I fumbled for the handle and opened the door.

"I want you out of the house tonight," I said, stumbling

175

out on the wet pavement and slamming the door behind me.

Dazed and numb, I hurried down the street. Then a train suddenly hurtled past on the track behind the row of terraces, shaking the ground beneath my feet.

Chapter 26

After Joe left my world came tumbling down. I went about my days feeling like I'd been buried under a pile of rubble, numb and devoid of light and sound. The days turned into weeks. By the end of June rain was coming down in torrents and high winds surged all over the country. On the TV news woeful staycationers dripped on flooded campsites and the downpours and gales brought public transport to a halt. The political party UKIP and its leader Nigel Farage seemed to be on every channel spouting anti-immigration rhetoric and brewing a storm of their own. Conor O'Grady came to mind. The world was becoming such a dark and ugly place.

At work I just about managed to crawl to the end of term. I struggled to concentrate on my end-of-year marking and walked up and down the exam halls like a zombie. I attended leaving parties, thanking students for presents and cards with a feeble voice and vacant smile and I avoided the staffroom and Mary's concerned enquiries about my mental health.

July dragged by. I stopped going out and I ignored texts and calls from colleagues and friends. I became convinced everyone in Chorlton knew about Joe and Karen and my fucked-up life. I hung my head in hurt and shame and wore sunglasses when I went out even though there wasn't a hint of sun. I started shopping late at night in the twenty-four-hour Tesco in Old Trafford to avoid bumping into anyone I knew. I stocked up on weed and curled up on the sofa every evening with a fat spliff, Merlot and Johnny Cash at his maudlin best for company.

I ruminated a lot on what had happened in Ireland but decided to shelve any further plans to search for my brother. I was starting to lose the motivation to do everyday things. The thought of getting back on that emotional roller coaster seemed a daunting insurmountable task.

Joe moved into a friend's house on the other side of Chorlton. The only contact we'd had since our conversation outside Karen's house was a couple of perfunctory emails about stuff to do with the house. He sent another saying he had accepted a two-month project in Madrid. He'd found a flat in Salford Quays and the tenancy was due to start in September. He said it was for the best, that we needed time apart to decide what we really wanted. I replied saying I knew exactly what I wanted and it wasn't being married to someone who'd shagged my best friend. I made sure I was out when he came round to collect his stuff.

Though Joe had often worked away, it had only ever

been for short trips. I started to feel the loneliness. As August dragged on, the big house became hollow with only me in it. I found myself daydreaming about being pregnant and hearing children's laughter filling the empty rooms. I saw Tess sitting on the sofa in the extension with a grandchild in her arms. I saw Mikey pushing another on a swing. Late one evening I was smoking in the garden when I thought I heard Joe laughing at the TV in the front room. I leapt up and hurried inside. The laughter was coming from a group of revellers in the street outside and I sat on the sofa and cried.

I browsed for last-minute breaks online in the Spanish mountains and walking holidays in Greece. I thought I'd give Italy a miss on account of Karen being there. But lethargy took hold, guiding me to the fridge and the wine then back to the sofa and the TV remote and I never went anywhere. I did consider going back to stay with Julia in Westport. But I'd have to tell her about Joe and Karen and I wasn't ready to do that. It was too raw. Putting it into words would make it real.

My husband slept with my best friend.

It was such a cliché, it was laughable.

In mid-August, a postcard arrived from Karen. It was from an art gallery in Rome. On the front, a Caravaggio painting called *Penitent Magdalene* showed a contrite-looking Mary Magdalene bowed in sorrow. On the back Karen had written one word. "*Sorry.*"

Enraged by such a cowardly, tasteless gesture, I grabbed my phone and texted her.

Thanks for the card. Very appropriate. Like you and your mother, Mary Magdalene was also a whore. Do not contact me again.

That evening I deleted all digital trace of her: photos,

phone, email and social-media contacts. I then started on my old photo albums. I burned every picture in the kitchen sink: Polaroids from our school days, arty images from when we went clubbing and all the photos of her with Alexia. It hurt to do that but Alexia looked so much like her mother she had to go. I stood over the sink and watched our years of friendship smoulder and turn to ash. If only it were that easy to erase Karen from my mind. Instead she loomed large, like a searing migraine. I replayed the film of her and Joe fucking over and over until my head hurt.

Life dragged me through those summer months like a mother pulling an unwilling child to school. Then, on the Saturday of the August Bank Holiday, I decided to venture out before I completely lost my mind. I needed books for a research project so I set off for the John Rylands Library in town. I took the bus, getting off at the stop directly in front of Kendals on Deansgate. But as I stepped on to the pavement and saw the shoppers going in and out of the store's rotating doors, I started to feel odd. I felt unsteady on my feet and grabbed hold of a nearby lamppost. I had trouble breathing and my heart was racing like never before. All those feelings of panic I'd experienced on the day of the bomb started coming back to me. Tess, Joe and I were being swept along with the current of people away from the Arndale, a police horse was trotting beside us and the bride was running on the pavement opposite in her wedding dress. I started to shake uncontrollably and stood with my hands over my ears waiting for the explosion. Then a booming Yorkshire accent came from nowhere as a group of teenage boys jostled past me to get on the bus.

"*Oi*, lads, can't you see the lady's not well?"

A pair of tattooed arms plucked them out of the way and before I knew what was happening, I was being led to the bus shelter by a large woman with a peroxide head of frizz. She said her name was Mandy. As I sat on the seat my heart felt like it was about to explode out of my body. It crossed my mind that it might, that it was now my time, that I was going to die the same way as Mikey. I closed my eyes and saw him writhing in the middle of the road in Old Trafford, his face ashen.

"My heart," I said, clutching my chest.

"It's OK, pet. I'm a nurse," said Mandy. "I can't be sure but I think you're having a panic attack. I get them too. They're horrible."

She was right. She gave me a bottle of water from her bag and stayed with me until my breathing had returned to normal. Then she flagged me down a taxi.

I was still shaking as I stumbled through the front door. I didn't understand. I'd been back to Deansgate scores of times since the bomb and I'd never I experienced anything like that. Why it was it happening to me now?

Chapter 27

As if having a panic attack in the middle of Deansgate wasn't frightening enough, the next day I bumped into Bryonie Phillips. I was jogging in The Meadows. I hadn't been running since the day Mikey died but I thought some exercise might help my mental health. I'd also heard it was a healthier sleep aid than copious amounts of marijuana and a bottle of Sauvignon Blanc every night.

The Meadows was the local name for Chorlton Eees Nature Reserve, the conservation area on the edge of Chorlton that hugged the River Mersey. Tree-lined paths led you through woodland and fields teeming with wildlife. It was my haven. I loved being deep in the woods away from the sounds and smells of the city. On my walks and runs there I'd spotted a water vole, a brown hare and one time a kingfisher. Despite days of continuous rain that had left the area muddy and treacherous, the path by the river was busy with dog-walkers.

I dragged myself along at a snail's pace, my calves stiff and in need of oiling. It felt like they were carrying the weight of both my body and troubled mind, but I plodded on regardless, past sunflowers battered and bruised by the wind. The river was swelling, the sluggish brown water rising and curling. After a while, I stopped by a willow tree to rest and watch a heron swooping for fish in the river.

I spotted Bryonie about twenty feet ahead. She was wearing a yellow raincoat with matching polka-dot wellies and was being dragged along the path by her tawny-coloured spaniel, imaginatively named Brownie. I suddenly felt exposed, like I was standing there stark naked for all the world to see. I recalled her laughter that day at the Barbakan Deli and shuddered. It wasn't one bit rational but I became convinced Bryonie knew all my dirty secrets. She knew about Joe and Karen and she relished telling everyone in Chorlton about my fucked-up life. I was sure of it.

I glanced around for an escape route as she headed towards me, smiling and waving and grappling with her beast. The only thing to do was to head down the bank at the side of the path and into the woods so I went for it. But the incline was steep and I lost my footing in the mud. I plunged onto my backside in the sludge. I got up but slipped again, this time rolling down the incline and landing beside a nettle bush. When I looked up Bryonie was standing on the path. Charcoal clouds drifted above her head and she had one hand over her mouth trying not to laugh, the Hound of the Baskervilles barking at her feet.

It was a cameo that summed up just about everything about my life. I kept falling on my arse again and again while the world laughed. Stung, I limped away, leaving my dignity in the nettle bush.

The next day was Bank Holiday Monday. Determined to keep up with my daily exercise, I drove up to Alexandra Park in Whalley Range, parked and went for a walk. Families were gathered around the pond feeding the ducks. As I passed by I thought of Sundays there with Tess and Dad shortly before he died. We'd throw old breadcrusts into the water, buy 99 cones from the ice-cream van near the café and Dad would kick a ball about with Mikey. At four years of age my brother was already showing sporting talent. An image came to me of Tess lying on the grass beside me in a pink summer dress. Her blonde hair was piled messily on her head and I was putting lipstick on her full smiling lips. The memory warmed me and I clung on to it. What happened to her was not her fault. At times she was the best of mothers and we were a happy normal family once.

As I drove home, families everywhere seemed to be piling into cars with bags of food, foil-covered sandwich trays and bottles of something or other. Many were probably dreading a day with in-laws, parents and siblings in damp back gardens or overcrowded front rooms. Christ, how I envied them. I'd have given anything for a dull afternoon with Dad, Tess, Mikey, Paddy or Peggy. I thought of the empty rooms waiting for me at home. What was the point of a dream house without a family in it?

Sunlight was squeezing its way out from behind the clouds when I spotted Samira Khan at the traffic lights on Alexandra Road. She was heading in the direction of

Brantingham Road like she was in a hurry. I felt a stab of guilt. I'd been so caught up with everything that had happened recently I'd completely forgotten to contact her after Conor O'Grady's attack on Adeel. Conor had been due to stand trial but at the last minute Adeel had dropped all the charges. I sighed. I didn't particularly want a chat with Samira about the old days. But I gave into my feelings of guilt, pulled up beside her and offered her a lift home.

Samira was delighted to see me and accepted. What had happened to Adeel had obviously had an effect on her. She'd lost weight and the happy carefree sheen in her eyes had been replaced by a wary, subdued look. As I pulled up outside her house she invited me in for coffee but I made an excuse about having plans. We chatted for a while in the car instead.

"So, how's Adeel?" I asked.

"Completely recovered now. Back immersed in his politics."

"I heard he dropped the charges against Conor."

She sighed. "Yes. Conor's father Tom came to the house one day. He begged me to persuade Adeel not to go ahead. Said his son had been suffering from post-traumatic shock for years after a bomb attack in Northern Ireland had left him in his wheelchair. He said the army had abandoned his son and left him on shitty benefits and without any help for his mental-health problems." She shook her head. "The poor man kept apologising, Carmel. He was so desperate for his son not to go to prison. He said it would be the end for him. Apparently Conor has already made two suicide attempts. It was a difficult decision to make. Of course I wanted Conor to be punished and go to prison for what he did to Adeel but he is not well in the head. So I asked Adeel to drop the charges."

"*Wow*. That's an incredible act of kindness, Samira."

I thought about my experience with Conor. I wanted to ask her if she thought he could go on to attack someone else, but I held back.

"Adeel refused at first. So I said he could look after his own bloody kids then. He soon changed his mind."

I laughed. "You are terrible, Samira."

She grinned and the old Samira was back.

"I know. Anyway, how are things with you?" She squeezed my arm. "You are so pale and skinny. You need to eat more, Carmel."

"I'm fine," I lied.

After she'd gone into the house I suddenly remembered about her chats with Tess and what she'd said to me the day I found Dad's letter. "*So cruel to have her son taken from her like that.*" I'd been so consumed by what had happened with Joe and Karen I'd completely forgotten to ask Samira if Tess had ever confided in her about the baby she'd given away. I thought about knocking on the door and asking her but the moment had gone. Only a few weeks before, I would have dived in there straightaway with a list of questions. Finding my brother had obsessed my every waking hour then. But now the bottom had fallen out of my world and I simply didn't have the energy any more.

I started to drive off but pulled over again as I passed the old house. I stopped and stared. It had been completely transformed and was barely recognisable. Grey PVC windows had replaced the cracked wooden ones, the roof was newly tiled and the brickwork plastered over. The porch had gone, Tess's garden had been completely gravelled over and a Mitsubishi four-by-four filled the driveway. I was overcome by a strange mixture of loss and awe.

Then the front door opened and a dark wiry man in a pale denim shirt came out followed by a girl of about six or seven. She had ebony waist-length hair and was wearing a lemon dress. She stopped on the step and called out to her father, pointing down at her foot. He turned round, walked back to her then bent down to fasten her shoe. He straightened up and as he kissed the top of her head I heard myself say "Daddy", and something broke inside me.

Chapter 28

In the days that followed the darkness slipped through the front door when I wasn't looking and made itself at home. Inconspicuous at first, it started to follow me around then before long it was forever by my side. The darkness had a voice too.

"You are worthless," it said, as I lay in bed staring at the ceiling. "You are neurotic, you have no friends and everyone has left you. Nobody cares whether you live or die."

Getting out of bed and putting one step in front of the other to go downstairs became a monumental effort. As did showering and eating. I nibbled on bread and cheese, crackers and the odd apple. My appetite for wine did not diminish and I guzzled a bottle most days. I lost track of time. Hours would pass and I'd realise I hadn't stirred out of bed. I was sleeping up to fourteen hours a day and I spent a lot of that dreaming about the dead. I was clinging to Tess's lifeless body in the room where I found her, I was watching Mikey writhing in the road at Old Trafford and I was watching Peggy step off the road into the path of a speeding car. But when I dreamt of Dad he was very much alive. We were running on the beach hand in hand in Achill and laughing, I was snuggled on his knee in front of the gas fire, he was helping me unwrap a doll's pram on Christmas Day. Whenever he was present the fear and the angst wasn't.

The lovely home I'd spent hours cleaning and decorating was abandoned to dirt and dust. Filthy plates, mugs and glasses piled up in every room, bins overflowed and the post piled up. After two weeks I started ordering all my groceries online, I'd put in an order at the local dairy to deliver milk and online banking meant I didn't have to go out anywhere to pay the bills. I soon didn't feel well enough to leave the house and thanks to the internet I didn't have to.

Joe sent a few emails and Julia rang a number of times but I didn't answer the phone. A flurry of texts arrived from Mary. I'd agreed to attend a series of literary events and performances with her at the Manchester Festival the following week. I ignored her. The thought of an evening in a crowded theatre in town terrified me. I couldn't do it. I was terrified of having another panic attack like the one I'd had in Deansgate. It was becoming a Catch 22 situation. The fear of having an attack, not the actual attack, kept me at home.

When I didn't reply Mary sent more concerned texts, then one morning she turned up on the doorstep.

"*Come out with your hands above your head, I know you're in there!*" she hollered through the letterbox. She waited for a while then she left, after slipping a note through the letterbox begging me to call her.

I stared at it and thought about calling her but then the darkness had a word in my ear.

"She isn't really a friend. She doesn't enjoy your company. She's only doing it out of pity."

One morning I opened the drawer of my bedside table, took out the make-up mirror I kept there and held it up to the light. I looked at my face, something I hadn't done in days. Dark crescent moons hung under my red-rimmed eyes, my cheeks were hollow and my hair stood on end like I'd been plugged in. I was jaundiced and weak. I looked into my eyes. Nobody was at home. I averted my gaze. I'd seen that look before. When I looked again Tess was staring back at me.

Chapter 29

I sat up bolt upright when I saw him standing at the end of the bed. He looked tanned and relaxed in a linen shirt, loafers and well-ironed jeans. Our time apart seemed to be serving Joe well.

"Shit," I said, shielding my eyes from the brutal rays of late morning sun that interrogated my face. I glanced over at the alarm clock. Eleven am. I'd overslept. I was supposed to get up at nine, clean the house then disappear while he came to collect his stuff. He was back from Madrid for a couple of days and staying with his friend at the other side of Chorlton.

I slumped back onto the pillows. From the corner of my eye I could see him surveying the room: the huge coffee stain on the beige carpet, the empty packets of

Nytol, chocolate wrappers, wineglasses, the half-open drawers and array of dirty clothes scattered everywhere. Tracey Emin's bed looked neat by comparison.

"Mary Duffy got my number from work and rang me in Madrid," he said. "She's very worried about you. She asked if you'd been kidnapped."

I sniffed. "I've had a virus and I didn't feel like seeing anyone but I'm fine now."

He stepped towards the bed as if he was about to sit down. I flinched and he moved towards the window instead, leaning back against the sill. On the wall beside him was the sepia poster we bought on our honeymoon in Venice. Couples wearing masks were dancing at a carnival ball. We bought it in a small shop in an alleyway away from the crowds. We'd walked for hours in the sizzling heat that day and afterwards we sat outside the tiny bar next door and held hands over pool-sized gin and tonics. On the walk home the heavens opened in a tropical downpour and we got drenched. We were so much in love we didn't care one bit. I'd been looking at the poster and thinking of that day a lot. It reminded me of him and our marriage, the mask part anyway.

"You don't look well," he said.

"I'm fine."

"You don't look it. You're so skinny and pale." He gestured around the room at the chaos. "Look at this. It's not like you at all." He cocked his head to one side. "You've been through a lot, Carmel. Maybe you need to get some help."

I pulled myself up onto a pillow.

"So you're giving me fucking mental-health advice after what you did? Don't you think that's a bit like beating someone to a pulp then handing them a box of plasters?"

He said nothing and lowered his head.

Out of the window behind him a white ribbon of plane trail soared between two clouds. Was life really going on as normal when mine had come to a standstill? Were people taking holidays? Were they having lunch in the cafés on Beech Road and going to work on trams, buses and cars?

I closed my eyes. I wanted to hurt him, to tell him about that night four years before, how I'd been blown away by another man at the teaching conference. Billy O'Hagan he was called. He was from Galway, a widower, and he lived in Chorlton. He was witty and rugged and we drank late-night tequila shots huddled together in the cold on the hotel terrace bar. Then we ended up in his room where we kissed.

"I still fucking love you," Joe said.

When I opened my eyes he was still standing by the window and I could see he was crying.

"I made the biggest mistake of my life. I don't want us to split up."

I buried my head in my pillow, remembering the look of dismay on Billy O'Hagan's face when I put my hand on his and stopped him unbuttoning my shirt. "Sorry, I can't," I'd said, getting up. "I love my husband too much." Then I left when I very much wanted to stay.

Joe wiped his cheek with the back of his hand then he moved around the room, picking up some of my dirty clothes from the floor.

"My contract in Madrid's finished," he said, throwing them into the laundry basket. "I'm staying on in Tom

O'Brien's spare room until I can move into the flat in Salford. If it's OK with you I'd like to come round now and again and see how you're doing."

"Whatever."

I sank deeper into the refuge of my pillows. Rain started to patter on the windows. All my fight was gone and I hadn't the energy to say no. The darkness was rolling over me again like a fog, weighing me down and sapping me of everything, even my anger towards Joe. I closed my eyes. I was so very very tired.

Chapter 30

The fog of my depression eventually began to lift. I distinctly remember the moment it first happened. It was a bright October afternoon down in The Meadows.

Shortly after Joe's visit I took sick leave from work and went to my GP. She put me on a waiting list for CBT counselling and prescribed me anti-depressants. I was hesitant to take them at first, a little afraid of the side effects. But I was lucky. I had the odd headache, a bit of diarrhoea but none of the self-harming thoughts or other terrible things I'd read about.

Joe came by most days. He shopped, paid the bills and helped around the house. We didn't talk much, communicating only about functional stuff and circling around each other as though separated by glass. But I appreciated a human presence. It cut through the loneliness of the long tortuous days.

I was on my medicinal daily walk in the Meadows and sitting on a bench on the curve of a path opposite a stream. Mild sunshine sprinkled the woods and dotted the carpet of ivy at my feet. I was listening to Snow Patrol on my headphones when a middle-aged couple in pastel-coloured waterproofs appeared round the bend of the path. They were guiding a blonde girl of about three who was wearing a Peppa Pig raincoat. I guessed they were young grandparents from the adoring way they looked at the child, as if every step she took and observation she made was pure genius. A young runner in yellow Lycra suddenly appeared round the corner with a dog and as she flew past them, the ruby Cavalier barked and jumped up at the child. She screamed and hid behind her grandfather's sturdy legs. The dog's owner stopped and apologised. I watched as the three adults tried to coax the girl to stroke the dog who had been put on a lead. The girl wasn't having any of it, continuing to peer at the dog curiously as the adults chatted. Then without warning she stepped out from behind her grandfather's legs and stroked the dog's carmine coat. Delighted with herself, she did it again. Then she ran on the spot and clapped her hands, giddy with excitement. Her face was bursting with pride and joy as all the adults applauded. It made me smile, I mean really smile, for the first time in months and I felt something shift inside me.

When they'd gone I looked around the wood at the rich greens, honey-yellows and copper-reds of autumn. I was starting to focus and see colour again. It was like I'd been wearing the wrong pair of glasses without realising and then I'd put on my old ones again. Snow Patrol sang "You Could Be Happy" on my iPod and I walked home with a slight spring in my step.

Later that evening I rang Mary. She'd recently been promoted at work and was now my new line manager. I was delighted. When I invited her out to dinner the following evening to celebrate, she accepted immediately.

She'd been round the previous week and I'd told her everything over tea and cake and tears in my kitchen. She listened without judgement when I raged about Joe and Karen. She resisted the urge to give me advice and waved a dismissive hand in the air when I brought up the topic of work.

"I'm your new boss," she said, delving into a slice of the delicious homemade Victoria sponge she'd brought round. "Do as you're told and stay at home until you're well enough to come back."

When I told her about the search for my brother and the Mother and Baby Home scandals, I was surprised to learn she'd actually read quite a bit about the topic. She said she'd heard rumours about the illegal adoptions in the homes in Ireland years ago.

I was nervous about going out in public to a restaurant. I'd ventured out only once in the evening since I'd started feeling unwell. I took off to the cinema in town one evening but had another panic attack on the tram and had to come home. That was before the pills, though. They were helping a lot with my confidence. I was now able to go out to the local shops and to The Meadows for my walk which I could never have done before. But to be on the safe side I arranged to meet Mary at a restaurant on Beech Road in Chorlton only few hundred yards from home.

A onetime police station, the Lead Station had bare brick walls and wine bottles stacked high on shelves. There was a cosmopolitan menu and an outside eating space in an enclosed yard decorated with fairy lights and plants. It probably hadn't been used at all during the recent damp months. Apart from a couple of families with children and a young couple who looked like they might be on a date, the place was very quiet. On the way in I spotted one of Bryonie Phillips's cronies sitting at the bar. I panicked. But he was engrossed in his phone and didn't see me as I hurried past into the eating area.

We sat at a table looking out into the outside yard. Mary was in great form. In a fuchsia shirt instead of her usual black or navy, she looked tanned and happy after spending half-term hiking around Sicily with her German partner Monika. We chatted for a while about our former boss Pete whose job Mary now had. Pete had left under a cloud after rumours of an affair with a Polish MA student. I knew Maja well and liked her. Much more than Pete, who was hairy and dismissive and quietly full of himself. Both were married. I reminded Mary how I'd told her earlier in the year that I had suspicions about an affair.

"Remember I said something was going on?" I said, dunking a chunky chip into the bowl of hummus on my plate. "Shame I didn't have the same intuition about my husband and my best mate."

"Shame indeed." Mary narrowed her eyes. "So how are things between you and Joe?"

"Much the same. Except he's kinder now and I'm not as angry. As much as I try I can't find fault with him at the moment." I bit into a chip. "Apart from the bit about him shagging my bestie."

Mary said nothing, sprinkling salt and pepper over her plate and frowning down at her steak.

"Do you still love him?"

I sat back and sighed.

"Love doesn't actually seem that relevant right now, Mary. I'm letting him be around because I need him. All I know is it actually feels better to have his presence around now and again than be on my own dealing with depression, even after everything he's done."

"Fair enough. Do you talk about what happened at all?"

"Not really. I did mention marriage guidance the other day but he says he doesn't want to be made to feel guiltier than he already is by talking to a large woman in Birkenstocks."

Mary looked under the table at her feet and I laughed. Then she hovered the bottle of Riesling in my direction.

"Had my one glass for today," I said, shaking my head and putting a hand over my glass. "I can't take the downers that come with the hangovers any more."

"All the more for me then," She grinned, filling her glass. "And what about counselling? You heard anything?"

"According to my GP there's a four-month waiting list."

"Christ. Is it that bad?"

"Yep."

"What about going private? You have the money."

"It might sound a bit daft but I'm scared of spending it. I have to know what's happening with Joe first and if we end up selling the house. Therapy's not cheap."

"A good investment, though."

I put my knife and fork down, rubbed at my temples and sighed.

"It's not about the money, Mary. I'm putting it off because I'm scared."

"Of what?"

I leant over and lowered my voice. "If I start digging I might discover that I'm like her. Like Tess."

"In what way?"

"Manic depressive. Bipolar or whatever it's called these days."

Mary dabbed her lips with a napkin then frowned. "You're a worrier and a bit oversensitive by times but I doubt you're bipolar. I'm sure you'd know by now if you were."

"I'm feeling much better now but they say depression's genetic. What if isn't just one episode? What if it becomes permanent?"

She reached over and picked up her glass.

"Carmel, you've had a pretty tough time recently. Don't you think your depression is a reaction to everything that's happened to you? Remember when you said you thought something was triggered seeing the little girl with her dad at her old house that day?"

I nodded. "Yes?"

"Didn't it ever occur to you that you've never dealt properly with your father's death? That at the age of ten you were thrown into the role of looking after Tess and Mikey and you never properly grieved for him? Losing a parent at a young age is huge and it's something that's probably taken its toll on you over the years. Then recently a series of events happened that were out of your control. Mikey and Tess died suddenly, you were told you might have a heart condition, you discovered all that stuff about Tess and the baby then you found out

200

about Joe and Karen. Who the hell wouldn't get down after going through all that?"

"And Joe's parents dying."

"Christ, I forgot that." Mary gulped from her glass again. "I'm slitting my wrists here. Look, Carmel, you've suffered loss after loss. Circumstances have made you depressed. It doesn't mean you're bipolar. You've just unravelled, that's all."

I sat back. Unravelled. I thought about that time I found Tess's knitting between the sofa cushions in the old house, how it came apart in my hands, stitch after stitch, loosening and unhooking, the shape of it finally disappearing. Was Mary right? Is that what had happened to me?

I gestured at the passing waitress and asked for coffee.

"Did anyone ever tell you you've got a way with words," I said to Mary then. "Someone should give you a promotion."

Chapter 31

Julia's letter arrived on an unseasonably warm Friday evening in November. Like everything else that year the weather was topsy-turvy. Summer had been winter and now winter was turning into summer.

I'd just got in from work. I'd been back for three weeks. I still had my bad days but Mary had given me an easy timetable and overall I was glad to be keeping busy.

Joe was round and had offered to cook a curry. Amy Winehouse crooned on the music system, chicken korma bubbled on the hob and I was setting the table. To any onlooker we looked like a normal couple enjoying a Friday evening together.

He was holding a brown envelope in his hand.

"I forgot. This was on the mat when I came in," he

said. "Irish postmark. Looks interesting."

He searched my face. He was looking for some kind of clue about what had happened between us the previous day but I looked away. The memory made me uncomfortable.

I'd been sitting on the bed drying myself after a shower and listening to Paul Weller being interviewed on BBC Radio 6. Joe still used his key and I hadn't heard him come in when I was showering. He'd moved into the flat at Salford Quays. We'd been getting on well recently and he'd started coming over more regularly.

I jumped as he walked in the bedroom door and gathered my towel around me. Light filtered through the gap in the curtains over him and he looked good in a work shirt and chinos.

"Sorry. I needed to get a few things from the cupboard," he said, turning to leave when he saw my state of undress." I'll come back when you're done."

"No. Go ahead."

Averting his eyes, he walked over to drawers at the bottom of the wardrobe opposite the bed. He knelt down inches from my feet. He had his back to me and I could smell his apple-scented aftershave. As he yanked the bottom drawer open, a ripple of muscle spread along his right shoulder-blade. Without thinking, I reached out and ran a fingertip lightly down his back. He went completely still then turned round. I undid the towel and fell back on the bed. Soon he was kneeling in front of me, his hands on my thighs, his eyes travelling over my body like he was seeing it for the first time.

"You sure?" he asked.

I nodded and opened my legs. He bent down, his

tongue searching and teasing. I helped him undress quickly and pulled him on top of me. He entered me gently at first, moving slowly then pausing. He looked into my eyes and told me he was sorry. The moment he said it I saw them both fucking on our sofa, her long legs wrapped around him as he cried out her name. I felt sick inside. Yet I didn't ask him to stop. I went through the motions instead. Thankfully he came quickly. He apologised for that too and asked if we could talk afterwards. But I escaped into the bathroom and made an excuse about going out.

I cried on the tram on the way into work the next morning, wondering if that would be our last time.

Joe handed me the envelope. When I saw Julia's neat handwriting, I made an excuse and ran upstairs with it. I felt so bad. In the past few months Julia had left a number of answer-phone messages. In one of them she'd said she had something for me. I'd been meaning to call her back but she and Mattie had gone on a cruise. She'd sent postcards from Venice and Dubrovnik but she hadn't taken her mobile so I couldn't get hold of her.

I took the envelope into the bedroom. I stopped and stared down at Joe's clothes by the side of the bed. I threw them in the laundry basket then I straightened the duvet, sat down and opened the envelope. Inside was a photocopied newspaper cutting and a letter from Julia.

My dear Carmel,

We're back now after the cruise. We had great craic and met lots of interesting people. I ate too much though and now I can't do up my trousers!

I left you a few messages on the answer phone before we went away but didn't hear back from you. Is everything alright between us? I've been thinking about your last visit. I do hope you have forgiven me for not telling you about Tess's baby. I felt I had no choice but to respect your mother's wishes. I hope you understand.

I don't know if you remember me mentioning a woman called Nancy Corley on your visit? Her family were neighbours of Tess's parents in the village. Nancy used to nurse with me in the General in Castlebar. She is retired now and lives here in Westport. Anyways, not long after your visit, I bumped into her in Tesco and we got talking. I asked her if she knew what had become of Tess's brother. She knew he'd gone to London years ago and she said she'd seen an article about him in the Mayo News a few years back.

When I got home Gerry and I went online and looked for the article but we couldn't find anything. So the next day he went into the Mayo News offices in Westport. They were very helpful and gave him a copy from the archives. That's what I was ringing to tell you about it.

I hope you don't mind me sending it on to you.

Give me a call some time and let me know how you are getting on.

All my love to Joe.

Julia

xx

I felt terrible. It never occurred to me that Julia might think I was angry with her for not telling me Tess's secret. I resolved to ring her that evening.

I picked up the *Mayo News* cutting. I'd often seen copies of the paper in Julia's house. It was a local paper, filled with news from every nook and cranny in the West, from farmer's fairs to burglaries, obituaries, visits from local dignitaries and community sporting events.

My eyes were immediately drawn to the photograph next to the article. I gasped. A man in a tux and long white silk scarf was standing in front of a theatre billboard. Though probably in his late sixties or early seventies, the likeness was remarkable: the large grey-blue eyes, the square jaw under the snowy-white goatee, the stocky build. He even had the same unruly thatch of hair. He looked just like Mikey if he'd lived for another thirty years. It was uncanny and unsettling. For a mad moment I imagined my brother had come back and my heart leapt with joy. His death was all a mistake, a bad dream. Then I came to my senses and read the short article underneath the photo.

Mayo Man Snaps Up Top London Theatre Prize

Timothy Dempsey, a native of County Mayo, has been named Best Director in the Off West End Theatre awards. His adaptation of Sean O'Casey's *The Plough and the Stars* played at the Southwark Playhouse earlier this year. The *Guardian* described it as 'Harrowingly brilliant' and *The Times* said it was 'One of the finest pieces of theatre you'll see in London this year".

Dempsey, who left Mayo for London in 1965, told the *Mayo News* he was 'humbled and delighted' at his win.

Demspey has worked as a lecturer, playwright and theatre director for over fifty years and lives in Battersea with his partner. He has one son.

Timothy Dempsey. In all my Google searches for Tess's brother I'd looked for Tadhg Dempsey. Tadhg must be the Irish for Timothy. I picked up my iPad from the top of the bedside table and checked. Turned out it wasn't a proper translation, but a lot of people thought it was. I didn't know any of that. Maybe I wasn't as Irish as I thought. So Tess had lied when she told Mikey and me that her brother had ended up living on the streets in Kilburn. Had she done it so we would never try and trace him? So she'd never have to face him again after what he'd done all those years ago?

I looked at the photograph again. My uncle looked shy and retiring and seemed to shrink from the camera like a hermit crab. He seemed nothing like the cruel brother I'd imagined who'd handed over his pregnant fifteen-year-old sister to the nuns to placate his parents and his rich Protestant friends. I took in the elegant tux and the highbrow theatre setting and sighed. Tess's life trajectory after she came out of the home was one of poverty, mental-health problems and loneliness. Yet his seemed to have been full of wealth, glamour and fame. I resented that. Yet part of me felt emotional. Here was my uncle, the only living breathing member of Tess's side of the family, someone I'd never met. Despite what he'd done in the past I couldn't help feeling an excitement and a connection. He obviously loved literature and the arts like I did and he looked so much like Mikey it hurt.

I googled his name, the right one this time, and I was impressed by what I found. The list of links to theatre productions went back years and he had worked all over the UK. Synge, Behan and O'Casey were there as well as Chekhov, Ibsen, O'Neill and some contemporary stuff.

He'd also written a number of reviews and articles and was currently directing a Martin McDonagh play due to open at Battersea Arts Centre in a few weeks' time. I found no social media accounts which didn't surprise me as he was a little old to belong to the Facebook generation. However, I did find the contact details of his theatrical agent in Notting Hill Gate.

I thought again about Kathleen Slevin seeing the two men take my brother away from the Mother and Baby Home in the open-top sports car. Instinct had always told me Tess's brother was one of them. I remembered how Julia said that Tess told Dad that her brother was more attached to the Protestant family in the lodge than his own. The question was, did Timothy Dempsey know where my brother was now?

I put Julia's letter and the article back into the envelope and slipped it into the drawer of the bedside cabinet. Then I picked up my iPad again and found the contact details of Dempsey's theatrical agent. I hesitated for a moment, wondering if I was well enough to get back on that emotional roller-coaster search for my brother again. Then I thought of the promise I'd made to Tess and about everything she had gone through. I couldn't let her down. I made a screenshot then sent it to my phone.

Chapter 32

London was locked in a blood-slowing cold. The TV screen in the hotel bar said temperatures would plummet to minus two and snow was expected by late evening. Christmas lights twinkled in the windows of the half-empty bars and restaurants along the Southbank and a thin layer of frost shimmered on the ground. The Thames was the colour of a shiny green olive and the dome of St Paul's was blue-white against the black night sky.

I glanced at my watch. Ten to six. The play started at seven thirty. It would take a good hour to walk to the theatre in Battersea but walking was what you did in London, whatever the weather. I pulled my cowl scarf up around my face. I regretted wearing my new red Hobbs coat. I'd chosen it to make an impression but it was too thin and the cold stabbed right through it. Some of the performers along the bank were turning in for the night. Yoda was climbing out of his flimsy lime-green Jedi dress and reaching for his Puffa jacket, and an African steel band in earmuffs and gloves were handing round a bobble hat for cash and packing up. I dropped a pound coin in the cap of a homeless man sitting in a doorway, hidden in a hijab of scarves.

The day after receiving the article about Timothy Dempsey I'd sent an email to his agent in Notting Hill explaining who I was. I said I wanted to touch base after Tess's death and included my contact details. I mentioned nothing about trying to trace my brother. Three weeks on, after two further emails and a message on the agent's answer machine, I'd had no reply. If I needed any further proof that my uncle knew something about Donal's whereabouts this was it. Angry at his stonewalling, I decided to take matters in my own hands.

I kept up a brisk pace down the Embankment to keep warm, passing a young couple on a bench facing the Thames. They looked in their twenties, Latino and beautiful. His gloved fingers were entwined in her long dark hair and they were kissing. I stopped in my tracks, the memory returning like a push in the chest.

In the weeks after the Manchester bomb Joe and I fell for each other quickly. We spoke every other day by phone and every weekend without fail he'd come up to Manchester or I'd go to London. The sight of his pale denim jacket and boyish grin at the end of the platform at Euston made my heart somersault. The second I stepped past the ticket barriers he'd pull me to his chest and kiss me long and hard then we'd smooch shamelessly on the Tube all the way back to his shared flat in Shoreditch.

We continued our long-distance relationship for the next two years. Joe lived in the East End in a shared flat long before the East End was gentrified. We spent Saturday nights drinking with students and locals in The Bricklayers Arms or The Griffin or we'd wander to the Eastern Eye on Brick Lane for a cheap curry. Now and again we'd meet up in the Founder's Arms on Southbank with Joe's work colleagues from the tech start-up where he was a programmer. Sundays were always spent in Greenwich with Paddy and Peggy and a roast dinner or bacon and cabbage. I'd fallen for them as quickly as I had Joe. The atmosphere in his childhood home was calm and conflict-free. It was a revelation to me that family life could be so happy.

Though I hid it from my Mancunian friends, I'd also fallen in love with London. Up north many of us resented the capital because every government invested so much in it. Power and culture thrived while we got so little and we saw nothing of ourselves in the city's wealth and glamour. Yet at that time I couldn't help being wooed by the hustle and bustle of the place, the diversity, the history, the variety of arts venues and theatres. The view of the city from the Southbank on a summer night or Greenwich Park at dusk filled me with awe. Arriving at Euston on Friday evenings felt like pulling off a dark hood. I was liberated from Tess's black moods and Mikey to look after and those weekends with Joe were some of the happiest days of my life. I was in love and I was free. If I hadn't had Tess and Mikey to care for I'd have moved to London in an instant.

One Friday evening I was about to leave Brantingham Road to get the Euston train when Mikey fell through the door looking like he was plugged in on high voltage. He was as high as a kite, rummaging through drawers and bags and demanding money from Tess. Thinking I couldn't leave him alone with her, I rang Joe at work and told him I wasn't going to make the train. He said he was gutted as he had a surprise for me but he understood (he and Mikey weren't yet at the stage where they loathed the sight of each other). Joe said he'd have to go the Founder's to drown his sorrows. Shortly afterwards Mikey left the house again. Raging, I decided I'd had enough of being treated as a doormat. I went over the road to ask Rose O'Grady to keep an eye on Tess during the weekend then I got on the next train to Euston. I hugged myself at the thought of surprising Joe.

The Founder's was heaving with warm bodies when I bounded in, weighed down by my backpack. Joe's colleagues were sitting at the back of the pub on the patio. Phoebe, a brittle Chelsea blonde who had a habit of imitating my accent every time we met, pointed at the door with a tight smile. She said Joe was outside. Off I went, jostling through the pints and suits. I couldn't see him anywhere in the crowd. Then I looked further out towards the river, stopping in my tracks. He was sitting on a bench with his back to me next to a girl with long dark hair.

My legs weakened and I grabbed the arm of a large American standing next to me who roared with laughter, put me in a headlock and asked if I wanted a fight. When I'd wriggled free I slumped against the wall of the pub to get a better view. The girl was tall and lithe with a nose-ring. She was heavily made up and wearing a tight white minidress and had long tanned legs that seemed to stretch to the far side of the Thames. I looked down at my white legs, denim cut-offs and scraggy Van Morrison T-shirt. When I looked up again, Joe and the girl had their arms around each other. I lowered my eyes, convinced that was it. He had someone else on the sly all along. I felt like I was about to shatter into a thousand pieces and was about to turn and walk away when they pulled apart. The girl stood up and pulled on a pink jacket then Joe turned round and saw me. He got up, waving me over, his face lighting up. By the time I got to the bench a huge grin had spread across his face. He turned to the girl who picked up the small pink suitcase that lay beside her feet.

"Here she is. Bloody hell. She made it after all. Sinéad, this is Carmel, the love of my life."

He introduced me to his cousin who was over from Cork for a few days and staying with Pat and Peggy. He'd been hoping the three of us could spend the evening together but she was already late for her flight and had to rush off to get to Gatwick.

I watched Sinéad disappear into the crowd feeling both immense relief and self-loathing. When she'd gone Joe pulled me on to his knee, kissing me long and hard and telling me how happy he was to see me.

I hated myself. Why oh why did I always imagine the worst? Just minutes earlier I was about to walk away from him forever without even questioning what was going on. It was only later that I came to understand why I did things like that. Losing a parent early on in childhood often leaves you with an irrational fear of losing other loved ones, such as a partner or a child. Joe was my first real love and when I saw him that night on the bench with his cousin I automatically assumed I'd lost him. I came to the realisation that it was probably the same fear that had held me back from having a child for so long.

I smiled and held Joe's face in my hands under the clear moonlit sky.

"Was she my surprise?" I asked.

He shook his head and reached into the pocket of his suit jacket on the bench next to him. Smiling nervously he took out a small box and placed it on my bare thigh. A boat full of revellers sounded its horn on the other side of the river then he asked me to marry him. I said yes and he slipped the traditional Irish Claddagh ring on to my finger. It had a small emerald in the crown.

We married shortly after. Looking back we were so young, maybe too young.

As I walked up the steps onto the Albert Bridge, trying hard to hold on to that moment, to clutch on to all the love I'd felt for him in the intervening years. But his and Karen's betrayal got in the way. It was still there every day when I woke up, a dull ache that never went away.

The Albert Bridge was my favourite of all the London Bridges. That night her chains fanned out from her towers like a necklace shimmering against a black satin sky. I plodded on, arriving at Battersea Arts Centre just after seven.

Posters for Martin McDonagh's play, *The Beauty Queen of Linanne* lined the walls. 'Unmissable,' said the *Evening Standard*. The *Telegraph* described it as "Gloriously funny". That evening's performance advertised a Q&A session with the play's award-winning director, Timothy Dempsey.

I collected my ticket from the box office then hurried to the bar where I downed a large glass of red wine. My heart pounding, I made my way to my seat.

Chapter 33

My seat was three rows from the front of the stage. It had cost twice the price of my train fare but I wanted to make sure I had a good view of Timothy Dempsey. Digging my fingers nervously into the red velvet of my seat arm, I looked up at the ornate domed ceiling and noted the neutered accents and fine wool coats of the wealthy London Irish making their way to their seats. I could have been wrong but I guessed Dempsey had never frequented the pubs of Kilburn or danced in The Galtymore in his younger days. All of this was all a far cry from the Mayo backwater where he and Tess were raised. I scanned the heads around me for the fecund mop of white hair I'd seen in the photograph but I couldn't see my uncle anywhere.

I forgot all about him the minute the play started. Set in an isolated cottage in Connemara in the nineties, it told the story of a vicious war between a bitter widow Mags and her forty-year-old virginal daughter Maureen. The simmering violence, explosive outbursts and doses of insanity made me feel very much at home. The play spoke about emigration. Those who stayed behind in rural communities often ended up living embittered lives and those who left sometimes found it hard to cope with upheaval and change. The daughter Maureen suffered a breakdown in London after racist bullying by her English co-workers.

I immediately thought of Tess. Had running away from Ireland helped or hindered her mental health? After Dad died she'd become very unwell and had been abandoned by a lot of her friends in the Irish community. The stigma of mental illness sent them running and like a beautiful cracked porcelain doll she'd been left behind in the back room of a toy shop. Would she have been abandoned in the same way if she'd been living in a tightknit community like Mags and Maureen? Would there have been more kindness? Who knows? The play threw up many questions I'd been asking myself for years and I loved every minute. At the curtain call I was on my feet applauding with the rest of the audience. I'd almost forgotten my reason for being there. Then the lights dimmed, a hushed silence fell over the auditorium and Timothy Dempsey walked on stage.

He sat at the hewn-wood kitchen table that had been the centrepiece of the set. He was slighter and older than in the photo. Seeing him in such a typical Irish setting, surrounded by pictures of the Sacred Heart and the

216

Virgin and a backdrop of the Connemara mountains, unnerved me. A thin blonde with horn-rimmed glasses sat next to him and introduced herself as the theatre's artistic director. As she read out his bio, he lowered his eyes and crossed his legs, circling his right foot nervously in the air. Tanned, in an impeccable navy suit and pink shirt, everything about him suggested good taste.

He answered the director's questions in a quiet considered manner with a finely tuned sense of humour. In contrast to Tess, there wasn't a hint of Mayo in his accent. Both Tess and Dad had little desire to assimilate outside the Manchester Irish community and they'd never altered their accents to fit in. Dempsey on the other hand, could easily have been mistaken for an English country gent. After a while the director opened up questions to the floor.

"I thought the nature of the relationship between Mags and her daughter was a bit over the top," said a middle-aged woman with a Maureen O'Hara head of curls. "Do you really think women are that vicious to each other in real life?"

"They are in Leitrim," interjected an elderly man behind to much laughter.

A handsome young man with floppy of blonde hair took the microphone.

"I enjoyed your production very much," he said softly. "I'd like to know if you think there are still small-minded communities in Ireland today like the one portrayed in the play. Or do you think the country has moved on?"

Dempsey sat up and peered at the man, nodding enthusiastically.

"I think there's been a huge generational shift in attitudes. Most of it is to do with young Irish rejecting the values of the Catholic Church. The paedophile scandals and the Magdalene Laundries have sent them running. There's a lot of support for the upcoming vote for gay marriage and the lobby to legalise abortion." He sat back and cleared his throat. "Yet whenever I go back I can't help thinking the older generation are still quite a conservative lot. Especially in the small towns and villages."

I shifted in my seat. So he was a smooth-talking liberal now, was he? Agreeing with abortion and outraged by the Magdalene Laundries after what he'd done to Tess? I tutted and exhaled loudly to the annoyance of the man and woman sitting either side of me. A few more questions followed then the theatre director looked down at her watch and said there was time for one more.

Something took hold of me. I took deep breaths and tried to ground myself.

Then gathering every ounce of inner strength I had, I put my hand up.

With a racing heart I watched the microphone make its way along my row of seats. I clutched it immediately with both hands so no one could see how much I was trembling.

Then I spoke.

"I see that you are a native of County Galway like my mother, Mr Dempsey," I said, swallowing. "You mentioned the Magdalene Laundries earlier so I was wondering if you have any thoughts on the recent discovery of the mass grave at the Mother and Baby home in Tuam?"

Dempsey flinched, craned his neck forwards and looked at me. Then he shrank back in his chair. In the long silence that followed a mobile phone rang at the back of the theatre and someone sneezed.

"Mr Dempsey?" I prompted.

"It's a terrible tragedy for all those involved," he said quietly, "but I'm afraid I don't really know much about it."

I gripped the microphone tighter and tried to control the quiver in my voice.

"I think you do," I said, "I think you know an awful lot about it."

People turned and stared but to my great surprise I held my ground. The search for my sibling had been long and painful and I was finally face to face with someone who could give me answers. I'd been waiting for this moment for months.

"Maybe I should ask you about the illegal adoptions instead," I said. "About the babies who were trafficked from the Mother and Baby homes all across Ireland and sold on to families and individuals in the US and here in the UK? I suppose you don't know anything about that either, do you?"

Dempsey froze then crumpled back into his chair, exchanging a look with the blonde who started to shuffle the papers on the table in front of her.

At the sight of his tired-looking arm flopping over his chair arm, I stopped. He was an old man. He was also my uncle. I'd made my point but it was now time to leave. There was no need to humiliate him further.

I dropped the microphone on my seat, grabbed my coat and bag and stumbled towards the exit, treading on toes and apologising. A nervous-looking usher pushed open the door. Before going through it I glanced back at the stage. The director was telling the audience about a new play the theatre was about to launch and Dempsey was sitting with his chin on his chest like he'd suffered a gunshot wound to the head.

I ran down the corridor into the main reception area. Ushers were standing around and a security guard was talking on a walkie-talkie by a side door. I went through the main entrance and stopped at the top of the steps, a blast of cold night air chilling me to the bone. It was snowing heavily and a white blanket covered the ground. I watched the flakes swaying and drifting like feathers, dusting the road and painting a white rim on the roofs of the line of black taxis queueing up outside. Shivering, I pulled on my coat and wound my scarf around my neck. As I made my way gingerly down the steps, a burst of applause erupted behind me.

Chapter 34

Apart from a group of women at a corner table surrounded by Prosecco bottles and discarded wrapping paper, the wine bar was empty. I found a seat by the window, put my glass of Merlot down on the table and took out the theatre programme from my bag. My stomach was twisted with knots as I took off my coat, unravelled my scarf and sat down. I opened the programme and stared at Dempsey's photograph. I felt sick.

I'd never intended that to happen. I was going to wait behind after the Q&A and introduce myself in a civilised manner. But now I'd blown it good and proper. Dempsey would have nothing to do with me and I'd never find out what happened to my brother.

Out of the window I could see the theatregoers flooding

out onto the pavement. Some were getting into waiting taxis and others were putting up umbrellas and hurrying in the direction of the train station. Two teenagers in hoodies were having a snowball fight in the road. They were scooping snow from the roofs of the waiting taxis, launching at each other and ducking and weaving between the cars. I watched, the sight triggering the memory of another snow fight many years ago.

I was seven and we were in Mayo for Granny's funeral. Tess always found going to Ireland stressful but that journey had been particularly traumatic. The rough crossing, the treacherous drive from Dublin in ice and snow with a teething toddler in the back seat had sent her over the edge. She spent a lot of the time cooped up in the back bedroom of Julia's house in Westport. I was told to tell the mourners at Granny's house that she was laid up with a bad dose of flu.

Granny was my first dead body. She was laid out in the mysterious front room that had always been out of bounds to us kids. The cellophane had finally been removed from the sofa, the good china unlocked from the dresser and the Sacred Heart and JFK pictures dusted down. When I entered the room holding Dad's hand, my Cleveland cousins were playing tag around the coffin and "Black Velvet Band", one of Granny's favourite songs, was playing on the tape recorder on the sideboard.

Dad had forgotten to warn me about the open coffin and I was traumatised. Granny's face was yellow and sunken, her mouth a toothless hole. I was horrified as Dad bent over and kissed her cheek. Thinking I'd have to do the same, I let go of Dad's hand, turned and fled through the house and out the back door. The snow hadn't let up in days. It was inches deep in the field at the back of the house. The landscape was a carpet of white, dotted with the shadowy outline of grazing cattle, the sky navy blue. The next thing I knew my cousins had followed me and were charging past me to get outside. They started making snowballs, laughing and throwing them at one another and at me too. I hesitated, glancing over at the doorway where Dad was standing.

"Go on," he said, smiling. "Granny wouldn't mind."

We fought and played until our fingers and toes froze and our clothes were dripping wet. Then we returned inside, rosy-cheeked and exhilarated.

It was still snowing when we set off for Dublin to get the midnight ferry after the funeral a few days later. Our knackered Vauxhall Viva was making spluttering sounds and as we pulled into a petrol station in Athlone and Dad joked that we might not make it to the port. Mikey's teeth were playing up again and he was wailing in the back seat next to me.

"Keep the child quiet for one minute, would you?" Dad snapped at Tess as he fiddled with the tuner of the car radio and bent over trying to listen. The newsreader was talking about the fire in the Stardust nightclub in Dublin on Valentine's Day. Everyone had been following the story on RTÉ news in Julia's house every night. Forty young people had died. Julia told me the whole of Ireland was praying for them and their young souls.

Dad filled up the tank and went to pay. It was dusk and people were leaving the small church beside the petrol station after Saturday evening Mass. Some of the churchgoers were gathering on the petrol forecourt. I wasn't paying much attention to them. I was thinking about the young people burning to death in the fire. Did they jump out of windows? Did they turn into balls of fire? I'd been having nightmares about it.

Mikey had fallen asleep by the time Dad got back. Then Tess started to fidget and become agitated and smack her forehead. She whispered something to Dad.

"You're imagining things," he replied with a frown.

"It was her. The She Devil. I know it was."

"It was not. We're miles from Tuam. It was just someone who looked like her."

The snow was falling heavily and the windscreen wipers were going like the clappers. Dad was trying to concentrate on the dimly lit road as Tess started to rock back and forth.

He turned to her.

"Did you take your tablets this morning?"

"*It was her!*" she wailed, covering her face with her hands. "I'd recognise her anywhere. Dear God. She haunts me day and night. Will she ever leave me alone?"

The car suddenly skidded and Dad grappled with the wheel then yelled at the top of his voice. "*Would you shut up, you raving lunatic, or you'll get us all killed!*"

Tess went completely quiet and still. It was the only time I ever heard him say anything like that to her. Despite his attempts to apologise and make it up to her, she never spoke to him again for the entire journey home.

I stayed in the wine bar watching the snow for a while longer. When I'd finished my drink, I put on my coat and scarf and exited through a side door into the street. The view was like something from a Victorian film set.

Narrow and cobbled, the street was a row of small neat terraces with snow-covered roofs and front doors adorned with brass. It was dimly lit apart from a couple of old-fashioned streetlamps and the inviting orange glow from a bistro at the far end.

There was no way I was walking back to the hotel so I opened out my map to look for the quickest bus or Tube route. Unable to see clearly, I stepped back into the light of the pub. After finding my route I put the map back in my pocket and was about to step out into the street again when I spotted him hurrying past. He was walking shoulder to shoulder with a younger man on the pavement opposite. They were deep in conversation. The younger man was tall and broad with salt-and-pepper wavy hair. Both wore long dark overcoats and scarves.

Without hesitating I stepped out onto the cobbles and followed Timothy Dempsey up the narrow street.

Chapter 35

I pursued the two men in their long coats along the cobbles like I was chasing a pair of cloaked villains. The snow was falling thick and fast by then and their shadowy outlines weaved through the blurry curtain of white. I wondered if they were heading for the dimly lit bistro at the end of the street. Engrossed in their conversation, they didn't hear me approach. Then I called out Dempsey's name and they both turned, startled. The younger man put a protective arm on Dempsey's shoulder.

"*Leave him alone!*" he shouted in what sounded like an Italian accent. "*He doesn't want to talk to you!*"

Fiftyish and craggily handsome, I could make out a pair of dark eyes, bushy eyebrows and a scar running down his left cheek. He turned to Dempsey.

"Come on, Tim," he urged. "We're already late."

Dempsey hesitated and stayed where he was.

"*Stop!*" I shouted, hurrying towards them. "*I'm sorry about what happened back there! Please! I'm your niece – I'm Tess's daughter. I just want to talk to you. Please!*"

I suddenly shrieked as I lost my footing and went skidding on a patch of ice. My bag went flying but I managed to grab hold of a nearby lamppost to stop myself landing flat on my backside. I held on to it for dear life, slithering on the spot like a bad ice-skater clasping her partner's waist. By the time I'd steadied myself Dempsey was standing behind me with a concerned look on his face.

"Are you OK?" he asked as he bent and picked up the scattered contents of my bag, putting them back in it.

"I am now," I laughed, slightly shaken. "That was a bit Torville and Dean, though."

"Very impressive axel, I must say." He smiled and handed me my bag then turned back to the angry Italian who was frowning and folding his arms.

"See you in there in five, Stefano," he said.

Stefano made some kind of gesture of annoyance with his hands, flung his red scarf around his shoulder, then turned and walked towards the bistro.

"*Actors!*" said Dempsey, shaking his head and watching him go with an affectionate smile.

We were alone in the empty street with the snow falling silently around us. The city sounds were distant, and it felt like we were tucked in one of the few quiet crevices in London. Dempsey put his hands in his pockets and stepped from one foot to the other, tentatively searching my face.

"You've a look of your mother around the eyes," he said.

"People say I look more like my dad."

He swallowed. "I was very sorry to hear of Tess's passing."

"So you knew she'd died before you got my email?"

He nodded.

"A friend heard her obituary on Irish radio and rang me."

"The famous mid-west radio death-notices, by any chance?"

He nodded again.

"Can I ask why you didn't come to the funeral?"

He moved his head to one side.

"I ... we'd been estranged for so long. It felt wrong."

"She was your sister!"

He stepped back like I'd slapped him and I immediately regretted my sharp tone. I had to be careful. I'd already blown my fuse once. I couldn't risk doing it again if I was going to get him to tell me about my brother. He lowered his eyes to the ground. He struck me as quite frail, a very different man to the quietly confident theatre director who'd answered questions in front of a huge audience a couple of hours earlier.

"I'm sorry for what happened in the theatre," I said, brushing a fleck of snow from my nose and tightening my scarf around my face. "I didn't come to London to embarrass you. I just lost it."

He smiled weakly.

"It's the type of thing Tess would have done when she was young. She had a hot head on her too."

"She did?" I found it hard to imagine my fearful delicate mother behaving like that. "Look, Timothy, I'm not here for recrimination. I just want to find out what

228

happened to Tess's baby. I know you and James, his birth father, took him from the home."

Dempsey exhaled sharply and stepped back, his breath visible in the dim street light.

"It's very important to me," I went on. "I have no family now. My only other brother died not long before Tess, and Dad passed when I was ten. They've all gone from me. I want to know if I have anyone else out there belonging to me."

I omitted the fact that he too belonged to me but it hung in the air like an icicle.

He reached into the inside pocket of his coat. "When are you leaving London?"

"Tomorrow lunchtime. But I can stay longer."

He handed me a business card. "Meet me at the café by the boating lake in Battersea Park tomorrow morning at ten."

I frowned down at the card.

"How do I know you'll turn up?"

He sighed.

"I'm not a monster, Carmel. I'll be there." He nodded down at the card. "Besides, you have all my contact details now so you can stalk me if I don't."

As he turned to go he threw me a small smile. "I've been thinking about you a lot, Carmel. I'm glad you found me but I'm sorry, I really have to go now. It's a work dinner with the producer of my next play and I'm already very late."

"Just before you go. I need to know. Is my brother alive?"

Dempsey nodded.

"And you know where he is?"

"Yes, yes, I do."

As he walked away I watched his shadow fade in the whirling snow and the tail of his coat disappear through the door of bistro. Slightly dazed and still gripping his card in my hand, I made my way back down the street. As I passed the wine bar, the women from earlier clattered out of the door on to the cobbles, laughing and chatting.

"Goodnight," I said, a grin spreading across on my face.

"Goodnight," they replied, pulling on gloves and scarves and fake fur.

Emerging on to the High Street, I stopped and tucked Dempsey's business card into my purse next to Tess's old bus pass that I carried everywhere. I pulled it out and looked at her photograph under the streetlamp.

"I'm close, Tess," I whispered. "So very, very close."

Chapter 36

"Tess was a nervous child, very sensitive and hyper-vigilant. She cried a lot and had trouble sleeping. She'd wander around the house at all hours. My mother and father hadn't a clue how to handle her."

Timothy Dempsey and I were sitting on a low leather sofa in the café in Battersea Park. Two cappuccinos and a couple of half-eaten croissants lay on the glass coffee table in front of us. Elegant in a black polo-neck, well-cut trousers and tan leather ankle boots, he rubbed his right eye. He had dark shadows under his eyes, like he hadn't slept much either. I felt very relaxed in his company, like pulling on an old jumper I thought I'd lost but found again at the bottom of a drawer. His smile, his laugh, the rhythm of his speech, they were all disturbingly familiar. I asked him to tell me Tess's story from the beginning. But the more I listened, the more I realised he was choosing his words carefully. Instinct told me he was holding something very important back.

"When she was twelve or so she started mitching school. She'd take off down the woods with magazines she stole from the village shop. Mammy despaired and Daddy beat her. One time when she was fourteen she went to Dublin for the day without his permission. When she got back Daddy took off his belt and laid into her. I tried to step in but my father was a big man. She ended up in a terrible state. The poor girl was black and blue."

I flinched. "She never told me any of that."

"That was just the way it was back then, Carmel. There was a lot of ignorance about rearing kids. The strap or the stick featured highly. Tess was difficult and I suppose it was the only way they knew how to deal with her." He picked up his coffee and sipped. "Last night you mentioned that your father passed away when you were young?"

I nodded. "A freak accident at work. He slipped and fell into a pit and was buried under an avalanche of concrete. I was ten and Mikey was four."

"Jesus. I'm so sorry. I met him a couple of times when he and Tess were courting. He used to call at the house. He was mad for her. Awfully nice and he had a calming influence on her."

"Dad was the best. She went to pieces when he died."

I pictured her the day the police came round to tell us. She was sitting in his chair next to the radiogram with Mikey perched on her knee. She blanched with shock then told the officers to get out of her house.

"So tell me. When did she meet James, the baby's father?"

Dempsey shifted in his chair then crossed his legs to reveal a pair of bright yellow socks under his boots. He cleared his throat.

"At a party in the village. She was as crazy about him as your father was about her. James was nineteen, three years older than her. He was my best friend. Tess looked much older. She was a well-developed girl but very young in the head."

"I haven't any photos of her as a child."

"I have a few you can have. Oh, she was a beauty. A natural blonde. She had great style too. She worked in the drapery store and made all her own clothes with the discounted material she got there. I remember the table in our front room was always covered with taffeta and other kinds of material in bright colours and balls of wool. She knitted too."

"She always loved her clothes and her knitting."

"As soon as she and James hit it off she told your dad it was all over. James and I had been friends since we were small boys in the national school. His family were Anglo-Irish and they lived up at the Lodge, a big house on the edge of the village. His parents were lovely people. They were a lot nicer than the anti-English crowd in the village would have you believe. Most Protestants at that time wouldn't let their offspring anywhere near the local children but Dorothy and Ronald sent James to the local Catholic school early on. They were eccentric, liberal, easy-going types. I spent a lot of my childhood up there at the Lodge. James was an only child and Dorothy encouraged our friendship. She treated me like a son. She was a sprightly woman, twenty years younger than Ronald. She loved the outdoors and she was always out and about walking or fishing." Dempsey shook his head. "At home my father had me grafting on the farm and cutting the turf. I wasn't cut out for that kind of work. I hated it. Tess and I feared him. Your grandmother was awfully cold and very religious. She showed us no affection. Dorothy was much kinder. I much preferred being up at the Lodge. She understood the way we boys were."

Dempsey blushed then stared out of the window like he was locked in a dream. Three inches of snow had fallen on the park overnight. The blue-tinged morning light filtered through the branches of the trees lining the footpaths and a snow sculpture of a man dressed in a school tie and nothing else sat cross-legged on a bench opposite.

"So Tess got pregnant," I said, interrupting his reverie. I immediately regretted the impatience in my voice, remembering that I had to tread softly.

Dempsey turned back. "Sorry. Yes, yes. It was a huge shock. She and James had only known each other a couple of weeks.

"God."

"It only ever happened once." He spoke quickly, circling his foot nervously in the air like he had done at the theatre and finding it hard to hold my gaze. He coughed and his voice became wheezy. "I've thought an awful lot about your mother over the years. It doesn't excuse what I did but I was nineteen and barely more than a boy myself when it all happened." He coughed again. "When your grandparents found out about the pregnancy they were beside themselves. Then when they learned that the baby's father was James and a Protestant

234

who had no intention of marrying Tess, they were broken. Daddy was incandescent. I was forbidden to go to the Lodge but I used to sneak up there all the same. One day I was with James in his room when we heard the sound of gunshots outside followed by a dog yapping. We peeped out from behind the curtains and there was Daddy, standing at the end of the dirt track with a shotgun and Jack our sheepdog by his side." Dempsey sighed and shook his head. "I'll never forget it. He had on his best suit. His daughter was pregnant out of wedlock, he was humiliated and heartbroken but he still put on his Sunday best to come up to the Lodge. It was his last vestige of dignity."

He leant forward, overwhelmed by a bout of wheezing that lasted for some time. He reached into his pocket, produced a perfectly ironed white handkerchief and covered his mouth.

"Sorry about that," he said. "It's my asthma. It plays up in this weather and I came out without my inhaler."

I asked the passing waitress to bring some water and waited for him to recover.

He drank the water. "So where was I?" he said then, dabbing his mouth and carefully folding the handkerchief.

"Tess was pregnant and your father turned up with a shotgun."

"Yes. My parents wouldn't speak to James' family after that so I became the messenger between the families."

"He didn't shoot the messenger, then."

Dempsey laughed. "Very good. No, he didn't. Anyway, your grandparents pushed for marriage but James said no. Dorothy and Ronald said Tess and James and the baby could go and live at the Lodge anyway, but they didn't know what Tess was like or how difficult or erratic she could be. Everyone, myself included, didn't think she was mentally strong enough to bring up a child."

I sat back and sighed. "She brought up two. She had her moments but she was a very loving mother."

Dempsey covered his face with his thin mottled hands.

"With hindsight I know what we did was very wrong, Carmel. But it was a different world back then."

"That's what I keep hearing. It was a different world back then. Seems like an excuse for appalling cruelty to me. Some families actually allowed their daughters to keep their babies."

"In rare cases, yes. Usually by keeping it a secret and pretending the grandmother was the mother. But in a lot of cases it was the local priest who made the final decision. Father Tobin told your parents Tess had to leave the village because she'd brought shame on her family. He came to the house one morning and he and I took her to Tuam. There was no questioning his word and even if we'd fought for Tess to keep the baby, we'd have been powerless against the will of the Church. I know now we were wrong but we genuinely thought we were acting in her best interests."

He bent down and scratched the back of his calf.

"You acted in the best interests of you, your parents, James, his family and the Catholic Church, I wanted to say. Tess and her baby didn't enter the equation. You handed Tess in to the nuns knowing they would sell on her baby to strangers so people wouldn't point at you in the street and talk behind your back at Sunday Mass. Tess wanted to keep her child as did most of the women in those homes. She suffered crippling mental health problems because of it. You played a part in ruining her life.

236

But I said none of it, turning my head to the window and looking out instead. The sun had started to melt the snow sculpture and water birds were flocking to the boating lake where the ice was starting to break.

When I turned back Dempsey was looking at me closely.

"How did you find out that James and I took the child from the home?"

"I traced a woman who was working there as a maid. She saw you. She remembered James' sports car."

A coffee machine whirred in the silence that followed.

"Were you and James together at that point?" I asked.

Dempsey blushed and fiddled with the polo neck of his jumper.

"Not at that point. I had feelings for him but it took James longer to come to terms with his sexuality."

"So Tess was his trial run?"

"It wasn't that simple. We were all very young and ignorant and confused."

He started to splutter and gasp for breath again and I handed him the glass of water. He gulped it down.

"I need to go home for my inhaler," he said, taking out his handkerchief again. His wheezing was worsening and he looked distressed. "Would you mind coming with me? It's only a ten-minute walk."

"Not at all." I said, helping him put on his coat. And I didn't mind. I could get a later train if necessary. I wasn't going anywhere until he told me the whereabouts of my brother.

237

Chapter 37

Dempsey and Stefano lived in a three-storey town house behind Battersea Park. Tucked at the end of a quiet road, it had a moss-dappled facade and a gravelled front garden lined with flower beds. Green-and-rust mosaic tiles lined a decent-sized porch with hanging baskets on either side of a butterscotch front door. Estate agents would have gushed about its secluded but relatively central location and slapped a price tag on it close to a million.

Dempsey and I had shuffled through the melting snow for over half an hour to get to there. He had to keep stopping to regain his breath and was wheezing and coughing badly. By the time we got to his front door I was starting to get worried. His face was drained of colour and I was practically holding him up. I contemplated calling an ambulance but he assured me he'd be fine as soon as he got his hands on his inhaler. He kept on apologising and he was still saying sorry as the pair of us fell through his long narrow hallway. Gesturing at me to make my way into the kitchen, he disappeared into a room on the right that looked like a study.

The kitchen was spacious and airy. A glass box structure had been added to what must have once been a very pokey room. Light flooded in from all angles and sliding doors opened out onto a small patio and long garden. I sat down at a mahogany dining table. The room was show-home tidy: the cream marble worktop sparkled, a row of shiny kitchen utensils hung above the Aga like soldiers standing to attention and lemon walls were lined with framed posters of Dempsey's theatrical successes. There was also a picture of an Italian production of Dario Fo's "Can't Pay Won't Pay" that I guessed had something to do with Stefano.

When Dempsey's coughing died down, I heard his footsteps in the hall then going up the stairs. I glanced at the clock above the door. If I was going to get my scheduled train I'd have to set off for Euston in twenty minutes.

Dempsey returned a few minutes later with a weak smile and a bit of colour back in his cheeks. I declined his offer of coffee and insisted on keeping my coat on even though the room was toasty. He relaxed into the seat opposite me with a glass of water and I glanced down at my watch. Taking the hint, he launched back into Tess's story.

"Not long after Tess went into the home, James' mother Dorothy decided she wanted to keep her grandchild and bring him up herself. The baby had actually been earmarked for adoption to an American couple but Dorothy was determined. There was no stopping her. She was in her early forties at the time and a very fit woman." Dempsey coughed weakly. "So she paid the nuns a sum of money. And James and I collected him and brought him home to the Lodge when he was few months old."

I shook my head slowly. "Christ. So the nuns sold her own grandson back to her."

"For about three times the going rate."

I moved my chair back, the scraping sound making us both wince.

"So he was raised in full view of everyone in the village but nobody bothered to tell Tess?"

Dempsey looked down at the table and rubbed the tip of his forefinger along the grain of the wood. "Nobody knew where she was, Carmel. She'd cut off all contact after she left the home."

I folded my arms across my chest.

"I don't believe that for a minute. Someone, a friend or a cousin must have known she was in Manchester. Someone could easily have found her if they'd looked."

"People didn't want to get involved. They were terrified of the priests and the nuns. There was always a conspiracy of silence where they were involved. The villagers didn't talk."

"And my grandparents?"

"They chose not to know," he said, sipping his water. "The child was a bastard in their eyes and they wanted nothing to do with him. Dorothy told James she bumped into my mother one time in the village with the baby. Your grandmother took one look at the pram and crossed over the road."

"Christ!"

"Oh, our mother was a piece of work, alright. James and I went up to Dublin to study at Trinity shortly after we brought the baby back to the Lodge. Dorothy brought him up for the first three years of his life before the accident. She was driving home from Dublin after James' graduation ceremony. It was a night of heavy rain and we told her to stay the night in a hotel. But Ronnie wasn't well at the time and she wanted to get back to him. She was hit by a lorry just outside Mullingar and killed outright."

"God!"

"She was the loveliest woman. James and I were devastated. We were in a relationship by then and about to move to London. James was desperate to leave Dublin. He said it was claustrophobic and homophobic. He was starting to get acting roles and wanted to try for jobs in the West End. We'd just got back to our lodgings after buying the tickets for the ferry to Holyhead when we got the news about Dorothy. James' father was in the early stages of dementia and couldn't look after the child so James and I took him with us to London."

"What? You and James raised him in London?"

Dempsey's face clenched, like a door shutting. "It has been known for gay people to bring up children, Carmel."

"I didn't mean it like that."

"Yes. James and I brought him up. Well, it was me, mainly. James spent most of his time partying on the Kings Road and Carnaby Street with his actor friends while I was left with all the childcare. I got a job lecturing at King's College so I was able to fit everything around school hours. Then when your brother was fourteen, James upped and left one day for Los Angeles.

He got a part in a TV soap and never came back. He sent birthday cards and money for a few years afterwards but then nothing."

He turned to the glass door that led out into the garden and cupped his hands under his chin. A black cat stared in from the patio table then it ran away, leaving pawprints on the snow-dusted wrought iron.

"James was the love of my life. He was beautiful and dangerously charming and I was heartbroken. But he wanted fame and a glamorous life more than he ever wanted a family." He turned to me. "I never once resented your brother. I loved the bones of him. As far as I was concerned, we were father and son."

"And Tess?" I tugged at my jacket collar, my face and neck hot. "In all that time, you never thought of looking for her?"

"I did everything in the boy's best interest, Carmel. I really did. First he'd lost Dorothy, then James. I was all he had left. He was in his teenage years which were proving difficult for him. He needed stability and Tess wasn't the most stable of characters. The last thing he needed was his mother to turn up out of the blue." He lowered his voice. "And if I'm honest I couldn't bear the thought of losing him."

"So what did you tell him? About Tess?"

Dempsey sighed. "That she died having him."

I got up and paced across the room.

"His name was on the list of children who died in the Tuam home," I said.

Dempsey lifted his head, startled.

"What?"

"When the scandal broke, a list of all the children

who died in the home was published. Donal Dempsey was one of the names on it. Age of death two months. Cause of death heart failure."

Dempsey went pale. "The nuns." he said.

I nodded and rubbed at my neck. "Yes. The nuns. They created a fake death certificate to cover the fact they'd sold him on." I sat back down. "Tess knew all of it. Not long before she died she read about the mass grave then she got hold of the list of the children who'd died. I don't suppose for one minute she was expecting her baby to be on that list." I glared at him. "I mean, why would she? Her brother and her family and the local priest had all assured her he would be adopted into a good family, hadn't they?"

Dempsey flinched then frowned. "But surely to procure a death certificate, they'd need a body?"

I nodded. "That's something I can't bring myself to think about. Anyway, the cause of Donal Dempsey's death on the list was heart failure. It was something the nuns just made up. Like I told you earlier my younger brother Mikey actually did die of heart failure. After his death we discovered he had a hereditary heart condition. Familial Hypertrophic Cardiomyopathy."

Dempsey nodded.

"You've heard of it?" I asked.

"Unfortunately I have."

"Tess was a carrier. She blamed herself for passing the gene on to Mikey and she never got over his death. Imagine how she felt when she found her baby's name on that list and learning he too had died of heart failure. She put two and two together as I did when I read it."

He sat forward with his hands over his face.

"She thought she'd killed both her sons," I said.

He stood up, tears running down his cheeks.

"Sorry, you'll have to excuse me for a moment."

"I don't have time. I have to get to Euston to get my train. Please. Just tell me where he is."

Walking over to a drawer by the Aga, he took out a large white envelope.

"Ellie, my daughter-in-law, always sends me photos," he said, sitting back down "She knows I prefer prints to digital. This is the most recent." He pulled a large photo out of the envelope, placed it in front of me then wiped his eyes with the back of his hand.

"This is Daniel with his son Tim and the latest addition to the family. They don't have a name for her yet."

I picked the photo up, my hand shaking. I blinked. My brother was smiling back at me. His long sandy-coloured hair fell loosely onto his shoulders and he was cradling a new-born in his arms. I looked closer and did a double take, every muscle in my body slackening. It was him without a shadow of a doubt. It was Dan, the bloke from the fundraiser in the Irish Club. Sitting next to him was the same tousled-haired boy I'd seen him with that day in Achill.

"Daniel?" I said, still staring down at the photo. "You said his name was Daniel not Donal?"

"Yes. When we got here I changed both our names to the English versions. It made life easier. Tadhg was always impossible to say or spell so I became Timothy. Donal became Daniel. He has his father's surname, Sheridan. Most people call him —"

"Dan," I said as the photo slipped from my hands.

Chapter 38

The café in the Whitworth Art Gallery was an elegant oblong of glass and steel overlooking Whitworth Park in town. It had recently been added to the old red-brick gallery and sitting in it gave the sensation of being suspended, a bit like being in a tree house. I'd been there many times and was delighted when Dan asked to meet there. I chose a table with a view of the giant metallic tree sculpture in the grounds. The artwork had been created on the spot of an old tree that had died. It was meant to represent loss and renewal and the ghost of what had gone before.

Plates clattered, a coffee machine whirred and Richard Hawley sang "Open Up Your Door" in the background. I concentrated on the words to stop my rising panic. I'd stopped taking the antidepressants but I'd popped a couple of beta-blockers earlier to calm my nerves. Outside the grass shimmered with a late January frost. It had been two torturous months since I made my discovery in Timothy's kitchen in Battersea but now the waiting was over. I was finally going to meet my brother.

When I saw Dan Sheridan staring back at me from the photo, I was left speechless and in a state of shock. Almost a year had passed since the fundraiser and my memory of that night was hazy because I was drunk. I remembered not being able to pin down his accent, him saying he had Mayo and Achill connections and I vaguely recalled him saying something about his son but I couldn't remember what.

How? I asked myself. How had our paths crossed that night? And again that day in Achill? Was it pure bizarre coincidence? Surely it had to be something more than fate or happenstance. I started to think Tess had a hand in it from the grave but then I told myself to cop on.

As I sat in shock across the table from Timothy, I listened to him talk about Dan and his son Archie.

"Like your brother Mikey, both Archie and Dan are carriers of Familial Hypertrophic Cardiomyopathy. Dan and Ellie found out a couple of years ago when Archie was in hospital for a routine operation. He's in perfectly good health but he has to have regular tests. Dan too."

I thought of the smiling boy I'd seen eating ice cream that day in the car park in Achill. Then I remembered that Dan had told me he raised funds for the British Heart Foundation in Manchester because his son was in and out of the cardiac unit at the children's hospital. But he didn't go into detail about HCM. I'd have remembered if he had. He didn't tell me that he was a sufferer, either. I sat back and shook my head slowly. So it wasn't bizarre coincidence or destiny that had brought us together at all. We were both at the fundraiser because we were tied together by our genes and by HCM. But the meeting in Achill? After Dan emailed me to arrange to meet we exchanged a couple of emails. When I told him about seeing him in Achill he was as incredulous as I was. He said that his wife Ellie had recently inherited a cottage on the island from her aunt. They were back and forth a lot working on it. He also said that the shop where I'd seen him was the busiest hub on the relatively remote island so if we two people were going to bump into each other anywhere it would be there. I often went back to Achill when I went back to Mayo. It was my go-to place as it held so many good memories for me from the days when Dad was alive. After visiting the Mother and Baby home and feeling the keen loss of my baby brother, Achill was the natural place for me to head to that day. I cycled in search of solace and healing, having no idea what else my day would bring.

A few days after I left Battersea, Timothy travelled to Dan's home in Altringham and told him the truth about his past. He also told him I'd been trying to trace him and passed on my contact details. A week later Dan sent me an email, saying he wanted to meet but needed time. He said he was finding it hard to process everything he'd just been told. Timothy and I exchanged a number of phone calls. In one call he told me Dan had cut off all contact with him. He was heartbroken and started to cry, saying how much he and Stephano missed having contact with Archie, Dan's son, and the new baby. Two long months passed. Every morning when I woke up I reached for my phone and checked my emails but there was nothing from Dan. Then, just as I'd convinced myself that it wasn't going to happen, he got in touch.

I glanced at my watch. He was ten minutes late. Lifting my latte to my lips, I somehow missed my mouth and splashed coffee on my top. Swearing under my breath, I picked up a napkin and rubbed at the stain. Mary had helped me choose my outfit the day before. Jeans tucked into boots, a cream silk top and pale-blue patterned scarf. She was so excited when told her I'd found my brother and was curious to meet him. Joe was happy for me too. He was still living in the flat in Salford then.

In the playground below the window a blonde boy of about ten in school uniform was standing inside a giant hamster wheel, stretching his limbs and attempting a 360-degree turn. A younger boy turned the wheel and fell about laughing as the older boy toppled over again and again. I grinned. The boy inside the wheel had a look of Mikey when he was little. I glanced at the empty chair beside me. What would I have given to have him sitting there with me. A clatter of plates and when I turned my head I saw our brother striding through the café entrance towards me.

Chapter 39

Dan gave a nervous laugh and said, "We mustn't keep meeting like this."

I stood up and we hugged awkwardly, his stubble catching my cheek. He smelled of cigarettes. His hair was more auburn than I remembered. He was more angular too, all elbows and sharp edges like a bicycle frame. I'd put him in his late forties when we first met. He was actually fifty-six but he looked good on it.

We stood still and stared at each other for a moment, our arms falling by our sides like we'd forgotten what to do with them. His cheeks were flushed and I was relieved to see he looked as terrified as I felt. He unravelled a mustard scarf and slipped off his burgundy Puffa jacket. Underneath he wore autumnal colours that complemented his hair, a dark yellow-and-green check shirt and burgundy jeans.

As we sat down Tess's face came to me. It was as clear as day. She was wearing bright-pink lipstick, she'd just had her hair done and a bright smile lit up her face. I suddenly felt overcome. Tears started to pour down my cheeks and I couldn't speak. It was all too much. I was overwhelmed by the pure and utter joy of my brother's presence.

I wiped my eyes with the back of my hand. "Sorry," I said. "I've been searching for you for quite a while. It's been quite a journey."

He stared down at the table, uneasy at my show of emotion. Composing myself quickly, I asked him about his journey getting here.

"Tram from Altrincham into town then I walked."

"Altrincham. I can't believe we've been living six miles from each other all these years."

He shook his head. "Me neither. Seems so cruel."

He ordered an Americano from a passing waiter and I ordered another latte. We made strained small talk about the café and the gallery and the relative advantages of living in Chorlton and Altrincham.

When our coffees arrived, Dan leant forward and stirred his slowly. "I was devastated when Tim told me about Tess." He stared down into his cup. "I've spent my whole life thinking about her."

"Did Tim and your father ever mention her at all?"

"Not really. I started to ask about her when I was five or six when I saw all the other kids with their mothers at the school gates. Then one day when I was seven James sat me down and told me that he and my mother were in a relationship but they weren't married. He said she'd died when I came out of her tummy. After that they never mentioned her again. I was very young and for a long time I thought it was my fault she'd died. To be honest, Carmel, finding out it was all a lie has floored me. I feel robbed, like someone stole my winning lottery ticket and claimed it as theirs."

I cleared my throat. "How is Timothy now?"

Dan turned sideways in his chair to accommodate his long legs then he rested his hands in his lap. "Fine as far as I know. Ellie talks to him, but I haven't spoken to him for a while."

"That's a shame. Despite everything I can't help liking him."

"It's very complicated."

His tone was sharp and it felt like a rebuke. I shrank back into my chair and in the brief silence that followed a plate smashed at the far end of the café. We both jumped.

Dan sighed. "Tim was a good father and a wonderful grandfather. But we're not here to talk about him." His face suddenly opened up like a flower. "Tell me about Tess. What was she like?"

"Beautiful. Funny. Child-like."

"Favourite singer?"

"Big Tom. Jim Reeves."

"Favourite Song?"

"'I Love You Because'. Dad used to put it on the radiogram and they'd waltz around the living room after a few sherries."

"Must have been hard for you all when your dad passed."

"It was. He was from Mayo as well and he adored Tess. They were really happy together."

251

"It makes me happy that she was loved. Did she go back to Mayo much?"

"Every year when Dad was alive." I hesitated. I wasn't sure I wanted to tell him about all the dark years when she rarely left the house. "She loved driving in Connemara and visiting Ashford Castle in Cong village."

"Home of *The Quiet Man*."

"Her favourite film."

Dan shifted in his chair. "Tim mentioned she had some mental-health issues?"

I swallowed, choosing my words carefully, wanting to do her justice and not paint her in too many dark tones.

"She did but her problems didn't define her. The times when she was well she sparkled."

"Was it to do with what happened in the Mother and Baby Home? A PTSD type thing?"

"It's hard to know. Timothy seems to think she had some issues when she was young. But then he did say he and Tess had quite a violent and uncaring childhood. Tess was never formally diagnosed but I think she was bipolar. She had highs and lows. Who knows if it was nature or nurture? It was probably a mixture. It so often is."

He chewed on a thumbnail. "I went through a period of depression when I was a teenager. I took drugs to make it go away."

I nodded slowly. "It's a monster of a disease."

He looked at me closely. "You too?"

"One episode. Very recently. I've never felt anything like it in my life. I've always been a bit anxious but I unravelled for a while. I had a lot going on. Tess and Mikey died, I was looking for you and then I discovered my husband had slept with my best friend."

"Sorry to hear that." He frowned. "Your friend. Was she …?"

"The woman with me at the fundraiser? Yes."

He reddened and looked away.

I sipped my coffee. I'd hardly touched it. "Do you mind if I ask you something, Dan? Do you think what you went through as a teenager was anything to do with not having a mother? It can't have been easy being brought up by same-sex parents back then. Did you ever feel different and singled out?"

He paused. "Of course. But I'd always known James and Tim were in a relationship and that Tim was my uncle. I'd grown up having two loving parents. I'd always felt loved and wanted and I was cool about it. I wasn't depressed about not having a mother. The depression seemed to come out of nowhere. Maybe it was hormones. It's never come back, touch wood. But what you've just told me about Tess and yourself makes sense. Maybe it's genetic."

He shook his hair back off his face and frowned. A thick silence settled over us like a fog and he stared out of the window. I knew that meeting him again was never going to be easy for either of us but I could see he was finding it much harder than me. Gone was the ease and banter of our first meeting. He was clenched shut like a clam, opening up only now and again. Or maybe he simply didn't like me. I started to wonder if we were going to have any kind of relationship at all.

I tried to steer the conversation in a different direction.

"So have you done much research into the Mother and Baby homes?"

"Loads. I read everything about the mass grave I was

253

supposed to be buried in, about the illegal adoptions and the government commission. Everything."

It was approaching lunch time. The café was filling with academics from the university nearby and arty types in black and horn-rimmed glasses with copies of the *Guardian* under their arms. We ordered a club sandwich each though I wasn't particularly hungry.

When the waitress had gone Dan sat back and folded his arms.

"In some ways I count myself lucky, Carmel. Yes, I was trafficked but at least I ended up with my birth father and my uncle. I think about all those poor sods who were never told the truth about their adoption. Imagine waking up when you're sixty and finding out that the parents whose names are on your birth certificate are not your birth parents like you thought but complete strangers. How fucking awful is that? Their lives must seem like one big lie."

"I'm sure many loved their adopted parents and didn't feel cheated but, yes, you're right. For many it's identity theft, plain and simple." I sighed and finished the last of my coffee. "So are you going to look for redress or anything from the Irish authorities? There are organisations in the Irish community here in Manchester that can help with that kind of thing, you know."

"I'm not sure. It might implicate Tim and I don't want that. At the end of the day he was a good father."

Dan looked down and circled his finger on the rim of his coffee cup. "I've come across so many online survivors groups in my research. I can't believe how many of us there are out there. Tens of thousands all around the world. Victims of the Mother and Baby homes, the Magdalene

Laundries, the industrial schools. So many fled Ireland."

I nodded. "Shame put them on a boat. If you ask me the diaspora is full of brave adventurous types who wanted a liberated life away from the oppression of church and family. But there are also a lot of walking wounded among them, people who are shadows of the people they might have been. And the ones you found are the brave ones who've spoken out. So many took their secrets to their graves."

Our sandwiches arrived. I picked at mine. I thought about what Karen said that day at the library, about not building up my sibling in my mind so he or she didn't disappoint, like her dad had disappointed her. I'd done everything she said not to. My expectations about Dan had been way too high and now I was coming down, disappointed by his lack of warmth. We chatted awkwardly for a while longer then I remembered the gift bag by my feet.

I picked it up and put it on the table. "I almost forgot. This is for you."

He lifted a fuchsia scarf from the bag.

"She wore it a lot," I said. "Pink was her favourite colour."

"Thank you." He turned it over in his hands like it was made of precious glass then he put it back in the bag. He took out the photo. It was taken at Josie O'Grady's wedding in '96, the week after the Manchester bomb. Tess was wearing the suit we'd bought at Marks and Spencer's and she had a small plaster on her forehead where she'd been injured. Mikey was sixteen, filling out a grey double-breasted jacket and holding up a pint of Guinness.

Dan stared at it without speaking. "She was very

beautiful, wasn't she? And I assume that's Mikey? God, he looks like Tim."

"Doesn't he? You'd have liked him. Everyone did. He was a lovable rogue. Tess adored him. I think she saw him as your replacement."

Dan continued to look at the picture. "He died so young."

I put a hand on his arm. "I'm sure you and Archie will be fine. You're both being monitored. Mikey didn't know he had HMC. And your little girl? Has she been tested?"

"She's got the all-clear."

He moved his arm away and I sat back.

"Thank God."

"Tess didn't look much older than that when I met her that time."

I frowned and leant forwards. "Sorry?"

"When I met her at another fundraiser at the Lowry Hotel. I told you that night at the Irish Club. Don't you remember?"

I felt myself redden. "I'm sorry. I was very drunk. I can't remember much about that night at all."

"You were with her. It was at the Lowry Hotel. We were queuing to get tickets in the foyer. I was standing in front of you and Tess. You were chatting to someone else and when I heard Tess's accent I turned round and asked her where she was from. We spoke very briefly about Mayo. I've gone over and over those few minutes a million times in the past few months."

I sat back, my hands flopping by my sides. "My God, *you met her.*"

"I thought you knew."

I shook my head in bewilderment. His voice was shaky and I could see he was close to tears. Slipping the photo into his pocket and grabbing his coat and scarf, he said he needed to go outside for a smoke.

When he'd gone I sat still, not knowing whether to laugh or cry. I dug hard into my memory for the encounter at the Lowry but I couldn't remember a thing. I closed my eyes and I imagined it instead. A few accidental minutes of banter after a lifetime of longing. How cruel life could be, tripping us up with such bittersweet moments.

Sometime later I was making my way to the bathroom through the glass corridor that connected the café to the gallery. I was still thinking about their meeting. I stopped halfway and looked out when I spotted Dan below. He was sitting on a bench in the garden. Enclosed by a cloud-shaped hedge, it had been created as a place of healing and the herbs and plants were tended by vulnerable people from local communities. In the summer it was crowded with peonies and poppies. An installation of coloured neon lights hung overhead on the gallery roof spelling out the words "*Gathering of Strangers*". Hunched forwards, elbows on his knees, Dan was holding his head in his hands. Then, as if suddenly remembering he was late for something, he jumped up and hurried towards the exit and out into the street.

Chapter 40

Two weeks after I met Dan at the Whitworth, Joe rang me at home. It was a Friday evening and he wanted to know if a letter had arrived for him from the hospital. Though he'd moved into the Salford Quays flat three months previously, a lot of his mail was still being delivered to the house. He was waiting to hear about an appointment for a cycling injury. He sounded croaky on the phone and said he'd been off work for a couple of days with a bad dose of something. I offered to drive round with the letter. Why wouldn't I? He'd looked after me when I was unwell the previous summer and we were getting on OK. I didn't hesitate to return the favour. I put some salad in a Tupperware box, wrapped up the dish of lasagne I'd just taken out of the oven and got in the car.

I shivered as I waited outside the entrance of Joe's waterfront building for him to buzz me in. It was an icy evening with a thin layer of February frost on the ground. Once former dockyards, Salford Quays was one of the country's first major examples of urban regeneration. As far back as I could remember the entire area had been one vast building site. Then one by one, the Lowry Theatre and Hotel, the Imperial War Museum and the shopping centre had opened up. More recently the BBC and Media City arrived, bringing jobs for locals, reluctant southerners forced to transfer up from London and celebrity sightings. Nowadays the Quays bustled with young hipsters living in glitzy high-rise residential buildings with names like Grain Wharf, Merchants Quay and Imperial Point.

"Why the Quays?" I asked Joe when he first told me he was moving there. "It's full of youngsters."

"Steady on," he replied, open-mouthed. "I'm only forty-two."

"Why not stay in Chorlton where your friends are?"

He stared down at his hands. "Too many memories."

It was my first visit to the flat. My heart dipped as I entered. Joe's bike took up most of the narrow hallway and the living room was depressingly pokey. Though he'd been there for months, he still hadn't unpacked properly. Unopened cardboard boxes, plastic storage containers and holdalls were piled high everywhere. Dirty dishes and plates filled the sink and cans and takeaway cartons lined the worktop in the tiny galley kitchen to the side. Despite the ridiculous rent he was paying, the furniture and fittings looked flimsy and cheap.

He was curled up on the sofa in his tartan dressing gown under a blanket. Used tissues, pill packets and medicine bottles covered a glass coffee table next to him. He didn't look well at all. His face, slightly jaundiced and hollow, lit up when he saw me.

"It's very cosy," I said awkwardly.

He threw me a wry smile and sniffed into a tissue. "I got the short straw when it came to houses."

The fact that I'd been living in the dream house that Paddy and Peggy had paid for wasn't lost on me. Joe hadn't objected so far. But then how could he? He'd slept with my best friend.

"You look shit, by the way," I said, going into the kitchen and moving his laptop off the worktop to make way for my dishes. "You need to eat something."

I heated up the lasagne in the microwave, put the salad on plates and poured two glasses from the half bottle of Viognier I found in the fridge. We ate on the sofa with our food on our knees, listening to Radio XFM on the digital radio on the table. Joe asked how my meeting with Dan had gone. I told him I'd been disappointed, that I'd built my long-lost brother up too much in my imagination.

I scooped up my lasagne. "He's finding it all a bit too much. I'm not sure we even get on. I thought meeting him was going to be this amazing happy ending. I suppose subconsciously I thought he'd replace Mikey. But he's much more complex. They're very different people."

"He seemed nice enough at the fundraiser." Joe cocked his head to one side and grinned. "Not that you'd remember much about that night."

"Stop it." I felt myself redden and slapped his knee playfully.

Joe wolfed down the last of his food, placed his empty

plate on the coffee table and sat back on the sofa.

"Mikey was unique," he said. "He and I had our differences but even I could see what a lovable scoundrel he was. Nobody could ever replace him in your eyes, Carmel."

"I know," I said, sighing and putting down my fork. "He was far from perfect though. I've been thinking a lot about something you said outside Karen's house that time."

Joe winced.

"Something about me enabling Mikey and Tess."

He held up a hand.

"I didn't mean —"

"No. Let me finish. I think you had a point. Well, maybe not Tess so much, but Mikey, yes. I bailed him out a lot of times when it would have been better to let him deal with the consequences of his actions. But I always had this idea it was my duty to step in and protect my naughty kid brother all the time because we didn't have functioning parents. Even when he was a grown man." I looked Joe in the eye "And you were also right about the day of your dad's funeral. I should never have left you to go and see Mikey in court. That was very wrong of me."

He sighed then slowly slid his hand along the sofa cushions and put it over mine. It was febrile to the touch and I left it there for a few seconds before pulling it away.

"None of that excuses what you did, though."

His head dropped forward onto his chin. "I get it, Carmel. I really do. I didn't just sleep with anyone, I slept with your best friend and it was something you can't forgive. I know I've blown it. But you have to know this. What happened with Karen was only ever about sex.

Nothing else. With you it was only ever about love. And sex." He stood up slowly. "I've loved you since the day I met you and I always will. Now if you'll excuse me I need to go for a slash."

As he disappeared down the narrow corridor into the bathroom I got up and went over to the sliding door that led onto a tiny balcony. I opened it and stepped outside, clenched by the cold night air. Frost shimmered everywhere and the lights from the Millennium Bridge reflected in the dark water, forming a turquoise shape like a giant peacock feather. A tall thin woman in a long coat was walking her dog along the canal bank.

I turned at the sound of voices. On the balcony to my right a young couple were pouring something from a bottle into glasses and laughing. For some reason I thought of Billy O'Hagan. We'd sat on the rooftop terrace bar that evening after the conference on a night not too dissimilar to this one, huddled in coats and drinking tequila shots. I was warmed by the memory. I looked back at the woman walking her dog. She reminded me of Lowry's matchstick figures. She was looking out over the river and there was something desperately lonely and sad about the way she lingered with her head bowed.

I looked back into the room. Joe was shuffling back through the piles of boxes in the direction of the sofa. As I stepped back inside The Cure's "Friday I'm in Love" was playing on the radio. It was our song; we used to listen to it on the Friday train to Euston or Piccadilly when we first met and were travelling to visit each other. Joe caught my eye briefly then bent down and turned the radio off.

I started picking up plates and glasses from the table.

"You off then?" he sighed, lying down on the sofa and tucking the blanket around him.

He closed his eyes and I stared at him as I'd done so many times over the years as he slept next to me.

"Why don't you go and pack a bag?" I said. "Then we can go home."

Chapter 41

There'd been showers on and off all morning but they'd stopped just in time. A mild September sun crept out from behind the clouds, honey-coloured rays dropping through the side window onto the worktop. I picked up my champagne flute. A mountain of gaily wrapped presents, cards and gift bags were piled high in the corner and a pink balloon saying "*On Your Christening*" was floating above the hood of the stove.

"See you've tidied up at last," I said, holding up my glass to my brother.

"Cheeky." Dan grinned and topped me up from the bottle in his hand. He was wearing a crisp white shirt and blue polka-dot tie that Ellie had forced on him. With his hair neatly greased back, he looked like a schoolboy uncomfortable in his Sunday best.

The large open-plan kitchen was humming with Dan and Ellie's bohemian friends and Ellie's family who were over from Achill. They were a garrulous lot, a mixture of hoteliers, academics and musicians. We'd spent the previous night carousing in the bars in the Northern Quarter in town and I was slightly the worst for wear. Dan and Ellie's seventies pre-fab was tucked in a cul-de-sac behind an industrial park in Altrincham. The house looked much healthier now than when they'd moved in. I'd helped them paint a couple of the rooms including this one. Gone were the piles of Ellie's score sheets and cello cases, sample paint pots and brushes. The boxes of books lying everywhere had found shelves, the baby toys had found a home in a lovely oriental trunk, and the posters and prints stacked by the door had been mounted on the sunflower-yellow walls. My favourite, a splash of vivid greens and yellows called *Achill Horses*, hung over the bright orange sofa that Ellie and I had found in a charity shop in Chorlton. Neither Dan nor Ellie were particularly enamoured with the house. Ellie earned very little as a jobbing cellist and with Dan's teaching salary it was all they could afford in the catchment area of the local grammar where they hoped Archie was heading.

Dan headed to the door to greet a woman with dreadlocks carrying a baby in a sling. She was wearing hiking boots despite the heat. They hugged and she handed him a cloudy bottle of something home-made which he put in the fridge. Children ran in and out of the garden barefoot and I'd detected a faint whiff of dope from the front room earlier. The talk all around the room was of Brexit and the EU referendum. Three months on after the June vote, everyone was still reeling with the shock and uncertainty of it all.

Ellie's cousin Declan picked up his guitar and started singing Elvis Costello's "Oliver's Army". He had a great voice and everyone stopped talking and listened. I was immediately transported to Karen's living room in Hillingdon Road when we were in our teens and a wave of sadness and regret dropped over me. It was in her top five all-time favourite songs. When Dee was at the pub she'd put it on and we'd drink Merrydown cider and pogo around the room singing at the top of our voices. I sighed heavily as I recalled our recent encounter in town.

It was mid-August and Joe and I had just come from an appointment at the baby clinic. He'd taken the bus into his office and I was heading to my car I'd parked in one of the roads behind the university. I was popping in to work afterwards to pick up some research papers and have a coffee with Mary.

I was halfway across Oxford Road and there she was standing twenty or so feet away on the pavement edge, facing me.

She was surrounded by a river of students in gowns and hats who were flooding out of the university buildings with their friends and family. She looked stunning in a grey figure-hugging dress and heels, her hair braided. Her arm was placed proudly around Alexia's shoulders and they were posing for a photo. The man taking it was the same man I'd seen in Alexia's Instagram post some weeks previously.

Though I'd deleted both Karen and Alexia from my Facebook and Twitter accounts, I hadn't deleted Alexia from my Instagram. I rarely used my account but I was bored one day in the clinic waiting room and I started scrolling idly through when I saw the photo of Karen. She was sitting on the thick knees of a rugged-looking man with salt-and-pepper hair and stubble. They were smiling at each other, surrounded by lemon trees, bougainvillea and blue skies. He had a look of Idris Elba and she was wearing a yellow sundress, her bare arms entwined around his neck. I tried to remember the last time I'd seen her looking so happy. Underneath Alexia had written.

Mum and George in his plush pad in the hills. Guys, get a room.

By the time I'd crossed the road my heart was about to implode in my chest. I looked around for an escape route but it was too late. Karen had already seen me. Alexia moved away to talk to another student and Karen said something to George and quickly made her way towards me.

I felt the panic rising and my flight instinct kicked in. I was about to run back across the road but instead I rooted my feet to the ground. *No, you don't*, Doherty, I said to myself. *This time you stay*.

She stood about a foot away from me, searching my face. A flicker of something crossed hers, pain, pity, regret. Maybe all of those things or perhaps none.

"Carmel," she said with forced cheerfulness. Then she raised her arms as if she was about to molest me in some kind of embrace. I was enraged. How could she think she could hug me as if nothing had happened? I wanted more than anything to give her an almighty whack across the face. But how could I? Behind her Alexia's face was smiling and laughing. She was enjoying her big day, I was her godmother and I was never going to ruin it despite what Karen had done. Instead I turned and hurried away, tears pouring down my face.

I was still shaking when I got into work. Mary got me a coffee from the vending machine in the staffroom and took me outside to calm down. We sat on the low wall outside our building in the sunshine.

"Do you think you'll ever be able to forgive her?" she asked.

I shook my head and sipped. "I really don't know, Mary. It's not just because she had sex with Joe. Sometimes when I look back over our friendship I wonder if it only worked because she was in charge. In many ways I think I've always been Karen's lackey and done what she wanted. Julia said as much when I was in Ireland recently. I think Karen was a bit of a control freak and took advantage of the fact that I was angsty and needy and manipulated me sometimes."

But, as the months passed, I started to regret not speaking to her that day. I regretted not asking her to meet up for a coffee and not giving her a chance to make amends. And it's a feeling that's chipped away at my heart ever since. She was in my life long before Joe and we've been through too much together to throw all those years of friendship away. So I contacted Alexia on Instagram and asked for her mum's address. It's taking me a while but I am composing a letter.

Declan finished his song to loud applause. Ellie whistled and clapped from the table in the middle of the room where she was handing out slices of pizza. I caught her eye and we raised glasses.

I'd found a near perfect sister-in-law in Ellie Lavelle. Razor-sharp with a heart of gold, she was one of those women who did a million things at once and never complained about her lot. Dan and I had her to thank for the relationship we now had. Without her it might never have happened.

The day after our awkward reunion at the Whitworth, Dan emailed and apologised for his sudden departure. He said he was emotionally all over the place and wasn't sure he was ready to have a sibling relationship. Then, with Kissinger-like diplomacy, Ellie took charge. Over the next few months she encouraged and coaxed us together, organising coffee mornings, birthday dinners and days out with the kids. It worked. Over time the unease Dan initially felt melted and we started to bond.

It felt good to have a brother again but Dan was no Mikey. Joe was right when he said Mikey was special. He had a charisma and easy-going way about him that charmed people within minutes of meeting him. Dan, on the other hand, was more cerebral and reserved, a much more difficult nut to crack. He was very different to the man I met at the fundraiser. And yet I was grateful to have him in my life. He, Ellie, the kids and Timothy had restored to me the sense of belonging I had lost after Tess and Mikey passed. They'd filled the black hole around me and made me feel tethered again.

On a sunny April afternoon in Southern Cemetery on what would have been Tess's seventy-first birthday, Dan asked me to be godmother to my beautiful niece. We'd just finished tidying the leaves around the headstone and I was replacing the dead roses in the metal vase with the fresh lilies we'd brought.

"Nothing fancy," he said as starlings and thrush sang in full throttle overhead, "Just a small humanist ceremony at the house."

"What? No priests or holy water or white christening gowns?"

He smiled. "Afraid not."

"Heathen." I stood up, brushed down my jeans and beamed at him. "Thank you," I said, "I'd be honoured."

As we walked back through the tree-lined avenues to the car, Dan said he was happy to see Tess among her own in the Irish part of the cemetery. The family plot was situated beside a copse of birch trees. Tess, Mikey and Dad had Connollys, McGraths and Dunleavys for neighbours and the surrounding graves were covered in the tricolour and Mayo and Galway football flags. Dan said she would have felt at home. Though I didn't say so, I wasn't so sure. I didn't think Tess had thought of Ireland as home for a very long time. If anything her country had exiled her in shame and made her homeless.

People were starting to move outside into the garden as more guests arrived. I filled up my glass and joined Timothy who was sitting by the window at the far end of the room. He looked a little lonely and out of place. Elegant in a cream linen suit and grey silk shirt, he stood out among the crusties like an orchid in a bed of weeds. Stefano was in Italy at a family funeral and couldn't make it.

The morning had not been kind to Tim. His face was pale and puffy-eyed. He'd asked me to take him to the grave and once there he'd wept at length. He'd sat in silence on the drive back. I suspected the realisation of what had happened to Tess all those years ago was hitting home. He was such a private man, I didn't like to probe. But I did know that he was a good man and full of remorse.

I pulled up a chair next to him as shouts erupted from

the garden. Younger children were flinging themselves across the bouncy castle and my nephew Archie and his friends were playing a game of rugby. Timothy and I turned to watch. Rosy-cheeked and tousled hair flying, as Archie darted across the lawn with the ball I thought of Mikey.

"I hear he's captain of the school team." I said.

Tim nodded, his face brightening as it always did at any mention of Archie. They were incredibly close. At the cemetery the day he asked me to be godmother, Dan told me he could never be estranged from Tim.

"It would kill him," he said. "Archie too. They adore one another."

Archie touched the ball down on the lawn and raised his arms in victory.

"Did I ever tell you Mikey played rugby for the England Under-21's once." I said.

Tim turned and looked at me.

"Are you serious?"

"Oh yes. He was a rising star. Then he had an accident and never played again. It broke him. Tess once asked him if he'd ever play for Ireland but he wasn't having any of it. He said he was English. That he was no Tony Cascarino."

Tim laughed. "Tony Cascarino. The fake Irishman." He glanced out of the window "You never know. Archie might play at Lansdowne Road yet."

"You never know. Do you know if the kids got their Irish passports yet?"

"They did."

I frowned. "They aren't really going to go back and live in Achill, are they?"

Tim looked at me and shook his head slowly.

"No. I think it was the initial anger of the Leave vote that made them talk that way. Ireland and the UK have agreements in place that mean we have the right to settle and work in the UK but there's still a feeling of not being wanted. Spending half your life in a country, working hard and paying your taxes then to be told you're not really welcome. Stefano feels it badly. The latest is that he has to apply for citizenship. He's been here for fifteen years."

I shook my head. "It's so depressing."

I wondered what Tess would make of us getting on so well like this. Would Timothy have won her over as he had me? Would she have forgiven him like I had? At times I felt guilty about how much I liked his company. We called each other weekly, emailed links to plays and literary articles and I'd been to stay with him in Battersea a number of times. Over wine and Stefano's delicious fresh pasta dishes he entertained me with childhood tales of Tess and life as a gay father with a teenager in London in the 60s. He was a great storyteller with a quiet way of luring you in and a witty turn of phrase. I simply loved being in his company.

I looked out of the window at the other side of the garden where Joe was standing by the bouncy castle. Beer in hand, he was chatting to Damian, one of Ellie's cousins. Damian's son, a boy of two or three with a blonde pudding-bowl hair, suddenly appeared at their feet, waving an ice lolly in the air. Damian knelt down, unwrapped the lolly then kissed the top of his head. Joe looked on, his face a mixture of curiosity and deep sadness. When the boy had gone he raised his bottle and drank at length.

We started trying for a baby the minute Joe moved

back in. We went at it hammer and tongs but despite having sex at every opportunity for five months, I failed to get pregnant. Knowing we had no time to waste, we booked into a BUPA fertility clinic in town for tests. Going private meant we could get everything done quickly and the results were back within weeks. As feared my age meant my eggs weren't in great shape. I had about a five to seven per-cent chance of getting pregnant with IVF treatment. What we weren't expecting were Joe's results. His sperm showed up abnormalities. This, combined with my age, meant our chances of conceiving with IVF were even lower. When we told the consultant about our earlier pregnancy he shrugged and said it was probably a fluke, the way things were looking now it was going to be extremely difficult. When we left the clinic, Joe cried like he had all those years ago outside that other clinic when the scan showed we had lost our baby. But this time I cried too. I'd left it too late. Fear and indecision had kept me lingering too long.

I turned to Tim. "I don't know if I told you but Joe and I have decided to adopt."

"You have?" He gave me a tentative smile.

"We're not broadcasting it or anything yet but we've found an agency we like and we're going through the initial checks and vetting at the moment."

"Excellent news. I'm delighted for you both."

"We don't want to get our hopes up too much. We might not even be approved."

"Why wouldn't you? You'll make wonderful parents."

"It'll be a long haul, at least eighteen months before we even get a match and the chances of getting a baby are small. But I have to admit, I'm starting to get excited now."

Truth was, Joe and I been completely taken aback at the amount of hurdles and training and checks we had to go through going though: medical records, personal references, extensive criminal-record searches. They'd even brought up a police caution for shoplifting when I was fourteen.

Tim said, looking over at Dan who was holding my niece on his hip. "None of it will be easy but it'll be worth it in the end."

The unforgiving voice in my head, the one that was fading with time, wanted to remind Tim how he had become a father. It wasn't just that he and James had bought Dan, that they had simply walked into the Mother and Baby home in Tuam, handed a large sum of money over to the nuns and taken my brother home. It was that in the years that followed Timothy had never searched out Tess to tell her. Part of me was still angry about it but I would never say it to Tim. I had grown to love him too much.

Thankfully, the world was a different place now. No adopted child of mine would be sold to me for profit or denied access to their documents and medical records. My child's birth certificate would not be falsified so he or she could never trace their birth mother. She would not be locked in an institution, made to work as a slave for her keep and have her new-born ripped from her breast simply because she wasn't married. The child I adopted would have the right to have contact with his or her birth mother. Neither of them would live a lifetime of longing, thinking of each other every day and going stone mad with the pain of not knowing.

The clink of metal against glass. Ellie asked everyone

to move into the garden then we shuffled into a semi-circle around Janet, the humanist celebrant. Janet was Scottish and over six foot. The trousers of her lilac linen suit were too short and she laughed a lot. A few children escaped their parents' clutches and headed for the bouncy castle but no-one seemed to mind. After the family introductions, Janet gave a humorous talk about the importance of parenting, Archie read a piece about how he was going to be a splendid brother to his baby sister and Ellie read a Margaret Atwood poem called "You Begin".

Then it was my turn. Dan gave that look he had sometimes, like he was searching my face for something he'd lost. Then he handed me my beautiful flaxen-haired niece. She had fallen asleep on his chest and continued to sleep on mine. I inhaled her newness, the lemony smell of her curls, and the soft tulle of her dress. It felt both painful and joyful at the same time.

Then for a moment I lost track of what Janet was saying as I caught sight of them by the fence, hidden in the sun's shadow. Tess was wearing her pink suit, Dad had his hand on her shoulder and Mikey was saying something that made them all laugh.

Ellie nudged me back to the present. Janet was asking me what name had been chosen for my niece. I looked at Dan and smiled.

"Tess," I said, kissing the top of her head.

Then I glanced in the direction of the fence again. But they'd all gone.

The End

Manufactured by Amazon.ca
Bolton, ON

19125212R00160